THE BOOK OF HAVOC

THE LAST ORACLE, BOOK SIX

MELISSA MCSHANE

Night Harbor Publishing

This book is dedicated to the memory of
Mike Resnick, author of Santiago and many more wonderful science fiction books,
and Neil Peart, the greatest drummer ever and another very fine writer.
Their works were part of this book from the beginning, and I wish I could have thanked them in person for their influence on me.

1

I loved my bathroom, which was painted a soft rose-petal pink on three sides and had roses carved into the white molding at the corners. Wallpaper with a delicate pink stripe and bunches of pink rosebuds covered the fourth wall. It was as feminine as my office, with its heavy oak and brass desk, was masculine, and I liked the contrast. But I had to admit it was barely large enough to fit the ancient toilet, the claw-footed tub of dingy white porcelain, and the pedestal sink made to look like an Ionic column. I'd crammed a wicker shelving unit for storing towels and rolls of toilet paper between toilet and tub, reducing the available space for people further. Cozy, that's what it was. "Cramped" was such a negative word.

I wiped steam from the mirror over the sink and depressed the latch to swing it open, revealing my tiny medicine cabinet. "Excuse me," Malcolm said, reaching past me for his razor. I leaned to one side and removed my toothbrush from the hook inside the cabinet. His hair was still damp from his morning bath, and he wore a towel slung low around his hips, a sight I found more erotic than if he'd been naked altogether. I took a moment to admire the view. Then I began brushing my teeth, staying out of Malcolm's way as best I could.

The mirror fogged up again. Malcolm liked very hot baths. I swiped its surface again, spat, and rinsed just as a dollop of shaving cream splatted into the sink next to my toothpaste. "Sorry," Malcolm said.

"Just a minute," I said, swinging the mirror open again to put away my toothbrush. Malcolm paused, razor held halfway to his upper lip, waiting for me to finish. I wiped condensation off my wristwatch and cursed. "I'm late."

"So am I," Malcolm said, though he didn't hurry his shaving. I guessed hurrying with a razor was a bad idea.

I shut the mirror, then swung it open again, causing Malcolm to take a step back. "Sorry." I removed a tube of moisturizer, closed the mirror, and caught Malcolm staring at me, half his face still lathered up. "I'm sorry! I'll get out of your way."

Malcolm sighed and resumed his shaving. "Helena," he said, "this isn't working."

"What do you mean? What 'this'?"

"You know what I mean. This bathroom is too small for two people, particularly two people who need to wash at the same time. And bathing takes far too long. I miss my shower, Helena. And I'm not fond of reenacting *Mr. Blandings Builds His Dream House* every morning."

I leaned against the bathroom door and folded my arms over my chest. "What are you saying?"

Malcolm washed his face and dried it before responding. "I love you. I love living with you. And this apartment is beautiful. But it wasn't made to accommodate two."

Despite the muggy warmth of the bathroom, I felt a chill pass over me. "Are you saying you're moving out?"

He kissed me, pushing the hair back from my face. "I'm saying I want you to move in with me. To my apartment."

"Your apartment? But—"

"I realize it's farther from Abernathy's, but I can arrange for a car to take you here and back so you won't have to drive, if that's what you want. And it's a very nice apartment." He kissed me again. "With a very nice bed."

"But—" Leave my cozy little home, my hard-won independence? "You live with your mother."

Malcolm scowled. "I live *near* my mother. The same building. Not even the same floor. Never mind. It's not important."

"No, wait. I'm sorry. You just...caught me off guard. Can I think about it?" I took his hand and squeezed it. "You're right about how crowded this place is. But I feel connected to it. Leaving...would be a big adjustment for me."

"I understand." Malcolm put his razor away and stood facing me, clearly unconcerned that he was still mostly naked. It was a morning habit of his I appreciated. "We can discuss it over dinner. I'll be back by seven—late meeting with a new client."

"I'll have dinner ready." It was my night to cook, which meant I'd probably be ordering takeout from the Chinese place two blocks over. I really should learn to cook. "And I have to get dressed now."

The bedroom, at least, wasn't so crowded that we couldn't both get dressed at the same time, despite the clothing rack we'd brought in for some of Malcolm's suits. I put on my favorite summer dress, a pale blue knee-length shift with spaghetti straps and a white knitted shrug, soft and short-sleeved, and brushed out my hair. I eyed the rack, partially obscured by Malcolm's body. He was right; the apartment was too small for both of us to fit comfortably in.

I set my brush on the dressing table and checked my reflection in the very feminine mirror, its frame carved all over with roses that matched the ones in the bathroom. Silas Abernathy, former custodian of the oracular store, had lived here for a time, and I'd always assumed he was married, because the bedroom bore so many feminine touches. But he'd never mentioned a wife in his diary or in his book *Reflections*, and the more I thought about it, the less likely I found it that he'd lived here with a companion. Maybe Malcolm was right, and it was time for a change.

Malcolm had finished knotting his tie and was swiftly making the bed. I'd told him he didn't have to do that, but he'd given me a funny look, said "It makes the room look better" and gone on doing it every morning. It was true, it gave the room a tidy look that was missing from the days I lived alone and didn't bother making the bed, reasoning I'd just mess it up again at night. I helped straighten the pillows, then followed him into the kitchen, where I put a couple of English muffins in the toaster and poured some tall glasses of orange juice.

"I don't have time for breakfast, love," Malcolm said, but he hovered near the toaster.

"You're the boss. They're not going to start without you."

"They should, if we want to maintain our reputation." He snatched the muffin as the toaster popped, juggled it, then slathered butter on it and took a huge but careful bite.

I poured honey on mine and took a smaller, equally careful bite, then washed it down with orange juice. "You'd be closer to your office if we lived in your apartment."

"Which in no way influenced my request."

"I know. It's just something to think about."

Malcolm finished his muffin and gulped down juice in seconds. He kissed me lightly, said, "I love you. I'll see you tonight," and was gone. I checked my watch. Three minutes until ten. Since I only had to walk downstairs to get to my job, I figured I could take a little time to eat. Besides, Judy was probably there already, and could open up, and it wouldn't hurt the Nicolliens to wait a few minutes for their auguries. Did I really want to give up my one-minute commute for the sake of a few extra inches' space?

I trotted down the stairs, relishing the coolness of the air. Abernathy's had excellent climate control, but it didn't extend to my apartment on the second floor, which was usually hot and stuffy during the summer. My office was cool and dry—cool enough that I was glad of my shrug—and I took a moment to sort through the mail-in augury requests. I should have been down an hour before to make a start on them, but Malcolm and I had both slept late after a long Sunday party with my family, and I'd be behind all day. I sighed. Mondays were so challenging.

The office door swung open. "There you are," Judy said irritably. "There's a crowd out here wondering where the custodian is."

"I overslept," I said. "Sorry."

"Don't apologize to me. It's not like I had to make nice with a bunch of impatient Wardens who all think their auguries are more important than anyone else's."

"I said I was sorry."

Judy waved it away. "No, I'm sorry. My father just learned that Susan Mendez is dead, not just disappeared. That's three murdered magi in a week."

"That's awful. I liked Susan. Though I didn't know what to hope for—that she was alive, but a traitor, or innocent, but dead."

"Me too. After all that mess last April…" Judy's voice trailed off. She didn't need to say what we both knew: that magery, having faced its greatest challenge in the discovery of a cabal of traitors working with the invaders, was still reeling from the aftermath. Many magi had disappeared when the existence of the Mercy, as the traitors called themselves, had been revealed. The few who'd turned up again had turned up dead. It had been months, and until this last week we'd thought the Wardens had regained stability. The recent deaths said otherwise.

"I should get to work," I said. Judy held the door open wider for me, and we passed through the narrow passages made by the bookcases. Some of them were so narrow we had to go single file. Abernathy's was crowded, disorganized, and cluttered with books crammed in any old way, and I loved it. Today the fresh smell of lilacs, a breath of spring persisting into summer, drifted through the bookcases. It had become one of my favorite scents, and felt as if Abernathy's was saying good morning to me.

I emerged from the stacks to find six men and women waiting for me, all in a line, all holding slips of white paper. "Sorry for the delay," I said, and accepted the first augury request. "I'll try to be quick."

With the scrap of paper in my hand, I took three steps and was enfolded in the timeless silence of the oracle. The morning light, blue-tinged, illuminated the books so they appeared to glow from inside. I paced the corridors, looking for the book that would fulfil this augury request: *Where should I relocate to?* It was the sort of augury that could probably have been handled by the catalogue, but it wasn't my responsibility to tell my customers what they should do.

I turned a corner and found the book, outlined in blue light and tingling to the touch. *Broken Homes,* I read on the fat paperback's cover, and there was a map of some sort illustrated below the title. Maybe this would be an easy one to interpret.

I handed it over to the waiting woman. "$750," I said, turning to the man next in line. "Thanks for—"

The door swung open, making the bells above it jingle. My heart sank. "Good morning," Timothy Ragsdale said. He wasn't smiling. Experience told me that wouldn't last long. His smiles were the kind you usually only see on feral predators—narrow, toothy, and backed by a snarl.

"Good morning, Mr. Ragsdale," I said. "I didn't expect you until tomorrow." A belated streak of fear shot through me. If he'd come earlier, and found me not at the door at precisely ten o'clock…

"I hold your monthly inspection at my discretion. You shouldn't get accustomed to a schedule you made up." There went the smile. He knew he held all the cards and he relished it.

"You're right," I said politely. "Please feel free to look around. I have to fill these augury requests."

"You don't think your inspection is more important?" *And my valuable time* went unsaid.

"I'm sorry, Mr. Ragsdale, but according to Article I, Section B, subsection 2, paragraphs iii-vi, augury requests made in person must be fulfilled before any other of the custodian's duties. I realize monthly inspections aren't written into the Accords, but I think mine is a fair interpretation. Of course, I'll bow to your understanding if you think otherwise."

Ragsdale's smile fell away, and I kept my face carefully neutral. This was the third inspection I'd had to endure, having been punished with a year's worth of close observation by the Board of Neutralities for violating the Accords, and it bode fair to be as excruciating as the other two. Ragsdale had been furious that I'd, as he saw it, betrayed his confidence in me, and he'd gone from being my staunch supporter to wanting to see me dismissed. I had no doubt that if he caught me deviating in even the smallest way from adherence to the Accords, he'd bring me up in front of a tribunal. Based on what the Board chairman, Laverne Stirlaugson, had said, he'd be successful. Politeness, and a scrupulous obedience to the Accords, were my only hope of survival. Fortunately, I knew the Accords well —probably better than Ragsdale did.

"Go ahead," Ragsdale said ungraciously. "I'll have a look at your records."

"Thanks, Mr. Ragsdale." I escaped into the oracle before I could say anything he could take as an insult. I felt slightly guilty at siccing him on Judy and her meticulously maintained records, but there wasn't anything I could do about it, given that I couldn't be in two places at once. Maybe she could tell him about the most recent catalogue we'd produced, finished just a few days ago. It was the most tedious procedure related to the oracle and I'd started thinking seriously about ways to speed it up.

By the time I finished the last augury—two more Nicolliens came in after the first set—it was nearly lunchtime, and Ragsdale and Judy weren't in the front of the store. I finished taking payment, normally Judy's job, and waved goodbye. Then I put the ledger away under the antique cash register and leaned against the counter, taking in slow, deep, calming breaths. Judy was no doubt keeping Ragsdale busy and out of my hair. I owed her one.

I headed back toward the office, trailing my fingers along the shelves. They came away dust-free, and I was grateful I'd dusted Saturday after closing, because I was sure Ragsdale would make an issue of dusty books. He'd tried to make an issue of cluttered books that weren't shelved upright with spines facing out, but I'd been able to cite section and paragraph about Abernathy's organizational structure, or lack thereof, and he'd backed off.

I heard Judy and Ragsdale talking as I neared the office. It didn't sound like they were fighting, which I took as a blessing. Ragsdale wasn't supposed to be inspecting anyone but me, but I was sure if Judy pissed him off, he'd turn that against me somehow.

Judy was sitting at the computer, with Ragsdale standing over her shoulder and peering at the screen like a nearsighted crow in his dark suit and receding hairline. "You authorized this database?" he said.

My heart sped up with nervous anticipation. "I did."

"You realize electronic organization systems are against the Accords?"

Judy's mouth fell open. I had no doubt he'd been nice and admiring, getting her to show off the system she was so justifiably proud of. "I'm afraid I don't know that citation," I said, and opened the bottom drawer of my desk to remove a fat sheaf of paper connected by three enormous metal rings. "Would you mind showing it to me?"

Ragsdale's smugness faded. "Excuse me?"

"I'm committed to obeying the Accords, Mr. Ragsdale. Now, I do know that in Article IV, Section D, subsection 2, it says custodians of Neutralities are responsible for organizing their records in the most efficient manner for their Neutrality. And as the Accords were written more than seventy years ago, they don't actually say anything for or against computers. If there's a passage that says organization must be in analog form, I haven't found it. So I'd be happy for you to point it out to me, and we'll change our systems."

"It's clearly implied," Ragsdale said.

"'Implied' isn't good enough, or so the Board tells me."

Ragsdale cleared his throat. "You're not allowing Ambrosites and Nicolliens to mingle on the premises, are you?" It was a weak shot.

"Of course not. The Board made that change, and I'm enforcing it." *Even if I think it's idiotic.* "Is there anything else I can show you?"

He cleared his throat again. "I'm satisfied. For now." He brushed past me and out the office door.

Judy opened her mouth. I held up a finger and walked to the door, peered around it, then stepped out of the office and followed Ragsdale to the front door. I didn't actually think he'd do anything to hurt the store, but I wasn't taking chances.

Once he was safely outside, I turned to Judy, who'd followed me, and said, "That was remarkably painless."

"Only because you have the whole damn Accords memorized," Judy said. Her cheeks were flushed and her eyes bright with anger. "I should have known he wasn't really interested."

"Just nine more inspections, and he'll be off our backs."

"I'm not sure I'll survive *one* more inspection."

I let out a long, slow breath. "Let's eat. I know it's early, but I could use some comfort food and my mom made meatloaf yesterday."

"I thought I hated meatloaf until I tried hers. Please say there's enough for two."

We sat in the break room and ate meatloaf in peaceful silence. Chunks of sun-dried tomato made little taste explosions in my mouth, rendering the need for some kind of condiment unnecessary. I swigged some Diet Coke and said, "Are you doing anything for the Fourth?"

"Father always invites a crowd for his annual fireworks display. We rent a pavilion at our neighborhood park. I'd invite you—"

"—but it would just make things awkward," I concluded. Judy's father, William Rasmussen, didn't like me any more than I liked him. I was mostly sure he'd given up on trying to get Judy installed as Abernathy's custodian, but not for lack of feeling I was unworthy.

"Sorry."

"It's okay. Olivia is doing a display of her own and we're going to that. Not that I'll appreciate it." Olivia and Rasmussen were both paper magi, capable of producing extraordinary illusions, and fireworks—or, rather, the illusion of fireworks—were something all paper magi learned to do early in their training. I had to take it on faith that they were amazing, as I had the ability to see through illusions.

Distantly, the bells over the door jingled. I pushed away the remnants of my meatloaf and sighed. "I'm never going to get to those mail-in auguries, am I?"

"It's not like they're going anywhere," Judy pointed out. I rolled my eyes and strode off into the stacks.

I did another three auguries before one o'clock, when the store went still and quiet again. I rolled out my shoulders and stretched. Doing auguries, communing with the oracle, always left me invigorated, but today I felt weary, probably thanks to my late start. An early bedtime was indicated.

"Helena?" Judy said, her voice muffled by the bookcases. "You need to look at this."

I headed toward the office only to meet her halfway there. She was holding one of the mail-in augury requests and wore a baffled expression. "I was sorting out the payments from the augury requests and I found this," she said, extending the envelope to me. It was dingy white and smudged with what appeared to be engine oil, and a vivid array of stamps canceled in several places told me it was a long way from home. I couldn't make out the words on the postmark, but the stamps all said MEXICO on them. Judy had slit the envelope lengthwise, and I extracted the folded paper from inside.

Like most augury requests that came by mail, it was folded in thirds; unlike most, it was handwritten, the writing shaky and pointed. I squinted at it. "It's in Spanish."

"I know," said Judy. "I've never seen one that wasn't written in English. Even the ones that come from China and Nepal are in English."

"*¿Cómo derrota a los tejedores?* I can read it, mostly, but I don't know this word, *tejedores.*"

"Google Translate is your friend," Judy said.

It took only a minute to open a browser window and type in the short sentence. Judy and I stared at the results, mystified. "'How do you defeat weavers?'" I read aloud. "What's that supposed to mean?"

"Maybe it's wrong about *tejedores,*" Judy said. "It could have another meaning."

I did a little more searching and discovered that depending on the dialect, *tejedor* could also mean "knitter," "schemer," or "pondskater," which I learned was a kind of insect. "Schemer makes the most sense," I said, "but I'm reluctant to take this translation into the oracle when I don't know for sure which meaning is correct."

"Don't you think the oracle understands other languages? Just because we always get those requests in English doesn't mean that's the only language it speaks. Or doesn't speak. You know what I mean."

"I do." I scribbled the first translation on the piece of paper below the line in Spanish and above the return address, then focused on the address written on the slip more closely. "Aren't Mexican addresses usually really long? This is just—" My mouth fell open. "Judy, this came from the Hernandes Node."

"So?"

"So last December the Board shut the Hernandes Node down because the Nicolliens and Ambrosites were so at odds violence was breaking out all the time. The custodian, Ana Ruiz—I met her at the Conference of Neutralities and she said she couldn't control them. There shouldn't be anyone there." I turned the envelope over to look at the return address, but like most augury requests, there wasn't one —people never wrote them on the envelope, just on the augury slip. And there was no name above the address inside. "This is weird on so many levels."

"So do the augury, and see what it says," Judy said.

Paper in hand, I walked out of the office and into the timeless peace of the oracle. The scent of lilacs again welcomed me, and I felt a little tension drain out of my shoulders. "I'm curious about this one," I said conversationally. I had no idea if the oracle was alive or not, but there had been times it had responded to my words as if it understood them, and I liked to pretend it understood me. "Do people only write in English as a courtesy to me, or is that something you need? If I were a wood magus like Jeremiah, I'd speak all sorts of languages, but even that has its limits. And the Hernandes Node...I wonder if Ana is still there. She had to go *somewhere*."

Ahead, electric blue light limned one of the bookcases. I walked faster, turned a corner, and found the augury, a book lying on its face under a pile of cookbooks of the world, glowing blue. I shifted the cookbooks and removed the book from the shelf. As I did, the blue glow faded, and it tingled with an electric pulse in my hands. I flipped open the cover. *Miguel Moreton*, it read—then the silver ink vanished, and the page went blank, displaying only the title and author printed neatly in black.

Confused, I shut the book and turned it over to look at the spine and front cover. *Textiles of South America*, it read in gold-embossed letters. I opened it again. No silver ink showing the name of the recipient and the price of the augury. The tingling was gone, leaving me with nothing but an oddly cold sensation where my skin touched the slick binding. "I don't understand," I said. "Is this the augury or not?"

Slowly, like a cloud crossing the sun, the light changed from blue to red. "No augury," I said. "But it was an augury, for a few minutes. I even saw the name, Miguel Moreton."

My voice was swallowed up by the books, which stood still and silent around me. "You could be a little more communicative," I said. "Did you change your mind?"

The world held its breath. I paced through the corridors, looking for I didn't know what. Eventually I ended up in the heart of the oracle, a place where four bookcases formed a square. The oracle had communicated with me before from that spot, and I hugged the maybe-augury to my chest and turned in a slow circle, looking for moving books or letters of light or anything like what I'd seen there before. Nothing.

"All right," I said. "No augury. I just hope you're not falling under the influence of another illusion. I never want to go through that again."

I set *Textiles* on the closest shelf and took two steps away before hesitating. "I think I'll take this with me," I said, retrieving it and holding it close again. "Just in case you change your mind."

Judy was waiting for me at the front counter when I emerged. Beyond her, outside the plate glass window with ABERNATHY'S stenciled on it, a couple of men loitered near the front door. The Ambrosites were queueing up for their turn, which started at two o'clock. "Well?" Judy said.

"No augury."

"Then what's that?" She pointed at the book.

"It was the augury, and Abernathy's changed its mind. Or something. I'm just going to...hang onto it for a while."

Judy shook her head. "I hate when weird things start happening around here. The last time, I was arrested."

"I'm sure it won't come to that."

"That's not as reassuring as you'd like it to be," Judy said, and opened the door to the Ambrosites.

2

I climbed out of Malcolm's cherry-red Mustang and shut the door behind me. "I'm just not sure I'm ready," I said for what felt like the hundredth time. I hoped I wasn't getting on Malcolm's nerves. I was getting on *my* nerves, that was certain.

"I understand," Malcolm said for what I knew was the hundredth time. He no longer sounded like he understood. He sounded like someone whose patience was being tried to the utmost. It made me feel selfish and petty. Moving into his apartment should be no big deal, really, so why was I turning it into a Broadway musical?

I stopped and turned, putting my arms around his waist and resting my cheek against his shoulder. "I'm sorry."

His arms went around my waist and drew me closer. "For what?"

"For being resistant to change. It's just—it's my first apartment, and that means something to me. But you mean even more. And it makes sense, if we're going to live together, that we both make compromises. Not just you."

"Me?"

"You're the one who gave up his shower and his own closet. I haven't given up anything except exclusive possession of the remote control." I took a deep breath, savoring the woody smell of his cologne. "Let's do it. Let's live in your apartment."

Malcolm let out a sigh. "Thank you," he said. "You won't regret it."

"I'd better not. I've never seen your apartment and I'm taking it on faith that it's nice."

Malcolm laughed and released me only to take hold of my hand. "You can decorate it any way you like. And I'll buy you a cabinet for your archaic DVD collection."

"You must really have wanted this, huh?"

"You have no idea. But I didn't want to pressure you."

We walked across the soft grass of the park toward the well-lit pavilion in the distance. The scent of freshly-mown grass wafted up with every step. "You didn't," I said. "You were very patient."

"It's a virtue I learned from dealing with my mother, who will, I'm afraid, want to throw us a housewarming party."

"That's...unexpectedly nice of her."

Malcolm made a derisive noise somewhere between a snort and a growl. "It will be an excuse for her to examine you and your suitability to be the partner of a Campbell. She's given up on me and Andria, but you're still an unknown quantity as far as she's concerned."

"I don't mind. So long as we're not actually living with her, I can endure whatever she throws at us. Besides, don't you think it's a positive sign? That she's coming to terms with our relationship?"

"You're so optimistic," Malcolm said, squeezing my hand. "I sincerely hope you're right. She is difficult, but she's still my mother."

We'd neared the pavilion and the crowd of people surrounding it, talking in low voices. Somebody's iPod was playing low, pulsing rhythm and blues that resonated with my bones and matched the beat of my heart. It wasn't what I'd normally associate with the Fourth of July, but wasn't jazz the quintessential American music form?

"Malcolm, Helena," said Derrick Tinsley, a stocky, dark-skinned man with a cheerful smile. He held out a couple of bottles of beer in our direction. Derrick was the bone magus of Malcolm's invader-fighting team and a good friend. "Been wondering when you'd get here."

"We're not too late?" Malcolm asked.

"No. Plenty of time." Derrick saluted me with his own beer. "Your friend is here already."

"Viv?" I looked around. "I see her." She was hard to miss, at 5'10" with bright crimson hair. She was chatting with someone I didn't know. "I'm going to go talk to her."

Malcolm kissed me. "I'll find you later."

It still left me breathless that he could kiss me in public, that we were finished hiding from the world. Not even three months before, the Accords had said I couldn't have a relationship with a member of one of the magical factions. I'd stood in front of the Board of Neutralities and convinced them to change that rule. Even the sanctions they'd imposed on me for breaking it couldn't keep me from feeling triumphant.

I wove through the crowd to Viv's side and said, "I think this makes you officially a Warden."

"That's what Pierce said, too," Viv said, nodding at her companion. Pierce was a tall, fat man who looked annoyed that I'd joined the conversation. I started to introduce myself, but he muttered something I couldn't make out and walked away toward the pavilion. Viv sagged dramatically and took a long pull on her beer.

"*Thank you* for rescuing me," she said in a low voice. "He just would not take a hint."

"He was hitting on you?"

"With the subtlety of a sledgehammer wielded by Captain Obvious."

"Doesn't he know you're with Jeremiah?"

"Of course he knows. He and about half the Wardens I meet seem to think Jeremiah being a former traitor means I deserve better."

"Is that why Jeremiah's not here?"

Viv nodded and took another drink. "Well, that and him not wanting to be the only Nicollien in a crowd of Ambrosites. Olivia invited him, but he still gets the cold shoulder from a lot of people and challenges from a handful of those. It's going to be months still until things are back to normal, assuming they ever get that way."

"Viv, he's done so much to fight the Mercy. That has to count for something."

"There are too many people who lost loved ones to the Mercy, one way or another. He makes an obvious target." Viv grinned. "Though most people won't challenge him. It only took a couple of duels to prove that was a really bad idea. I love dating such a badass fighter."

"He certainly looks like he'd be easy to take." Jeremiah didn't look like a badass fighter. He looked like a stereotypical computer geek. People tended to forget that a wood magus, a front line fighter against the invaders bent on destroying humanity, wasn't a pushover no matter how many nerdy T-shirts he owned. "Did you decide on a new place to live?"

"Almost. He wants it to be someplace overgrown, to surround us with weapons if the Mercy come after us."

"That reminds me. Malcolm and I are moving into his apartment."

Viv squealed. "Oh, sweetie, that's so exciting! When?"

"I don't know. We only just decided tonight. Is it bad that I'm nervous?"

"Not bad. Weird, maybe. You've been living together for a while now, so I don't see why this would make you nervous."

The pavilion lights dimmed, then went out entirely. Light from the distant street lamps kept the darkness from being complete. It turned us all into moving shadows of varying degrees of light and dark, with the gleam of teeth and eyes the only thing to mark us as living. Viv gripped my hand. "Now *this* makes me nervous. You're practically invisible."

"So are you," I said, though Viv's skin was paler than mine—even in the summer, she never tanned, just went through an endless cycle of burning and peeling if she wasn't careful. We stood in the darkness listening to the shuffling movement of our neighbors, casting about for the first sign of fireworks. I wondered where Malcolm was. Probably it was better to let him come to me; he was the one with experience in sneaking around under cover of darkness.

"Welcome," Olivia Quincy's voice rang out. "Keep your eyes on the skies, and if we get rousted, Malcolm Campbell will do the talking."

"What does she mean, rousted?" Viv whispered.

"I don't know," I whispered back. "I doubt we're supposed to have beer in this park. Maybe if someone sees the fireworks? Big ones that fly high are illegal."

"Then how does she keep them secret?"

"I don't know. It's all illusions."

"It's a localized effect," Malcolm said close beside me, making me jump. "None of the illusions are visible farther than one hundred feet from Quincy. But it is a complicated illusion, so there's always a chance for mistakes."

I heard a pop, and suddenly the sky was full of scarlet sparkles. "Those aren't illusions," I said. More fireworks, gold and blue and silver, followed the first.

"This is just warming up," Malcolm said in a low voice. "The background, as it were."

The next one burst as the others had done, purple and green specks filling the sky. "Purple rose," Malcolm murmured in my ear. I quashed a moment's self-pity as everyone around me oohed and aahed.

"I'm sorry you can't see this," Malcolm said. Beside me, Viv's face was turned to the sky, a look of delight touching her features.

"It's all right." More explosions filled the night air, and Malcolm told me what I was missing: a kite that soared with the light breeze, a tree dotted with red apples that fell like raindrops to brush our noses, an old-fashioned sailing ship that shot a cannon salute with a distant *pip pip* sound. I could hear that, and wondered what had caused it that wasn't an illusion.

In my pocket, my phone buzzed with an incoming text.

That was odd. I couldn't think of anyone who'd be texting me at this time of night on the Fourth of July. They'd all be at parties of their own. I dug my phone out and glanced at the screen. Lucia. I swore under my breath. If Lucia Pontarelli was texting me, it was probably important custodian business.

DID YOU GET AN AUGURY REQUEST FROM THE HERNANDES NODE?

Huh. IT CAME YESTERDAY, WHY?

"Is something wrong?" Malcolm said.

"I don't know yet." An explosion of gold and silver turned into twinkling violet dust. My phone remained silent. Apparently that was all Lucia wanted. So much for important.

As I was putting my phone away, it vibrated again. HERNANDES NODE TAKEN BY THE MERCY TWO DAYS AGO, Lucia wrote. ALL PERSONNEL KILLED.

I sucked in a startled breath. THOUGHT IT WAS SHUT DOWN.

A long pause. "Helena," Malcolm said.

"Just a minute."

Bzzt bzzt. I'LL COME BY IN THE MORNING. TOO LONG FOR TEXT.

I put my phone away. "Lucia had some bad news about the Hernandes Node. She'll tell me the rest tomorrow."

Malcolm and Viv both looked at me with some concern, their faces lit blue and red. By the sound of the cheering, it was the grand finale. I caught a glimpse of the mundane fireworks just as they faded away and the lights on the pavilion came up. Olivia stood some distance away, laughing and acknowledging thanks. Scraps of folded paper surrounded her like scattered snowfall—the sources of her fireworks illusions. Olivia was unusual in her heavy dependence on actual paper for her illusions. It was slower, I knew, but also permitted more elaborate illusions. I wondered what Rasmussen's fireworks looked like. Probably not as good as Olivia's.

"What's the Hernandes Node?" Viv said.

"It's in Mexico. It was overrun by the Mercy. But it was supposed to be empty." I sighed and took Malcolm's hand. "I don't know what to think. I'm going to stop worrying about it."

"That's good, because the city display will begin soon, and we will have a perfect view of it from here," Malcolm said.

I let him put his arms around me and snuggled into the warmth of his body. Somebody dimmed the pavilion lights again just as distant pops heralded the beginning of the second show. It wasn't as elaborate as Olivia's, obviously, but it was still beautiful—more beautiful to me, I thought with a twinge of disloyalty, since it had no illusory component. Even so, I couldn't keep my mind from drifting back to Lucia's texts. How could the node be overrun if there was no one in it to be run over? And who was Miguel Moreton, who would have received an augury if the oracle hadn't changed its mind? I filed those questions away for tomorrow. If anyone knew the answers, Lucia did.

———

THE MORNING DAWNED GRAY AND WET, PROMISING A STORM LATER THAT day. "When would you like to move?" Malcolm said over breakfast. "Not that I want to pressure you."

"Sunday, since neither of us has work. I can pack in the evenings. I have to say I'm starting to feel excited about this."

"I'm glad to hear it. I'll have the apartment cleaned before the weekend. I think the cleaning service has been going over it weekly, but given that it was unoccupied, who knows how thorough they've been."

"I'm not sure I need a cleaning service." I enjoyed cleaning, or at least found it therapeutic, and the idea of having my space invaded by strangers made me feel uncomfortable.

"It will free up your time. The apartment's quite a bit larger than this place. But if you don't like it—"

"No, it's fine." I didn't think I should make a fuss over something I'd never experienced. And maybe I'd grow to like it. "Can we take a look at it some night this week?"

"Of course. Tomorrow night?"

We kissed at the apartment door and I waved goodbye to Malcolm, whose car was parked behind the store. Then I trotted down the stairs and into my office, where a pile of mail already lay, sorted into two stacks. They'd all been slit neatly open. I dipped into one and found it contained a check drawn on some bank in Kentucky for $5000. One of the things Abernathy's never worried about was delinquent payments. Anyone failing to pay for an augury would never receive another one, no exceptions.

I set it down and picked up the other stack, the one containing augury requests, sorting through it for stamps from Mexico. Nothing but domestic mail today, which was unusual. I squared the stack on the table and let out a sigh. I hoped Lucia would come in soon. I needed to know what had happened to the Hernandes Node, and who Miguel Moreton was. Maybe Lucia knew something that would enlighten me as to the oracle's mysterious behavior.

Judy was sweeping up when I came through to the front of the store. "When did you get here?" I asked.

"8:45. I couldn't stand being home one more minute. Father's on the warpath again over these missing magi. He's convinced the Nicolliens need to be proactive in tracking them down. Never mind that it's been ten weeks and if they haven't found them by now, it's not going to happen."

"I can see why he'd be upset, though. Most of the missing magi in both factions held positions of responsibility. It would make sense that he'd want to know what kind of precautions he should take, either to prevent his organization from being compromised or filling those positions."

"I hate it when you're reasonable." Judy steered the broom around and brushed the tiny pile of dust into an industrial-sized dustpan. "You're up early, too."

"We've been talking about our moving plans. I want to see the place before I move in on Sunday."

"You've never been to his apartment?"

She made it sound like something shocking, and I blushed even though it was stupid. "It just never came up."

"The Cheltenham is seriously posh. I'm surprised you weren't even curious to the degree of spending a couple of hours there."

The implied *a couple of hours of sex* made me blush further. "I just... really like my apartment."

Judy shrugged and carried the broom and dustpan away. "Nothing wrong with that."

I managed to get three mail-in auguries done before ten o'clock, when I opened the door for the first Nicolliens. Before I could take the first augury slip, the door banged open again. "Davies," Lucia said in her usual brusque manner. "A word in private?"

I glanced at the Nicollien, who had the look of someone who wished he were anywhere but here, and judged he wouldn't make a fuss over the delay. "All right," I said, and led Lucia back to my office. Judy was there, entering receipts into our accounting software. She pushed back from the computer when we entered, eyeing us both suspiciously.

"Don't worry about leaving," Lucia said to Judy. "Davies will just tell you everything later—no sense you going anywhere. What was the augury request you got from the Hernandes Node?"

"I can't tell you that," I said. "Confidentiality."

Lucia rolled her eyes. "At her discretion, the custodian can reveal confidential information on behalf of a criminal investigation."

"Is that what this is?" I asked, startled. "I thought the Mercy overran the Hernandes Node—and what does that mean, anyway?"

Lucia sighed and leaned against the tan melamine desk. "I expect the two of you to keep quiet about this. We're trying to contain the situation for as long as possible, which I doubt will be more than a few days. The Hernandes Node was shut down on the first of the year, as per the Board's orders. But you can't just make a node the size of a Neutrality stop working. So there were a few people left there to maintain the system and slowly bring it to full shutdown. A few more people, enforcers, to keep the factions from using it illicitly. Everything was going according to plan until two weeks ago tomorrow, when the Board liaison lost touch with the node. She went to investigate—and nothing's been heard of her since."

"Was she killed?"

"Presumably. The Durango Node sent investigators last week, and they reported the node was occupied. Miguel Moreton—"

I gasped. "Something wrong?" Lucia asked.

"He's the one the augury was for. Except then it wasn't. Who is he?"

"And they say *I'm* cryptic," Lucia said wryly. "Moreton was the head of the Durango Node's team, the one that went to see what was up with the Hernandes Node. He was killed in the fighting Monday afternoon."

I exchanged glances with Judy. "What fighting?"

"Durango Node's magi took on the occupants of the Hernandes Node on Monday," Lucia said. "They had their asses handed to them by the enemy. A few escaped to confirm it was the Mercy who'd done it."

"But I don't understand. If they were in so much danger, why didn't they call instead of mailing the request?"

"The Hernandes Node is smack in the middle of nowhere," Lucia said. "I doubt telephones are something they've got in abundance. And the Durango Node wasn't supposed to attack, just monitor and collect intelligence. No word on whether they disobeyed orders, or were jumped, but if Moreton sent you an augury request, it's likely he meant to be around long enough to receive it."

I bit my lip nervously. "The question was 'how do you defeat weavers?' Except it was in Spanish, so that's the translation. I hope Google wasn't off too far."

"Weavers." Lucia rubbed the bridge of her nose. "That makes no sense."

"It could also be knitters, schemers, and pond insects," Judy said.

"That's not much more helpful. I haven't come across any of those in the last three months."

"Oh, and this—" I said, taking *Textiles of South America* off the filing cabinet where I'd left it, "was the augury. Except the name and price disappeared as I was looking at it. Maybe because Miguel Moreton was killed?"

"That's awfully convenient, that he'd die just as you were looking at it," Lucia said, but she took the book from me and glanced over it, flipping through a few pages. She read the augury request, which was stuck between two pages the way we always did with the mail-in ones. "Textiles. Weavers. Too bad I don't speak Spanish."

"You think it means something?"

"Davies, at this point I see meaning in *everything*. I'm about ready to start jumping to conclusions."

"Will the factions attack the Hernandes Node now?"

"If they can," Judy said. "Meche Garcia and Antonia Sanchez hate each other so much they'd rather fight each other than the invaders. Father says Meche challenged Sanchez personally and they've fought three duels in the last year. He and a few other Nicollien heads have petitioned the Archmagus to replace her as the Nicollien leader in Mexico."

"I don't know," Lucia said. "Their animosity certainly makes things more complicated. We also don't know how strong the Mercy is. A lot of magi disappeared after the worldwide attack on the steel magi, but whether that accounts for all of them—or if some of them are still hiding in plain sight—"

"You said your test had eliminated all the traitors," I said. The magi in collusion with the invaders had a neurological marker showing they were traitors, but it occurred naturally in about one in three people—including me—so Lucia had come up with a test to determine who was actually the enemy.

"Here, yes, but not every place is finished with the testing," Lucia said. "The point is, we have no idea how many magi are traitors, or how many of the Mercy might be involved in the taking of the Hernandes Node. With Mexican magery in turmoil, finding out the truth might prove more challenging than just sending in teams. Which I'm tempted to do."

"Can you do that? Interfere in some other node's business?"

Lucia shrugged. "It's a case of acting first and getting permission later. But I'm not convinced it would be the best course of action. I'm waiting to see what the Board instructs. They could very well tell me to send my people in, in which case I don't want to anticipate their orders. And I'm reluctant to send anyone into a situation where we don't know what to expect." She straightened and shook her head. "Weavers. I'll keep that in mind. Moreton was smart, if erratic, and he wouldn't have sent that request if it hadn't been exactly what he wanted to know."

"We're watching for any more augury requests from Mexico," I said. "I'll let you know if anything related shows up."

"Don't be careless," Lucia said, shaking an admonitory finger at me. "If Ragsdale takes exception to your behavior—"

"I can quote the Accords at him."

Lucia snorted and led the way back to the front door, where I could see one of the Gunther Node's little white vans parked in Abernathy's magically reserved parking space. "Just—be careful," she said. The door shut behind her.

I turned to face the waiting Nicolliens. "Thanks for your patience," I said, accepting the first slip. "I won't be long."

But as I searched the shelves for the woman's augury, I couldn't help thinking about Moreton's augury. If the oracle wouldn't provide an augury for a dead man, did that mean its predictive powers reached beyond the store? What else did it know? I never had figured out all the reasons it wouldn't give an augury. It wouldn't answer anything beginning with the word "who," wouldn't help anyone commit a crime, but there were sometimes questions that struck me as perfectly innocent that nevertheless elicited the red-tinged light of "no augury."

I found the book and checked inside the cover, just in case. Name and price were there in silver ink, and stayed clear and crisp all the way out of the oracle. The memory of seeing it fade away, as if the pages were absorbing it, wouldn't leave my mind.

3

I withdrew the augury request from its white envelope, unfolded it, and caught the photo that fell out of it. An infant with wisps of blond hair escaping from the elasticized bow around her head beamed out at me. On the back, in blue pencil, were the words *She looks just like you! We're planning a visit in October—can't wait to see you.*

"Is that your niece? She's adorable," Judy said, taking the photo from my hand. "Though I don't get those bows. It looks like her head is being strangled."

"It does not. It looks cute." I read the augury request: *Which preschool should we apply to?* "What I don't get is the craze for enrolling a five-month-old child in the right preschool. She's got more than two years before it's an issue."

"If it's a popular one, you want to get on the waiting list immediately. I'm surprised Cynthia didn't enroll her ten minutes after learning she was pregnant."

The augury was, oddly, *What to Expect When You're Expecting,* which struck me as being a little late to the game. But the oracle knew best, I assumed. "I hope this doesn't mean Cynthia's pregnant again," I said as I emerged from the stacks.

Judy wasn't there. A man in a lightweight summer jacket and a fedora stood by the counter, his weight resting on the balls of his feet as if he were poised to run. In the time it took me to say "Welcome to Abernathy's, can I help—" I realized who he was. Ross Dunlop. He'd murdered my boss, had tried to murder me and destroy the oracle. I turned to run, my hand going for my phone.

"Don't move," Dunlop said, and I turned around, fearing he was armed as he had been before. His hand was in one pocket of his jacket, which bulged enough to make me sure my guess was right. "I don't want to hurt you, but if you let anyone know I'm here…"

I laughed, a little hysterically. Where was Judy? Where was *Malcolm*, for that matter? He was usually home by this time. "That's a change for you. Last time I saw you, you wanted me dead."

"Things have changed. I have information for Lucia Pontarelli. You're going to give it to her."

"Me? Why can't you—"

"Don't be stupid. If I approach Lucia, she'll have me bound over for trial. If she doesn't just kill me on sight."

"Then what's so important that you're threatening me?"

Dunlop glanced quickly from left to right, looking for I didn't know what—witnesses, maybe? "Several Ambrosite nodes in Honduras have been destroyed. I'm guessing the Nicolliens have suffered similar losses. The enemy is on the move, and Lucia needs to be ready."

"Destroyed? Wouldn't we have heard about it?"

"Latin America is in chaos. With the fighting between Nicollien and Ambrosite in Mexico, and the presence of the enemy—"

"The Mercy."

"As if I care what their name is. It's about to boil over."

"What's in it for you?"

"I'm a killer. I'm not a traitor. I had a great life down south until this war between Wardens and the Mercy destroyed it." Dunlop shifted his hand in his pocket. "Tell Lucia. And don't bother trying to find me. I ward-stepped here and now I'm going to find somewhere else I can live, far away from the conflict."

His body shuddered, going zig-zag wobbly like an out-of-focus image on an old television screen. "Wait!" I shouted. If I could keep him here, maybe someone would arrive who could call Lucia for help. "How much have they taken over?"

"I don't know," Dunlop said. His voice was scratchy, fuzzy-sounding and distant. "But they're on the move." His body flattened, spread thin, then he disappeared, leaving behind the sound of static. I ran for the door and shut and locked it, not caring that it was still twenty minutes 'til six. My hands were shaking so badly I had to clasp them together to still them. He'd ward-stepped into the store. That meant Abernathy's wards were vulnerable. Anyone could get in. Well, any stone magus, but still—

I fumbled my phone out of my pocket and called Lucia, saying only that Dunlop had appeared with a message for her. It was cryptic, I knew, but it would also push my call to the front of whatever Lucia used to determine in what order she'd return messages. Then I called Sally Johnson, a stone magus I knew well, and asked her to come over and check the wards.

"Helena?" I heard Malcolm's voice in the distance. "Did you want to eat before going to the apartment?"

I ran through the bookcases as fast as I could manage without bumping into them and threw my arms around him, knocking him back a step. "What's wrong, love?" he said, bearing me up.

"Ross Dunlop just held me at gunpoint," I murmured into his suit coat.

"He did *what?*" Malcolm held me at arm's length, examining me. "He didn't hurt you?"

I shook my head. "He wanted me to give Lucia a message—he ward-stepped in here—why didn't the alarm keep him out?"

My phone rang. "It's Lucia," I said, and snuggled into his arms. "Hang on."

"Now that's a blast from the past I wish had stayed gone," Lucia said. "I take it he left."

"He's gone."

"I notice he didn't have the balls to confront me directly. All right, what did he say?"

I related the conversation, feeling Malcolm grow tenser as I spoke. When I finished, Lucia said, "We've had no word from Mexico, good or bad, since Monday. I haven't wanted to push because the Board warned me off, but I think what they want just became irrelevant. If the Mercy are destroying or capturing the smaller nodes, they're likely planning a push to the greater Neutralities."

"But how are they doing it? How can they be so powerful?"

"They aren't facing an organized resistance down there. It's past time the Neutralities got involved. I'll contact Velazquez and Sandoval and see what they've experienced."

"I still haven't received any augury requests from Mexico or Central America. None from Chile or Brazil, either, and we usually get half a dozen from each of them in a week, minimum."

"I'd like to tell you not to worry about it, but it worries me. Just— let me know if you get any more strange requests." She hung up.

I sagged in Malcolm's arms and felt him stroke my hair. "The alarms aren't set to go off if someone ward-steps in," he said. "One is semi-mundane, for preventing intruders from entering the traditional way, and the other is magical, to keep invaders out. I blame myself for not thinking of the stone wards as a weakness. I wish I'd been here."

"Me too." I drew in a deep, ragged breath and smiled at him. "Good thing we're moving, huh?"

"I suggest we get something to eat, then explore the possibilities of our new home," Malcolm said. "I hope you like it."

"I'm sure I will." Right now my safe little apartment over the store didn't feel very safe.

––––––

THE CHELTENHAM WAS LOCATED NEAR THE EDGE OF THE PEARL District, across the street from a park the size of a postage stamp. I noted a couple of scruffy-looking men wearing backpacks and carrying bright blue plastic drawstring bags and wondered if they were homeless. It was probably judgmental of me to think that, just based on their appearance. But I couldn't help wondering, if they were homeless, if that park was where they'd spend the night, and how comfortable it might be.

Malcolm drove into an underground parking garage and parked in a numbered spot. "There are two spots per apartment, so you'll have a parking space to yourself," he said. "Nice and warm and no more running from your door to the car in the rain."

"It's not that far a run." I saw a shadow pass Malcolm's face and concluded, too late, that he was trying to make this experience enticing. "But I won't miss scraping ice off the windshield."

The elevator and stairs were a short distance away, the concrete wall painted a bright scarlet that matched the risers on the stairs. Malcolm took the stairs rather than the elevator—well, I was used to that, he always said stairs were faster over short distances. The metal door at the top of the short flight was also red. It made me think of kindergarten—an industrial neighborhood kindergarten, possibly run by women with iron-hard hairstyles and no sense of humor.

Beyond the door, though, was a foyer done in warm, welcoming colors, maroon and sage and goldenrod. A wall of glass with a glass double door gave a view of a wide walkway lined with planters, all of which were overflowing with greenery, those fat-leaved shrubs with green and yellow mottled leaves. The tiny park was visible at the end of the walk, across the street.

A second wall of glass defined the other side of the foyer. Malcolm held that glass door for me, and I entered a long, narrow room decorated in the same colors as the foyer. A tall desk of warm, dark wood faced the door, and a man dressed all in black—suit, shirt, tie, and shoes—hurried out from behind it to greet us. He looked like a maître-d who'd been pressed into service for a funeral.

"Mr. Campbell," he said, "welcome home." He had a faint Australian accent that struck me as out of place, but what did I know about luxury apartment concierges?

"Mr. Clark," Malcolm said, sounding at his most formal. "This is Helena Davies. We'll be moving in on Sunday."

Clark inclined his head to me, and I had to resist the urge to curtsey. "Ms. Davies, it's a pleasure. Mr. Campbell, should I arrange for movers?"

"I think we'll be all right," Malcolm said, "thank you."

"As always, please let me know if there's anything you need." Clark nodded again and returned to his position behind the desk. I followed Malcolm to a bank of three elevators, one of which slid open when he pressed the call button. The walls of the elevator were covered with a strange clear coating, in which were embedded thousands of clear blue bubbles, like someone had captured sea foam and compressed it. It fascinated me, and I touched it, half expecting to feel the same tingle I felt from an active augury. But it was smooth, glasslike, and I withdrew my hand, feeling sheepish.

The doors slid open on a hallway paneled in light cedar, the smell of which was overlain by a more flowery, clean scent. The two smells mingled pleasantly, which was a surprise. The low-pile maroon carpet gave the hall a warm, friendly appearance. It had the same high-end-hotel feeling the Grandison, where they'd held the Conference of Neutralities, had had, with half-glass wall sconces shedding a clear light over the extent of the hall.

Malcolm took my hand and we walked down the hall, past two doors, one on either side but not directly facing each other. I thought that might feel more private, if you weren't confronted by someone else's door every time you stepped outside. Or maybe that was just how the apartments were arranged.

The door we stopped at was numbered 406, and Malcolm opened it without producing a key. As a steel magus, ordinary locks meant nothing to him, but I wondered how I was supposed to get in. "I have a key for you, and we'll attune you to the security system before we go," Malcolm said as if reading my mind. Well, it was probably an obvious question.

A short hall with an elaborate light fixture that wasn't quite a chandelier, its curved bronze rods intersecting in mysterious ways, opened on a living room whose vaulted ceiling seemed too high for an apartment building. A wall of windows illuminated the space brightly, the gauzy drapes drawn back so no ray was prevented from striking the brown leather armchairs and Scandinavian-inspired square-framed sofas. I walked across the hardwood floor to lay a hand on the back of one of those sofas, upholstered in a cream-colored fabric that looked like tightly woven burlap, though the surface wasn't as rough and uneven as burlap would be. It was, in fact, unexpectedly soft, like goose down. Someone had artfully arranged chocolate-colored throw pillows on the sofas, and a plush rug matching the pillows made a nice island in the middle of all that wood.

"DVD player and cabinet here," Malcolm said, indicating a glass-fronted cabinet beneath the giant flat-screen TV. A freestanding fireplace defined an imaginary fourth wall beyond the armchairs. I sank down on the square leather ottoman in front of the fireplace and tried to imagine how it would feel to snuggle up in front of it on some cold November night. Pretty good, probably.

Malcolm took me through the dining area, with a table long enough to seat eight—who did he think we would be entertaining?—made of a reclaimed slab of oak stained dark so all the knots stood out in stark relief. Ranks of straight-backed chairs lined its sides, and tall glass vases filled with river pebbles and blades of grass like green spears stood at either end.

A square opening to the left of the table turned out to lead to the kitchen, where I had to stop and stare. My mother would have appreciated it. I was just intimidated. Two ovens, a six-burner glass-topped range, a stainless steel refrigerator you could hide a body in, and more glass-fronted cabinets, behind which I could see white bowls and plates and plenty of tumblers and stemware. "Malcolm," I said.

"I know," he said. "I'll show you how to use the important things, but don't worry, I don't expect you to suddenly know how to cook." He put his arm around me and squeezed gently. "Just be careful what buttons you push."

"Why?"

"Some things are connected to the security features, not to the kitchenware." He steered me to stand in front of the ovens and twisted one of the dizzying array of dials. The drawer beneath the oven slid open, revealing an assortment of handguns, each in its designated spot.

I gasped, then laughed. "Just how *Mr. and Mrs. Smith* is this apartment?"

"More than I'd like to admit. I confess, I like gadgets, and I indulge that preference here. None of it can hurt you, it's just that you won't find much need for it. I hope. I'll show you what you need to steer clear of, and we'll get your phone set up to control the climate and the lights."

"I'm starting to feel nervous."

Malcolm turned me to face him. "You have nothing to fear here," he said, his voice low and comforting. "This place has the very best security my company has to offer. It's true, I occasionally bring work home with me, but I guarantee you you're in no danger."

"I know," I said, and hugged him. "Show me the bedroom?"

The bedroom was *amazing*. Bamboo screens lined the walls, their translucent paper glowing in the late afternoon light. The king-size bed was piled high with pillows in seafoam green and white, the creamy pale carpet felt like stepping on a thick pad of moss, and a second television hung on the wall so two people could cuddle up on the bed and watch movies together. A sliding Japanese panel revealed the bathroom, with two round stone basins on the granite counter, a glass-walled shower stall, and a garden tub so deep there were steps going up to it. I thought of my beautiful little bathroom and felt only a mild twinge of guilt at letting the memory slip away. "No wonder you wanted us to live here," I breathed. "I've never seen anything so luxurious in my life."

"Don't think I resented—"

"Of course not. Home is wherever we are together. But we won't be stumbling over each other in this bathroom."

Malcolm put his arms around me and kissed the top of my head. "So, you like it?"

I suppressed my reservations about the kitchen. "I do. I can't wait to move in."

"I thought we might bring a load or two over before Sunday.

There's really not much to move. Mostly clothes." Malcolm turned me around in his arms. "Let me show you the closets."

I put my arms around his neck and pulled him down for a kiss. "Why don't you show me the bed instead."

He smiled. "I might have guessed you'd lured me up here for carnal purposes."

"Well, that bed *is* awfully nice. We should see how comfortable it is."

His hands went to the hem of my shirt. "I suppose my assurances mean nothing."

"You haven't slept here in three months. You might have forgotten."

I wriggled, helping him remove my shirt, then kissed him again, a long, slow, satisfying kiss. Malcolm shrugged out of his suit coat and threw it at the empty tub, yanking at his tie while I began unbuttoning his shirt.

In the distance, the door opened. "Hello? Are you here, Malcolm?"

Malcolm closed his eyes and cursed under his breath. I snatched my shirt and tugged it back over my head. "Who is it?" I whispered.

"Andria," Malcolm said. "I never did reattune the door to exclude her." He buttoned his shirt, but left the top button undone and the tie off. "I think she stayed out of my way to ensure I wouldn't."

"Malcolm? Clark said you'd come in." Andria's voice was high-pitched, like the twitter of a canary. I heard footsteps tapping across the wood floor. I quickly checked my reflection in the long mirror and finger-combed my hair, not that it would do much good. I quashed irrational feelings of jealousy and reminded myself that Malcolm had dumped her, so it didn't matter if she was pretty and well-groomed.

"I'll have to have a word with Mr. Clark about telling people my business," Malcolm murmured, then took my hand and led me out of the bathroom, through the bedroom, and into the short hall leading to the living room just as Andria appeared at the far end. She startled and put a theatrical hand to her lips. "I believe I've asked you not to enter my home uninvited," Malcolm said coolly.

"Now, Malcolm, don't be so stuffy," Andria said. Her long dark hair was pulled back from the perfect oval of her face, accentuating her fine cheekbones and elegant nose. Her smile was perfectly pleasant, but she only glanced briefly at me before turning her attention back to Malcolm. "Your mother has been trying to reach you."

"I know. I've been busy." Malcolm drew me forward, keeping a tight grip on my hand. "Helena, this is my cousin Andria Lemaire. Andria, Helena Davies."

The big eyes widened. "Malcolm's girlfriend! I was beginning to wonder if you were mythical. Really, Malcolm, why have you kept her such a secret? *Tante* Madeleine has good reason to be upset with you."

"Mother is always upset with me. It's her default state. Did you have a message from her? I know she's capable of leaving voice mail, so I'm not sure why you felt you needed to play go-between."

Andria took a few steps and put her hand lightly on Malcolm's arm. "Because now you can't pretend you didn't get it," she said, laughing in that trilling way I was starting to find annoying. "*Tante* Madeleine is hosting a dinner party on Sunday, and she insists you be there—oh, and of course you, too, Helena. Everyone will want to meet *you*."

Malcolm moved his arm away from her grip. "Thank you for the notice. We may attend, other concerns permitting."

"You can't possibly have anything more important than a family party going on. Even Ewan will be there. Stop being so surly."

"I am *not*—" Malcolm began, then visibly calmed himself. "If Ewan is coming all the way from Seattle, of course I'll want to be there. Now, if you don't mind..." He gestured in the direction of the front door.

Andria's gaze flicked over me again. Then she covered her mouth with one hand and giggled. "Oh, of *course*," she said, her trilling voice heavy with meaning. "I am *so* sorry I interrupted your... I'll just excuse myself."

My face had to be flaming red. Malcolm appeared unmoved. "Actually, there is one thing I want to do before you leave," he said, releasing me to take Andria's shoulder and steer her back to the front door. On this side, there was a complicated panel with a touch screen and a blinking green light next to the frame. Malcolm took Andria's right hand, not very gently, forced it open and pressed it against the screen. More green lights started winking. Ignoring Andria's protests, Malcolm pressed a series of numbers in the keypad, then hit Enter. The lights all went off. Malcolm released Andria, who pulled away indignantly.

"Who the hell do you think you are, manhandling me like that?" she demanded. The canary twitter had turned into a seagull's shrill croak.

"The owner of this apartment," Malcolm said, "and someone who doesn't like that you feel entitled to walk in here whenever you feel like it. The key, please."

He held out his hand. I thought Andria was about to claim she didn't have it on her, which was a total lie. But after a few seconds' hesitation, she dug a plain steel key from somewhere inside her purse and slapped it into his palm. "The backup key I'm sure you made, too," Malcolm said. Andria glared at him, and the two of them fought a silent battle for nearly a minute before she finally rolled her eyes and produced a second key, this one brass. "Thank you," Malcolm said. "Now, if you'll excuse us...?"

Massaging her right palm as if he'd slapped it, Andria turned and strode off down the hall in the direction of the elevators. Malcolm shut the door behind her and leaned against it, pressing his forehead against the smooth metal—it was metal?—of the door.

"I apologize," he said. "She meant to make you uncomfortable."

"She nearly succeeded," I said. "Is she always like that?"

"Often, yes. When she isn't conscious of putting people on edge, she's actually pleasant. She gets a thrill out of angering people while she remains calm. It can be interesting to watch her interact with my mother, so long as you aren't drawn into the conflict."

"I don't want to be. You know I don't mind going to dinner with your family. I have to meet them sometime."

Malcolm sighed. "I've been reluctant to introduce you. I'm afraid you'll think less of me once you've met them."

"Malcolm, I would never do that." I put my hand on his. "I suppose I should be attuned to the apartment. Is that like what you've done with Abernathy's back door?"

"Yes. Put your hand flat on the screen."

He did something mysterious with the keypad again, and all the lights pulsed green, then went back to a single blinking light. "The security system knows you belong here now, and will let you in. The lock is just a deterrent to casual intruders. Not that Mr. Clark would let anyone like that past the front door."

"Is that why there's a regular key instead of, I don't know, a palm lock or retina scan or something on the front door?"

Malcolm laughed. "The wards and attunement are far more effective even than technology. The key is symbolic. Well, not *just* symbolic, because it's a working key, but you understand what I mean."

He handed me the steel key, hesitantly, as if afraid I might reject it on the basis that it had been Andria's, but I took it confidently and kissed him. I'd meant it to be light and affectionate, but his arm went around my waist, and it became something deeper, more serious. I inhaled the wonderful woody smell of him and realized the same scent, much fainter, filled the entire apartment. This was his space, and he was as secure in it as I was in mine.

I let out a shaky laugh when we broke apart and said, "I thought Andria had ruined the mood, but I was totally wrong."

Malcolm traced the line of my eyebrow and kissed me again. "I'm glad you think so," he said. "Let's find out how comfortable that bed is for two."

4

Three familiars were parked outside when I came downstairs the next morning. All of them watched me through the plate glass window with ABERNATHY'S stenciled on it with identical looks of avid hunger. At least, I assumed they were identical; one of the familiars didn't have a face. Its body strained at its leash, though, and I heard a high-pitched whine coming from one of them. I shuddered and turned my back on them. Having been attacked by familiars who'd broken their bindings, I wasn't confident in the Nicolliens' ability to keep them in check, even leashed.

"I wish they'd destroy their familiars," Judy said, watching the three monsters through narrowed eyes. "The risk is just too great."

"Your father could make it an order," I said.

Judy shook her head. "He's not convinced they're any danger. I think, if the intelligent invaders can control them, they can turn familiars against us."

"But there's no evidence they can do that. Just speculation."

"I would have thought you'd be the first to call for extermination."

"Just because they scare me is no reason to act hastily. They're still useful in the Long War." I remembered my conversation with the invader that had worn a human as a suit, and added, "At the very least, they should be investigating the possibility that familiars might prove a weakness of the enemy."

Judy looked intrigued. "How?"

"I don't know. The one I spoke to said the invaders we fight are about as closely related to them as chimpanzees are to us. Couldn't studying the familiars, I don't know, reveal weaknesses they have in common with the intelligent ones?"

"That makes sense. I bet you're right, and there are Nicolliens doing that right now."

"Or someone at the Gunther Node. It sounds like the sort of thing Darius Wallach would be all over."

Judy picked up the wide-headed broom and headed off into the stacks. "I'll ask Father. If it turns out no one else has thought of that, he should know about the possibility. Though it makes too much sense for you to be the only one who came up with it."

I tidied up behind the cash register, then let the waiting Nicolliens in. If familiars proved to have some weakness they shared with their more intelligent, more terrifying brothers, I'd let them snarl at me as much as they liked.

The morning was uneventful. The mail arrived with no letters from Central or South America, which left me downhearted as well as fearful. Surely the Mercy couldn't have taken over an entire continent? The twenty-one Neutralities in South America had implemented the Board's directive to segregate the factions with no strife at all, so they should be able to put up a unified defense if the Mercy attacked, unlike the beleaguered Hernandes Node. But that assumed they weren't outnumbered or outgunned. Nobody knew the true strength or numbers of the Mercy. They might well be in a position to defeat node after node until they swept the length of South America.

Just after noon, Viv pushed open the door, followed closely by Jeremiah. "We brought lunch!" Viv said, holding up bags that smelled deliciously of spicy meat and cilantro.

"That smells divine," I said. "How are you off so early?"

"I swapped with someone who's going to a wedding this afternoon." Viv put her bags on the counter. "And it's such a pretty day, I convinced Jeremiah to join me for an indoor picnic."

"But I draw the line at sitting on the floor," Jeremiah said with his usual brilliant smile. Today's T-shirt had a picture of a malevolent eye and the words MORDOR FUN RUN in blocky letters below it. "So if you don't mind eating at the counter..."

Judy emerged from the stacks, her eyes wide. "Café Panama," she said. "My favorite."

"Fish street tacos," Viv said. Judy fell on the bag with a cry of exultation.

Food distributed, we stood around eating in happy silence. I leaned against the wall and took another bite of my sweet pork burrito. It was hard to maintain my unease over the missing South American augury requests when I had good food and good friends to share it with. The air was cool and smelled of freshly mown grass, only a little odd in this old store, sunlight flowed through the windows, and I was going to move into a luxury apartment in two days. I felt more relaxed than I had all week.

The door opened, making the bells jingle. Hastily I put my plate down and wiped my mouth. "Can I help you?" I said.

The woman eyed our impromptu party with annoyance. "I'm here for an augury," she said, waving a slip of paper in my direction. Her eyes fell on Jeremiah, and narrowed. "Jeremiah," she said.

"Lydia," Jeremiah replied politely. "How are you?"

Lydia's lips curved in a silent snarl. Ignoring him, she advanced on me. "Make it quick," she said. "I don't like the company."

"Right away," I said, forestalling the comment Judy was about to make, which I was sure would be something relating to the wisdom of being polite to the custodian. I just wanted to get the woman out of the store as quickly as possible. Jeremiah wouldn't provoke her, but I'd seen enough people aggress on him to know his behavior didn't always matter.

Safely inside the oracle, I unfolded her request. *How do I avenge my brother?* It gave me chills, though I didn't know why. The request, combined with her reaction to Jeremiah, made me feel as if something serious was about to happen in Abernathy's. I hurried through the bookcases, looking for the blue glow, feeling propelled by some unnamed urgency.

I had to climb the shelves to reach Lydia's augury, which was large enough to require both hands in getting it down. *Atlas of the World,* its blue cloth binding said, and half the back cover was missing, cut off vertically as neatly as if a razor had done it. Clutching it in both hands, I ran for the exit.

I emerged to the sound of shouting. "—think you have *any* business associating with us?" Lydia shouted. "You should have had the decency to run!"

"That's not who I am anymore, Lydia," Jeremiah said. He sounded as calm as Lydia was furious. I came out from among the bookcases to see the two of them facing each other down. Jeremiah had put Viv behind him, and Judy stood next to the cash register, holding her phone as if she wasn't sure who to call.

"You deny having betrayed us?" Lydia's voice went low, but was every bit as furious as before.

"I don't deny anything," Jeremiah said. "I chose the wrong path. I'm just grateful I realized my mistake before I did anything truly unforgivable."

"You think so? Who the hell are you, to decide what's forgivable and what isn't?"

"Lydia. I had nothing to do with Bryce's death—"

"*Don't speak his name!*" Lydia screamed. In a flash, two long knives were in her hands. Viv gasped. Judy began speaking into her phone in a low, urgent voice. I hoped she was calling Lucia. I hoped Lucia would miraculously break her no-answering-phones policy and send help immediately.

"He died because of damned traitors like you!" Lydia went on. "You think there's *anything* you can do to make up for it?"

"Bryce was my friend—"

Lydia screamed, a long, wordless sound, and leapt at Jeremiah. Quicker than I could follow, Jeremiah gestured, and suddenly he held a long wooden staff, carved all over with runic designs. It caught both blades and shoved them up and to the side, then whipped around to catch Lydia hard in the side. Air whooshed from her lungs, and she took a step back, out of his reach. "Don't do this," Jeremiah said.

His calm tone enraged her. Once again, she came at him, knives flashing, and Jeremiah deflected the first blow and dodged the second. Viv, far too close to the fight for my comfort, stood still as if she were frozen in place. Probably she feared being a distraction. Knives and staff danced together, an intricate weaving of wood and steel. Lydia got in a lucky blow, and Viv drew in a pained breath as a thin line of blood sprang up on Jeremiah's cheek. Jeremiah blotted it with the back of his hand. "You need to back off, Lydia," he said. "Let's end this."

Lydia grinned savagely. "Yes, let's," she said, and thrust once again for his chest. Jeremiah's expression went flat, emotionless. He whirled around, striking her elbow fast and hard, and Lydia cried out and dropped one of her knives. Without stopping, Jeremiah scythed the woman's legs out from under her, making her fall heavily to the linoleum floor. Before she could recover, he thrust the end of the staff at her throat. It sprang to life, small, flexible branches shooting out from the tip to entangle her neck. Lydia gasped and clawed at them, her face going red with the effort to breathe. Jeremiah stood over her, still expressionless.

"Jeremiah," I said, barely audible even to myself. He either didn't hear me, or ignored me, just stood there watching his victim struggle.

Viv stepped forward. "Don't," she said, putting a hand on his arm. He jerked, startled, then looked at Viv. "Let her go," Viv added.

Jeremiah glanced down at Lydia. He let out a deep breath, then withdrew the staff. The little branches retracted, leaving behind red lines on Lydia's skin. "Sorry," he said, though I wasn't sure who he was addressing. He spun the staff in both hands, making it whir through the air and then vanish. "I could have killed you," he told Lydia, "and maybe it means nothing to you that I didn't. But Bryce was my friend, and I wouldn't have had anything to do with the foul magic that killed all those steel magi even if I'd been asked to. Believe that, or not. Just don't come after me again. And don't even think about threatening Viv."

Lydia pushed herself up on her elbows, breathing heavily. "Don't think this settles anything between us," she rasped. Nobody moved to help her as she got to her feet, collected her knives, and staggered out of the store, leaving behind her augury.

Nobody moved in the silence she left behind. The cheerful tones of the "Funeral March" startled all of us out of our paralysis. Judy answered her phone. "It's all right, she's gone," she said. "No, he didn't —everyone's fine—you don't really think that, do you?" A long pause in which I could hear the tinny, distant sound of Lucia's voice. "Unless you're going to have bodyguards trail Jeremiah, I don't see how that would help," Judy said. "All right. No, it's really all right. Thanks." She hung up. "Lucia wants to put enforcers in the store. I told her that would be pointless, since Jeremiah's almost never here."

"I apologize," Jeremiah said.

"For what?" said Viv. "It's not your fault people can't get past what you've done. What you're trying to make amends for."

"And it's not like you started the fight," I said. "Didn't you say yourself that you weren't going to hide, no matter how much antagonism you faced? This will pass."

"Malcolm still has Wardens challenging him over the death of Amber Guittard," Jeremiah said. "It's been almost a year since that happened. How much worse is what I've done?"

"One or two in the last month. That's not a lot." But I didn't sound very convincing.

"Maybe I need to leave, let this blow over," Jeremiah said. "But I feel I can still do so much more good here."

"And I don't feel like losing my job," Viv said. "You'd better not be about to tell me you'd leave me," she warned him when he opened his mouth. He shut it immediately.

I retrieved my burrito, which was still warm. "Don't go. You're not a coward and you aren't guilty of half the things people accuse you of. And we need what you know about the Mercy."

"I think I've told Lucia everything I remember. I wish I knew why

South America has gone silent. I was never involved in the Mercy's larger plans, just my small part in them."

Judy stuffed half of one of her tiny tacos into her mouth. "That's still more than enough," she said when she finished chewing. "And you identified so many other traitors. Who knows, maybe we just haven't asked the right questions yet to unlock more secrets."

Jeremiah shrugged. "I'll stay," he said, "but I won't come here during the day anymore. Just in case."

"But you shouldn't—"

Jeremiah shushed Viv. "It's a sensible precaution, even if it shouldn't be necessary. I don't mind."

Viv looked mulish. I said, "Thank you. I appreciate it. But if you need an augury, don't let them stop you coming in."

"It's just the way it has to be," Jeremiah said.

We finished our lunch in silence, with no other people coming into the store, then cleared away the mess and said goodbye to Viv and Jeremiah. Watching them walk away, Judy said, "I would never have bet on them lasting more than three weeks."

"Why not?" I felt defensive on Viv's behalf, though Judy's comment hadn't sounded judgmental.

"Differences like theirs don't make for a long-term relationship. They ought to drive each other crazy. But they don't. I wish I knew why."

The wistful tone of her voice made me feel awkward, like I'd stumbled into a conversation she was having with someone else. "I guess who they are underneath all that is what keeps them together. They're both fiercely loyal, they both believe in being open with each other...things like that."

"I guess." Judy straightened and turned away from the window. "We've got thirty minutes before the Ambrosites start showing up. I'm going to enter receipts. That ought to count as my good deed for the day."

"You get paid to enter receipts. It's not like you're doing it out of the kindness of your heart."

"I don't think I get paid enough for that. When am I eligible for a raise?"

I should have done more mail-in auguries, but instead I spent the time until two o'clock flipping through Lydia's abandoned augury. Should I hang onto it for her? The title page still read, in silver ink, *Lydia Harrison, $350.* I didn't know what the correlation between importance of question and price of an augury was, but I did know the really vital ones, like ones for locating a missing child, were handed out for free. So I guessed, if someone had a big question like how to avenge a dead brother, and the price wasn't too steep, it was either easy to interpret or the oracle was taking pity on the recipient. I looked at the brightly colored maps and wondered what they might mean to Lydia. To me, they were nothing.

I flipped through the pages to the first map of South America. I only knew the locations of a few of the Neutralities there, but the ones I knew weren't scattered evenly throughout the continent. I idly plotted them out with my fingers: Espinoza, on the Chilean coastline; Rojas, in tiny Uruguay; Mendoza, in Peru. Then, farther north, Velasquez in Honduras, Sandoval in Nicaragua, and the lost Hernandes Node, in Mexico. My world history teacher, Mrs. Fox, would be so proud of my growing geographical knowledge.

I turned back a few pages to the map of Asia. I knew even fewer of these Neutralities than I did the South American ones, but then there were more to know in that vast continent. Lucia said there were probably more nodes big enough to be Neutralities than we were aware of, given how uninhabitable many parts of Asia were. If the Mercy managed to take them over, we might never find out about it.

My finger hovered over the Pondicherry node, which I'd originally remembered because the name didn't sound at all Indian. Its custodian, Marya Prajapati, was a regular user of the oracle...so why couldn't I remember the last time I'd received a request from her?

I hurried into the office. "Can you look up Marya Prajapati and tell me the last time she asked for an augury?"

A few deft keystrokes brought up the customer database. "Prajapati...looks like it was two weeks ago," Judy said. "That's long, for her."

"Maybe it's nothing."

"Or maybe the Mercy have struck again."

"I'll tell Lucia." I got out my phone and scrolled through my contacts. "Though I don't know what she'll do if there *is* a problem."

Having left my message, I strolled back to the front of the store. A couple of Ambrosites were chatting by the front door, but I decided not to let them in early. If Ragsdale found out about it, he'd have my head for displaying partiality, even though I was really only displaying impatience.

My phone rang. "Prajapati isn't picking up on her private line," Lucia said. "I wish Neutralities weren't so damned isolationist. If there's a problem in Pondicherry, we all ought to know about it."

"Is there someone else you can call?"

"Chowdhury at Devarakonda, but it's four in the morning there, and if I wake him for what turns out to be nothing...I'll call in a couple of hours. It won't make that much difference—and let's hope those aren't famous last words." She hung up unceremoniously.

I put my phone away and walked to the door to let the Ambrosites in. As soon as I finished with these auguries, I was going to go through the database to see if any other Neutralities had gone suddenly silent. I prayed my suspicion was wrong.

5

I sat on the end of the bed and watched Malcolm hammer a nail off to one side of the flat screen TV. The bed was taller than mine, and soft, but solid, letting me sink a few inches into it before supporting my weight. I loved the seafoam green of the duvet cover and how it coordinated with the pale dusty gold of the walls. "Should you really be putting holes in the wall?"

"It's our apartment, love, we can do what we like," Malcolm said, setting aside the hammer to pick up the framed print of a samurai warrior I'd brought from the study in my old apartment. "And someday, when we decide to redecorate, there will be spackle." He hung the warrior in one smooth action and stepped down from the short stool. "Even?"

I crawled back toward the pillows, centering myself, and gave the picture a considering eye. "Even. I don't know how you do it."

"Luck, I think. It's certainly not magic." Malcolm scooted toward me and reclined on the many pillows, his arms behind his head. "It's like they were made to go there."

"I think it's a good omen." The warrior and his companion, a lovely geisha, now hung on either side of the TV, a perfect complement to the Asian décor of the bedroom, with its bamboo screens and faux paper lanterns. I lay back and looked up at the distant ceiling. It wasn't real yet, that this was my bedroom, though the prints helped. I wondered how long it would take before I stopped feeling like this was just an elaborate, lengthy sleepover.

Malcolm rolled over on his side and put his hand on my hip. "That took much less time than I'd thought. You travel light."

"Well, your kitchen is already fully stocked, so we didn't have to pack the dishes." It had been an unexpected pang, leaving behind the things my mother and I had bought for my first kitchen. Even if I didn't know how to cook.

"That reminds me. I have a gift for you." Malcolm rolled off the bed and left the room. I sat up and waited for him to return with a wrapped package, book-shaped, with a big red bow. "Keep in mind that I have no expectations of you," he said, handing it to me.

"You're making me nervous." I tore off the wrapping paper and stuck the bow to his head, making him laugh. I held the thing at arm's length. "A cookbook."

"You're always talking about how you should learn to cook," Malcolm said. "As I said, this isn't my subtle way of suggesting you do so. Just an assistant if you decide you want to."

"*How to Boil Water.* Malcolm, do you have any faith in me at all?" But I laughed and flipped through it. "This looks...pretty good, actually."

He let out an exaggeratedly relieved breath. "I was afraid you'd be offended."

"Why is everyone so sure I'll be upset if it's suggested I learn to cook? Thanks, Malcolm." I kissed him lightly. "And now I'm going to shower. I feel sweaty after hauling all those loads. You can join me if you want."

Malcolm smiled wickedly. "You're going to *love* the shower. And everything that comes after it."

———

CLEAN, DRESSED, AND THOROUGHLY RELAXED, I PERCHED ON ONE OF

the kitchen stools at the central island while Malcolm made ham and cheese sandwiches. I flipped idly through the pages of the cookbook, making note of recipes that looked interesting. "I'll have to go to the store tomorrow after work," I said. "Maybe we shouldn't count on me making food right away. We could be eating awfully late."

"No worries," Malcolm said, handing me a plate. "Just make a shopping list and Mr. Clark will send someone. It will be purchased and put away before you come home."

"Wow." For some reason that struck me as far more decadent than anything else in this apartment, including the bidet. "I just...wow. That's really nice."

"It's part of the service. The cleaners come on Friday morning and the deep cleaning happens on the fourth Thursday of every month."

"I've never had a cleaning service before."

"Ours is a very casual thing. My mother has a live-in maid and cook. That is, a maid and a cook, two different people."

"She has *room* for that?"

"She lives in the penthouse apartment. It's two stories tall and has four bedrooms and two sitting rooms, in addition to a full dining room, an entertainment room, a den, and I've forgotten how many bathrooms."

"Did you live there growing up?"

"No. She moved here after my father died. Ewan and I moved in to the building to be a support to her. Though it was immediately clear the kind of support she wanted meant the two of us being on call night and day."

"I'm sorry if this is rude, but why didn't you move out when you learned that?"

"Because I like this place, even if it is a trifle upscale." Malcolm took a bite of his sandwich as if cutting off the conversation. I wasn't sure what else to say, so I started thinking up possible new topics. But after a moment, he went on, "And I suppose there is still a part of me that would feel guilty at abandoning my mother. She...changed, after my father's death. She used to be more warm and loving, but afterward...it was almost a year before the two of us could have a civil conversation."

"I'm sorry."

"Some of it was my fault. I was angry at everything and everyone, and we disagreed on the direction the company should take. About the only thing we had in common was our hatred of Nicolliens, which only made us more bitter at the world and didn't make either of us happy. Ewan was caught in the middle, which made *him* angry..." Malcolm took another bite, this one smaller. "I'm looking forward to seeing Ewan tonight. I haven't spoken to him in a few weeks and I'm interested to hear how his team is working out."

"So who will be there tonight?"

"If Andria was telling the truth about it being a family party, it will be us, Mother, Andria, Ewan, and probably Ewan's girlfriend Cathy. If she was playing me, it could be any number of high-ranking Ambrosites, though not Ryan Parish. He and Mother don't get along. She wanted me to take the leadership when Serena left."

"That's a relief." There was something Madeleine and I had in common; Parish and I didn't get along well either, though I respected his leadership abilities. I briefly wondered if Madeleine Campbell blamed me for being the indirect cause of Ryan Parish's elevation.

"In either case, tensions will likely be high, and Mother may want to test you, see how you react under pressure. You're not from an old Warden family, which makes you an unsuitable partner for a Campbell, in her eyes. On the other hand, you're the custodian of a named Neutrality, which offsets the other and means she won't snub you outright. Just...be prepared to smile and nod a lot. She'll come around."

I finished my sandwich and washed it down with the last of my bottled water, which was practically the only thing in the fridge. "I'm trying to think of a way to ask you a potentially offensive question."

He raised his eyebrows. "Ask."

"If your mother is...like she is...then what did your father see in her?" Malcolm had loved and respected his father deeply, but I had trouble reconciling what I knew of Alastair Campbell with anyone who could love a woman like Madeleine.

Malcolm nodded slowly, as if he were acknowledging a telling blow. "My father worshiped her," he said. "He treated her like a queen, and he would never allow either of his sons to disrespect her. And she responded well to that. She was kinder, more human, around him. As I said, she used to be more affectionate, and I never felt rejected by her when I was young. I remember watching them one night, coming home from some party or other, and the way he looked at her—I was about eight, I think, and not interested in girls yet, but it still made me shiver to see how much emotion was in his eyes and his smile that night."

He took a long drink from his bottle, and added, "She cared about Ewan and me, but I think my father was the only person my mother ever truly loved. That's a terrible thing to say about your own mother, but it's true. And losing him was a greater blow to her than I could imagine. Some of my anger toward her came from realizing that nothing I did was going to be able to replace him in any way—and that she didn't want me to even if I could. Once I understood that, I was able to feel compassion for Mother, and that led to our current state of understanding."

"Which is—what?"

"Well, once I made it clear that I would not be marrying Andria, and Mother began speaking to me again—"

"She stopped speaking to you?"

"For two months."

"Didn't that bother you?"

"Of course. But I'm not going to live my life to suit her. And she had her heart set on the match. She just needed time to work through her disappointment, and it didn't hurt me to give her that."

I wasn't so sure it was as benign as all that. I tried to imagine my mother not speaking to me for two months for going counter to her wishes and came up blank. "You're more generous than I would be."

Malcolm shrugged. "At any rate, once we got past that, we started communicating about the things we both cared about. The company.

The Long War. She's a stone magus and capable of great magic, though she hasn't fought with a team in decades, and I found I could share my team's triumphs with her and have her contribute to strategy discussions. We have topics we avoid, like her plans for her children's romantic futures, since I think she's manipulating Ewan and Cathy and she, as I said, thinks anyone but Andria is unworthy of me. But in general we're able to spend whole evenings together without it coming to blows."

"You're exaggerating about it coming to blows, right?"

"Yes. Though occasionally these parties end in a roaring argument."

"I was already worried, but now I'm seriously dreading tonight."

"Don't be. Mother has good manners. She won't overtly come out and accuse you of entrapment."

"Malcolm!"

"Sorry. I was trying to lighten the mood. You really don't have anything to worry about. She'd consider it déclassé to be rude to you when you're a guest in her home. And if I'm wrong about that, we'll just excuse ourselves." Malcolm took my hand and squeezed it. "Though I wish it was your family we were having dinner with tonight."

"So do I," I said.

———

I SETTLED MALCOLM'S DIAMOND SOLITAIRE PENDANT AROUND MY NECK and tucked away a stray lock of hair. The new bathroom was perfectly lit, and I had my own mirror, which...well, it wasn't like I'd never had my own mirror before, but the beveled edges and how they caught the indirect light made it feel almost like one of those celebrity makeup mirrors with bulbs circling it.

I put on a pair of pearl eardrops I'd been given as a high school graduation present by my grandparents and hoped they were fancy enough. Then I scowled at my reflection. I didn't care what Madeleine Campbell thought of me. I wasn't born to money like

Andria and I didn't have a magical lineage. I loved Malcolm, and he loved me, and that was more than enough for both of us.

"That expression will make you fit right in at the Campbell dining table," Malcolm said, coming to stand behind me. He ran a gentle hand down the side of my neck to my shoulder, then settled his arm around my waist. "You look beautiful tonight."

"Thank you." I converted my scowl to a smile that became genuine when I saw how he looked at me. I was wearing a red blouse with filmy sleeves and a white skirt that flared out around my knees when I moved. I turned around and put my arms around his neck. "It can't be all bad, can it?"

"Of course not. You haven't met Cathy—she's very nice, if a little quiet. My objections to her relationship with Ewan are purely for her sake, because my mother is overbearing and manipulative, not because I don't like Cathy. She's not a magus, but she owns an architectural firm we Wardens use often. Her company builds wards right into the foundations."

"That sounds interesting. But I thought you said once that you weren't sure if Ewan really cares for her. How does she feel about him?"

Malcolm shrugged. "It's just a suspicion, and probably an unworthy one. Cathy and Ewan seem happy, and they're still together even though Ewan moved to Seattle, so I could be wrong. Maybe I'm just annoyed that my mother's manipulations ended up bringing together two people who genuinely care about each other. Am I a bad person for wishing she'd failed?"

"I don't think you're a bad person," I said, drawing him close to rest my forehead against his. "I think you and your mother have unresolved issues, that's all."

"So I'm a mama's boy?"

"You're whatever the opposite of that is. Not a mama's boy at all."

Malcolm kissed me. "I am sometimes strongly reminded," he said, "of why I fell in love with you."

"Oh? Why is that?"

"You have the most generous heart." He kissed me again, slowly, making my knees wobble. "And the most beautiful smile—yes, that one."

I hugged him, feeling my cheeks go rosy with pleasure. "And I love *you*," I said, "because no one has ever seen me the way you do, and I like who I am when we're together."

I heard him sigh. "I suppose it's too late for us to come down with some horrible illness."

I swatted his backside lightly. "It's just a couple of hours, and then we can come home and snuggle up in this wonderful bed."

"You can count on it," Malcolm said.

We held hands as we walked down the hall to the elevator, then silently rode up to the penthouse level. The foyer looked just like our floor, maroon carpeting paired with cedar half-paneling, but there was no hallway, just a single door facing the elevator with two brass sconces on either side. Malcolm knocked twice, but made no move to open the door. "Courtesy," he said when I gave him a curious look. "The penthouse is attuned to me in case of emergencies, but otherwise I pretend I don't have an open invitation. It's—"

The door swung open. A dark-skinned woman wearing a traditional maid's uniform, down to the white frilly cap, curtseyed and held the door open farther for us to enter. I bit my lip to stifle a smile —it was my nervousness, and the feeling that I'd walked into a 1930s screwball comedy, that brought it on, and I didn't want the woman thinking I was laughing at her—and walked with Malcolm into a round, marble-domed room with creamy white walls and long, trumpet-shaped wall sconces of black iron.

A dizzying pattern of black and white tiles made a maze of the floor, something I found impossible to look away from. Was it a black path on a white background, or white on black? Whichever it was, it ended at the center of the room where a glossy black pedestal table bore six or seven prism-shaped vases containing rose and gold azaleas, the only touch of color in the room. Even the wall art was black on white—or white on black—photos of striped grass in shade, blown up until the blades were grainy.

Two doorways framed in black opened off the entry. The maid

indicated we should follow her, though no doubt Malcolm knew where to go. She led us through the doorway on the left, down a hall painted the same creamy white and hung with photos matching those in the entry. It was the sort of place a zebra could hide in. The floor tiles, at least two feet square, made a diamond pattern of black and white that clashed, in my opinion, with the art. I kept my gaze fixed on the far end of the short hall, where the evening sky was visible through floor to ceiling windows. Low clouds caught the sunset light, turning into a cotton-candy skyscape of blue, purple, and pink. It was so beautiful I couldn't stop watching it, even after we entered Madeleine Campbell's formal sitting room. One of them. Malcolm had said she had two. One was more than enough for me.

This one reminded me of a half-eaten tub of vanilla ice cream I'd once accidentally left on the counter overnight. In the morning it had been completely melted, soft-looking and warm and, when I'd touched it, creamy and smooth. The room had that same soft, unfocused look, though it smelled not of room-temperature cream, but of fresh linen. The carpet had no visible nap and a pad easily an inch and a half thick, into which the spindly legs of the ivory-painted and upholstered sofas and chairs sank. Something that seemed more sculpture than light fixture, even though it glowed softly from every one of its amorphous limbs, hung low overhead. I thought it might have been a flock of birds, but I resolved not to say anything in case I was wrong and might look like an idiot.

Madeleine Campbell rose from one of the sofas and came to greet us, her hands extended. "Malcolm," she said, her voice lightly accented and unexpectedly deep. I'd only "met" her once, when I'd invisibly visited Malcolm in the hospital last spring, and if I hadn't been in her home I might not have recognized her.

Malcolm took her hands and let her air-kiss him on both cheeks. "Mother, I'd like to introduce Helena Davies."

"Ms. Davies, what a pleasure. Please call me Madeleine," Madeleine said. I accepted her hand, which clasped mine rather than shaking it, and managed not to curtsey. Madeleine was taller than I was and more formally dressed, wearing a pink chiffon gown that matched her fingernails. Her black hair was piled high on her head and pinned there with clips studded with sparkling pink stones. "Ewan and Cathy have not arrived yet—Desdemona, please tell Ms. Lemaire my guests are here." The maid bobbed a curtsey and left the room.

"Malcolm, would you mind serving us? I will have my usual martini. What would you like, Ms. Davies?"

"Please, call me Helena," I said, barely stammering, "and I'll just have some white wine, if that's all right."

"Of course, anything you like. Thank you, Malcolm."

I stood helplessly in the middle of the room while Malcolm silently handed us drinks. The wet bar was almost invisible at the side of the room unless the cabinet was open, but it was sizable and once I'd seen it, I couldn't think of anything to say that wasn't a comment on how much liquor Madeleine seemed to need. Madeleine sipped her martini and said, "I am sorry we have not met before this. I find I have little use for Abernathy's, so I have never been there."

I took a slightly larger drink than I'd intended and swallowed my annoyance along with a hasty reply. A lot of Wardens didn't use Abernathy's, for all sorts of reasons, but usually that fact didn't piss me off like it did when Madeleine said it. "I find I'm still meeting new Wardens, even though I've been custodian for a year and a half," I said, as politely as I could manage. "I suppose it's fortunate Malcolm *does* have a use for the oracle, or we might never have met."

"I agree," Malcolm said. He held a bottle of beer—where had he found *that?*—and took a long drink. I caught sight of Madeleine's expression; she was not happy with her son. Was it the beer, or something else? I sipped my wine and prayed Malcolm wouldn't tease his mother to the point that she'd forget her good manners.

Footsteps tapped lightly along the white and black tiles, and Andria appeared, dressed in a mint green dress that looked like Grecian robes, down to leaving one shoulder bare. She smiled pleasantly at all of us. "Malcolm, be a dear and fix me a martini," she said. "Helena, I love your blouse. That color suits you."

"Thank you," I said.

"You *have* to tell us all about yourself," Andria said, coming forward to draw me down to sit next to her on one of the sofas. "Really, Malcolm, it's like you're ashamed of her, how secretive you've been."

"It's not Helena I'm ashamed of," Malcolm said, handing Andria a glass. "And I don't think it's polite to grill your guests."

"If she is to be part of this family, I think we are entitled to a little curiosity," Madeleine said. "You do not mind, do you, Helena?"

"Of course not," I managed. "I, um, I was born in Portland, I've lived here all my life—"

"Tell us about your family," Andria said.

"My parents live in Happy Valley. I have an older sister—"

"Ewan," Malcolm said. I turned in my seat to see Ewan Campbell, a thinner, more elongated version of Malcolm, enter the room. A plump young woman, her red hair in ringlets around her shoulders, had her hand hooked around his elbow. "And Cathy. It's good to see you again."

"Hey, Mal," Ewan said, reaching out to shake Malcolm's hand in what I thought was a strangely formal gesture between brothers. I rose to offer him my hand, grateful for the pause in the grilling. "Helena. Nice to see you again. This is Cathy Zumwalt, my fiancée."

"The custodian of Abernathy's," Cathy said. Her voice was high and sweet, but where Andria's sounded like the twitter of a dozen canaries, Cathy's was more like water rushing over a streambed. "It's like meeting Warden royalty."

Her smile, friendly and amused, made her comment funny instead of biting, and a little of the tension I was carrying melted away. "I wouldn't think of myself like that," I said, returning her smile, "what with being relatively new to the world." I glanced at Malcolm. Fiancée? Malcolm looked briefly stunned, but said nothing. I decided not to exclaim in wonder, since Ewan had made it sound like it was common knowledge. But if Ewan hadn't told his own brother...

"But it must be wonderful, having such a close attachment to the oracle." Cathy accepted a glass of wine from Malcolm. "Is it hard work? I'm afraid I don't know anything about it."

"Oh, let's not grill Helena about work," Andria said lightly, as if she hadn't been grilling me just moments earlier. A look of annoyance crossed Cathy's face swiftly, and her hand closed that much tighter on Ewan's coat sleeve. "I still want to know about your family, Hel. You have an older sister, and...?"

"Um...a younger brother," I said, annoyed at the casual *Hel*. "He's starting at the University of Oregon in the fall. My sister works in New York City. My father is a software developer and my mother works from home." I rattled off the details, feeling like a contestant on a game show where the real questions would begin at any moment.

"That's interesting, Hel. Don't you think that's interesting? And Nathaniel Briggs hired you out of the blue. Is it true he wanted a patsy to cover his blackmail racket?" Andria's twittering voice went smooth, and her eyes were wide and innocent, belying the nastiness in her words.

"*Helena* is the best custodian Abernathy's has had since Silas Abernathy," Malcolm said, his voice cut with steel. "However she came to the position."

"I don't know why Mr. Briggs hired me," I said, gripping my glass firmly so the angry trembling of my fingers wouldn't betray me, "but it turns out I was the right choice for the job."

"I should think so," Ewan said, "if you were able to become the oracle to fight off that invader. Mal said it was enormous. How did you do that? If it's not impolite to ask."

I could sense Andria fuming and wondered briefly what the hell she thought she was doing. Trying to make me uncomfortable? And some host Madeleine was, letting it continue. "It's not impolite, but I don't know if I can explain. It felt as if I gave the oracle permission to transform me, but that might be wrong. Everything happened so quickly."

A chime rang out over my last words. Desdemona stood at a

doorway at the far side of the sitting room. "Dinner is served," she said, her words inflected with a heavy Spanish accent.

"If you will all join me," Madeleine said, and we all set our glasses down and trooped after her. Malcolm took my hand and tucked it into the crook of his elbow. His muscles were tight with tension, and when I glanced at his face, I saw barely contained anger there. I tugged on his arm and, when he looked at me, gave him a reassuring smile. Malcolm's jaw unclenched, and the corners of his mouth turned up slightly. I looked at Andria, ahead of me a few paces. I knew too little of her to have any idea why she might want to insult me, but if it was as simple as the jealousy of a spurned woman, she was wasting her time.

Ahead of her, Madeleine turned her head slightly to address Ewan, saying something I couldn't make out. She'd been polite so far, but I didn't think I could count on that state of affairs to continue. Already this dinner party felt like international diplomatic warfare, with me as disputed territory. The food had better be excellent.

6

———

I hadn't understood why Malcolm had called his mother's dining room "full" until we passed through a doorway wide enough to admit three at a time and I saw it in all its glory. Not one, but two chandeliers dripping with faceted crystal shed their brilliant light over the walls, which were painted a dark, rich plum that kept the room from being truly overwhelming. I regretted my rather casual attire immediately. This was the sort of room that demanded evening dress and, possibly, a necklace of diamonds as big as your thumbnail.

A table long enough to seat twenty but set for six filled the room, which had floor to ceiling glass windows the whole length of one wall. Gauzy curtains obscured the view of downtown Portland just now coming to life on a Sunday evening. They blurred the cotton-candy clouds filling the distant horizon, giving me the impression of a world seen through a veil. I felt the warmth of soaked-up sunlight coming off the windows as I passed and realized I'd felt chilled since entering the apartment, though I hadn't heard an air conditioner and there were no ceiling fans. The windows were a welcome reminder that there was a world outside this rather narrow, unfriendly one.

The six place settings were grouped at one end of the absurdly long table. Though I'd had dinner with Harry and Harriet Keller many times, most of them formal, I'd never seen gold-plated silver-ware before. Nor china gilded along the edges. It struck me as, not fancy, but tacky, and more of my tension slipped away. Maybe this was how the truly rich ate, but if that was the case, I didn't have much respect for their taste.

Ewan held his mother's chair at the head of the table for her before doing the same for Cathy and taking a seat at his mother's right hand. Malcolm, pointedly ignoring Andria, held my chair so I was seated at his mother's left, then perfunctorily seated Andria and took the chair between us. I kept a close eye on Madeleine, reasoning that following her actions would keep me from looking like too much of an uncultured rube.

A door opened in the plum-colored wall, and a man in full wait-er's livery, complete with white gloves—*did they actually do that anymore? I suppose the rich can demand what they like*—emerged carrying a silver tureen from which came the most delicious smells of roasted red peppers and fresh cream. I quickly put my napkin in my lap and watched the waiter serve Madeleine a thick red bisque that made my mouth water.

Having served Madeleine, the man backtracked to Cathy's place and went around the table, serving Andria last. I wasn't sure this was especially good etiquette, but what did I know? I *did* know to wait until everyone was served before taking my first bite. It tasted every bit as good as it smelled. Madeleine's cook was excellent.

Another man in identical livery entered the room, carrying a bottle of wine. He showed it to Madeleine, who nodded, then he filled all our glasses and disappeared again. I sipped; it was a nice chardonnay that I thought went well with the bisque. I'd become more of a wine connoisseur thanks to those dinners with the Kellers, as Harry Keller was a self-proclaimed wine snob who had quite a cellar. But I was probably always going to be a beer drinker at heart. Good thing Madeleine didn't know that.

"Helena," Madeleine said, as if my thinking of her had drawn her attention. I startled and my spoon rang out against the china. "You have been Abernathy's custodian for...how long?"

"About a year and a half."

"And it has been an exciting year and a half, *non*? Murder, attempted destruction of the oracle, attacks by traitor magi...nothing half so exciting ever happened when the Briggs family ran the store."

"Do you have a point, Mother?" Malcolm said.

Madeleine's eyes widened. "I am just saying we live in interesting times. Have you heard that saying, Helena? The Chinese say 'May you live in interesting times.' Only it is not a blessing, it is a curse."

"You think magery is under a curse, then?" I said, and sipped my soup.

"I do not believe in curses. But we are certainly seeing disaster after disaster, especially with what is happening south of the United States."

"What's been happening there?" Cathy asked.

"I thought everyone had heard about it," Andria said, in a tone of voice that made Cathy's cheeks redden. "The capture of the Hernandes Node by the Mercy, how they're spreading throughout Mexico and beyond. They appear to be unstoppable."

"Not unstoppable," Malcolm said.

"But they certainly demonstrate fighting techniques we're unfamiliar with," Ewan said. "I've heard rumors that their steel magi know tricks no one's ever seen before."

"That's frightening," said Andria, though she looked more excited than afraid. "What happens when they decide to move north?"

The waiter returned to remove our bowls, and I closed my mouth on a reply. Surely we shouldn't speak so freely of Warden business in front of non-Wardens? But Madeleine said, "I am sure the efforts of northern magi will be more than enough to repel the traitors," and I guessed by Malcolm's non-reaction that these probably Wardens themselves. So instead I tried not to be irritated at Madeleine's casual assumption of American superiority, if not outright racism.

"The South American magi are fighting well," Malcolm said. He sounded as irritated as I felt. "The Mercy simply have advantages."

"Like what?" asked Cathy.

"They were once Wardens, and they know our secrets. Many of them were in positions of authority and know the techniques and strategies we use. I'm sure some of those smaller nodes were overwhelmed primarily because the Mercy knew the access codes for entry. We're trying to change our defenses, but that takes time."

"Campbell Security finished its review of the Gunther Node protections, yes?" Madeleine said to Malcolm. For the first time that evening, she sounded professional, not at all as if she had a secret agenda.

"Two days ago," Malcolm said. "Most of the wards in the city have been rekeyed. Howard Lancaster asked me to give you his thanks for your participation."

"There is no sense my staying retired when the future of magery is at stake," Madeleine said, waving that off. The waiter set down a plate of caprese salad in front of her, then gave one to me. I took a bite; too salty. So much for Madeleine's fabulous cook. Well, you couldn't be perfect all the time.

"Malcolm told me your firm handles warded properties here in the city," I said to Cathy, to distract myself from the overly salty tomatoes and mozzarella. "Are you an architect?"

"I am. Though recently I've come to specialize in retrofitting wards to old buildings, or more specifically, identifying good sites for wards in old buildings." Cathy tasted her salad and made a tiny face of disgust. "Abernathy's is the longest-warded building in Portland, in fact."

"That makes sense, if there weren't any Wardens here before the oracle arrived."

"There were Wardens here," Madeleine said. I watched her take a bite of her salad, curious about her reaction. Nothing. Maybe she liked over-salted food. "Not many. Enough that they could arrange for the purchase of that old building, and warding it before the oracle took possession."

"I don't understand how it all works, but I'm grateful for the wards," I said before remembering the appearance of Ross Dunlop in the store just days before. "Though I wish they weren't always running down, or whatever you call it."

"The proximity to the oracle drains a ward's efficacy rapidly," Madeleine said. "If you were a magus, you could tell when they need to be restored." She was back to sounding dismissive.

"If Helena were a magus, she couldn't be Abernathy's custodian and wouldn't care one way or the other," Malcolm snapped.

Madeleine raised one eyebrow, a gesture that made her look feline. She said something in rapid French. Malcolm's left hand, resting on his thigh beneath the table, closed into a fist. "Not all your guests speak French, Mother," he said, his pleasant, calm tone at odds with the tension in his hand.

Madeleine glanced at me with a tiny smile. "My apologies. I sometimes forget myself. English is not my first language."

"That's all right," I said, hoping to keep the conversation on a polite heading. "I wish I'd studied French in high school. I took Spanish instead, and I don't remember much of it."

"It is not a thing Americans do often, learn another language to the point of fluency," Madeleine said. "Unfortunate."

I examined her words for hidden pitfalls and found nothing objectionable. "I agree."

"I said only that it is a pity the custodian cannot be a magus. How much better able you would be to defend your charge," Madeleine said.

"I suppose there would always be pressures on your loyalties if that were so," I said.

Madeleine's smile broadened, as if I'd said something amusingly naïve. "Better to have someone with no loyalties at all?"

Malcolm pushed his mostly untouched salad plate away and said, "Cathy, do you and Ewan have a date for your wedding?" with the air of a man deflecting a conversational bullet. It spared me trying to figure out what oblique insult Madeleine had intended.

Cathy looked relieved at the question. "September first," she said. "A nice autumn wedding. Just something quiet, immediate family only—" She flicked a glance at Madeleine, and I got the sense that the size of the wedding was a hard-fought battle between them.

"That sounds lovely," I said. "Where will you live?"

That prompted a glance at Ewan, and I kicked myself for coming up with a not-so-innocuous question. "We...haven't decided yet," she said. "Ewan's hunting team is in Seattle, and my business is here...it's complicated."

"I understand that. Malcolm and I had some difficulties settling on where to live. I love my apartment over the store, but it's just too small for two."

"And his home here, it is not good enough for you?" Madeleine said.

"Um...of course it is. Or we wouldn't have moved in. It's beautiful." I felt as if every word was a shovel digging me in deeper.

"I agree," Andria said. "I *especially* like the master suite."

That was more than I was willing to put up with. Rubbing it in my face that she'd been with Malcolm before me! I drew in a breath to blast her with something harsh, not that I knew what that would be, and Malcolm put his hand on my leg and squeezed hard. "You'd find it much changed," he said to Andria, "as Helena has made it her own. But then you always did have trouble accepting...change."

Again, I couldn't see Andria around Malcolm, but by the way Ewan's face went completely expressionless, her silence was one of stunned fury. I put my hand atop Malcolm's and squeezed it gently in thanks. "I think the kitchen is beautiful," I said cheerfully, "even though I'm no cook. Yet. I think it's something I might take up."

"Feel free to ask my cook for advice," Madeleine said, as calmly as if Andria had never spoken. "He is quite experienced."

The waiter took away my salad plate, barely touched. "Thanks, I'll remember that," I said. "My mother is an expert cook, too, and she's always wanted to inspire her children to follow in her footsteps, but none of us have."

"Does your mother run a catering business, then?" Madeleine said.

"No, she sells knitted and crocheted children's clothes online. She just loves cooking."

"Children's knitted clothing. Your family seems...very nice," Madeleine said with a half-smile. It felt like a jab, but so subtle I couldn't call her on it. I leaned back as the waiter deposited a plate bearing a delicious-smelling salmon filet in front of me. The tangy scent of lemon wafted to my nose. One of my favorites. I took a bite. Ah, the cook had redeemed himself. Flaky but not dry, with the sauce accenting the flavor of the fish instead of masking it.

"I love my family," I said, refraining from putting a heavy emphasis on "my." Madeleine's behavior was odd, but she hadn't been overtly rude—at least, not in English—and I could be civil. Though if Andria said one more nasty word, I was going to attack her with my dessert fork.

Silence fell as we all applied ourselves to our food. I ate placidly, not feeling a need to carry the conversation. Let Madeleine play the hostess. Besides, the fish was delicious, and it seemed wrong to diminish that by talking around it.

"I hear Ryan Parish has been called south to consult with the Ambrosite leader of Central America," Ewan said, clearly not feeling the love. "Do you know anything about that, Mal?"

"Ryan hasn't discussed it with me," Malcolm said, "other than to instruct the teams to continue operations as usual."

"Parish shows you no respect," Madeleine said. "You are the foremost hunter of your generation. You should advise *him*."

"I prefer the position I have, Mother," Malcolm said. "It leaves me free to run the company."

Madeleine made a dismissive noise. "Why did the oracle choose such a brute, Helena?"

She caught me with my mouth full. I hastily swallowed and said, "I don't know why the oracle decides what it does."

"How can you not know? Do you not have a connection?"

"Well, yes, but it's not like it tells me things." This wasn't entirely true, but I didn't feel like explaining the way the oracle had communicated with me in the past. "I'm the oracle's hands, so it really only guides me to the extent it needs, and that doesn't mean I have to understand."

"So you could make a mistake."

I blinked. "I'm sorry?"

"If it does not communicate directly, you might misunderstand."

"Madeleine, if this is about Ryan Parish, I assure you I didn't make a mistake." Where was she going with this?

"I am simply trying to understand, *non*? I want to know if it is possible for the custodian of Abernathy's to make a mistake about an augury."

She sounded genuinely curious, but I felt something else was going on. "I...don't think so. The oracle's guidance is always very clear. You'd have to see it yourself to understand."

"But there was the attack by the Mercy—the illusions—"

"That confused the oracle, not me. Did you have a specific augury in mind?"

Madeleine pushed her plate away. "I requested an augury last year I believe was incorrect."

"Mother—" Malcolm said, his voice a warning.

"What augury?" I asked, though I felt I already knew.

"The Accords were very clear. You had no business being attracted to my son," Madeleine said. "I asked to learn who his true life's companion should be. You could have falsified that augury out of a desire to see him separated from someone far better suited—"

"*Mother!*"

"That's enough," I said. Strangely, her insane logic, if you could call it that, didn't anger me the way Andria's smug comment had. "Madeleine, I don't falsify auguries for any reason, and if I did, the oracle would reject me. I'm sure to you Andria seems like a better choice for Malcolm, but isn't it up to him?"

"We're leaving," Malcolm said, rising and throwing his napkin on his plate with some force. "Helena?"

"It was nice to meet you, Cathy," I said, "and good to see you again, Ewan. Madeleine, I'm sorry."

"Don't you dare apologize to her," Malcolm said, his jaw clenched.

"I'm not. Madeleine, I'm sorry you're so obsessed with running Malcolm's life you don't want him to be truly happy. But I'm not going anywhere. Get used to it." I took Malcolm's hand, and we left the ornate dining room at something less than a run.

Malcolm swore under his breath as we passed through the apartment. "Slow down," I said, tugging on his hand.

"Not until we're safely home," he said. "Damn it, I can't believe she did that. Helena, I am so sorry."

"It's all right. It was too ludicrous to be hurtful. No, really," I added as Malcolm turned an incredulous look on me. "She had to be ignorant to even suggest it."

"You're far more generous of spirit than I am." Malcolm stormed out of the elevator and slammed the front door open when we were still five feet away from it. He tore off his jacket and tie and flung them on one of the sofas. "She's still obsessed about that. I thought I made it clear that I would never marry Andria. And she—" He cursed again at length. "You should not have been exposed to that."

"I told you, it doesn't bother me." I sank down into one of the leather chairs. It was warm and butter-soft, and I trailed my fingers along its arm. "I'm just sorry your own mother behaved that way."

Malcolm dropped onto the sofa opposite me and leaned back, staring up at the ceiling. "I have never more wished my father were alive than right now."

"I wish I could have met him."

"So do I." He sighed. "At least we were able to finish most of the meal before it all imploded. I don't think I could muster the energy to prepare food."

"Let's eat ice cream and watch a movie in bed," I suggested. "Something mindless and fun. *Bringing Up Baby*?"

"You," Malcolm said, "have excellent ideas."

7

Despite the relaxing evening—or possibly because of too much ice cream—I spent a restless night, waking from nightmares I didn't quite remember to gray skies and rain beating the windows. It was early for me, not quite six o'clock, so I left Malcolm sleeping and got myself a bowl of cereal. I sat at the central island in the vast, impersonal kitchen and turned the pages of my cookbook, idly making a list. Spaghetti with meatballs and a salad, that ought to be easy enough, even if the instructions for cooking spaghetti were offputtingly long. And I did so know how to boil water. I hoped that part of the book was a joke.

"You're up early," Malcolm said, bending over to kiss my cheek. "No eggs?"

"I didn't feel like anything heavier than Cheerios this morning. Bad dreams."

"Oh? What about?"

"I don't remember. I was running from something, or to something, and there were things in the shadows. It was just unsettling. Who do I give this list to?" I waved it at him.

Malcolm got out a skillet and began cracking eggs into a bowl. "The concierge at the desk downstairs. They'll handle the rest."

"It feels so decadent."

"It saves you time, and your time is precious to me."

"To me, too. But this will take some getting used to."

Malcolm smiled. "I intend to pamper you as much as you'll allow. Don't make that face—it gives me pleasure to make you happy. You wouldn't want to deprive me of that, would you?"

I smiled back and shook my head. "I guess not." I wasn't sure I needed to be pampered, but if it made Malcolm happy and didn't hurt me... I shoved my disquiet aside. This was our home now, and I belonged here, even if on some level I felt I didn't.

I drove across town to the store, trying not to feel odd about doing so. It had been a year and a half since I'd had to drive to work, and I'd never done so from this direction. As I parked behind the store, I laughed at myself. *Turns out Andria's not the only one not good with change, huh? Well, as you told Madeleine, get used to it.*

I had left early, unsure of what traffic would be like, but Judy's car was parked in the lot behind the store already. Sometimes Judy's work ethic exhausted me. Or maybe she just wanted to get away from home again. It must be hard for her, staying neutral in the home of the Nicollien leader, especially with how...active William Rasmussen was. I wondered if the Nicolliens in Central America had called on him the way the Ambrosites had Ryan Parish.

Judy was intent on the computer screen when I opened the office door. "Good morning," I said.

Judy startled. Swiftly she minimized whatever she was looking at. "You're here early."

"Woke early. What are you doing?"

"Just...you know, online things." Her face was carefully blank, so blank I was suspicious.

"What online things? Personal things? You know I don't care if you do personal stuff at work."

"No, just things."

"Judy, you're acting weird. What's really going on?"

Judy glanced at the monitor, which displayed the background of a fantasy starscape. Her shoulders slumped, just a little. "Fine. I was updating my profile."

"Profile? For what?"

Judy moved the mouse and a web page came up. I leaned over to look at it. "BeMatched.com? A *dating site*?"

"Thanks for making this better by sounding so calm and accepting."

"No, it's just...I don't know what I expected. Why do you have a profile on a dating site?"

"I'm trolling for victims for my organ trafficking ring, Helena. Why do you think?"

"I'm not doing this right, am I?"

"Not even a little bit."

I turned around and left the office, then entered again, shutting the door firmly. "Good morning, Judy, what are you doing? Oh, a dating site? Wow, that sounds fun! Meet anyone interesting yet?"

Judy's scowl wavered. "I only just joined yesterday. I was finishing my profile questionnaire when you came in. They use it to determine your compatibility with others. Once I submit it, they start sending me matches, and I can choose which ones I want to talk to. It's pretty basic."

"That's...actually pretty brave of you. Does it go the other way around? They send your profile to guys?"

"I guess." Judy slumped in her chair. "I know, I'm pathetic and desperate."

"No, you're not! I just didn't think you—I mean, I thought you met plenty of guys already. What about the one you said you were interested in before you came to work here? With the Accords changed, you're free to date him."

"He's moved on already. And it was never serious, just...anyway, most of the Nicolliens are in awe of who my father is, and that spills over onto me. The Ambrosites hate my father, and *that* spills over onto me. And I don't know if you've noticed, but most of the men working for Lucia are either old, married, or gay. So the available pool is both small and shallow."

"I see. Yeah, that's tough." I chewed my lower lip in thought. "Aren't you worried about dating a non-Warden? It's a big secret to keep."

"True, but if I make a real connection with someone, I'm not afraid to tell him the truth. I'm going to worry about it later."

I wasn't so sure that was a good idea, but it wasn't any of my business. "You'll tell me when it sends you those matches, right? Because I think, as your friend, I have a right to help you weed out the bad ones."

A smile touched Judy's lips briefly. "That could be fun."

I heard the distant sound of the door rattling. "Mail's here. Time to do some real work," I said.

It was going to be a beautiful, hot day, the skies clear of clouds, the sun reflecting off the pavement to make things hotter. I sorted through the augury requests, and gasped. "Argentina. Finally, something from South America!"

"That's such a relief. Hurry, open it," Judy said.

I slit the envelope and removed the sheet of folded paper. Typed, and in English. *How can we increase the production of* sanguinis sapiens? "This is from the Covarrubias Node," I said, reading the return address typed below that sentence. "It's so normal. I expected...I don't know. Something to do with the war."

I turned the envelope over and read the postmarks. "It was sent seven days ago. The same day the Hernandes Node was overrun."

"So?"

"So nothing. It's just a weird coincidence. But it might explain the normality, if the Mercy wasn't on the move yet." I went back to opening envelopes. "I just wonder what things are like there now."

"If there's no augury, that ought to tell you something."

The office phone rang, startling both of us. It was a beige lump older than both of us put together and hardly ever rang. We kept it for the rare occasions someone would call with an augury request instead of mailing it in. I picked up the handset. "This is Abernathy's."

"I have an augury request." It was a man, his voice smooth and cultured-sounding, with a strong Hispanic accent. "Can you receive it?"

"Certainly, sir. Could you wait just a moment?" I dug in the shallow central drawer of the desk for a pen and paper. "Go ahead. First your name, then the question."

"My name is Diego Galarza. The question is, 'Where are the missing keys?'"

I wrote it down and repeated it back to him. "Will that be all, sir?"

"That is all." He gave me an address in Colombia that I copied down below the question. "You will send it today, yes?"

"It will be in the mail by this afternoon."

"Thank you, Ms. Davies." He hung up, leaving me feeling unsettled. Of course people knew the name of Abernathy's custodian, but for him to address me by it when I hadn't identified myself...it felt like he knew secrets about me I didn't share with anyone.

Then it registered. "Colombia!" I said. "Damn it, I should have thought to ask him if everything was all right."

Judy read the augury silently; it was upside down to her. "That seems like a pretty innocuous question. Things can't be so bad if that's all he wants to know."

"It must not be urgent, if he's willing to wait a week or more for the mail to deliver the augury." I folded the scrap of paper in half and put it with the rest of the mail-in auguries. "I'm going to do the South American ones first. I can't help being curious what the oracle's response will be."

It was nearly ten o'clock by the time all the auguries were sorted. Ignoring the Nicolliens lining up outside, I took the Argentina request first, afraid of seeing the red light of "no augury." But the sunlight had the same blue tint to it I was used to. I found the augury easily enough and set it on the counter with the augury request slipped between its pages. I ought to call Lucia and tell her about it— not the question, obviously, but the fact that we'd received word from one of the silent Neutralities.

I eyed the front door, wondering if I dared do Galarza's augury and make them wait a minute or two. Sighing, I opened the door and welcomed them in. The Accords were clear on precedence of augury requests, and while I wasn't as much a stickler for the rules as Ragsdale wanted me to be, I certainly wasn't going to break them on a whim. I smiled, and accepted the first Nicollien's slip of paper.

The Nicolliens all wanted to talk about South America, but since no one knew anything more than what was already public knowledge, the discussion just kept circling around to speculation about what the Mercy was doing down there. I kept my mouth shut about Argentina and Colombia. If I added to the speculation, Lucia would use me for target practice. I said only that I was sure the Neutralities could handle themselves, which wasn't entirely true, given that the Hernandes Node had fallen and the Durango Node had taken a beating. But it was better than giving into inappropriate and premature despair.

After the store had emptied at around 12:30, I picked up the folded paper and turned it over and over in my hands. Maybe I could put it off until after lunch. I was hungry and I wanted my peanut butter and honey sandwich. No, I'd promised Galarza his augury would go out this afternoon. I glanced over the paper one more time, put it in my pocket, and walked into the oracle.

Instantly, the light went dim, as if a mass of clouds had rushed to cover the sun. I almost stepped back outside to see if that was true, but remembered in time that leaving before finding the augury would invalidate the request. I walked into the stacks, sidling through the narrower corridors, looking for a blue glow. The air felt heavy, not muggy, but tangibly bearing down on me. It felt like a duvet, light and fluffy when you first crawled under it, but increasingly heavy as its weight settled on you. Only this didn't stop at the gentle pressure of downy feathers, it continued to press down on me like a backpack someone kept adding iron cookware to. My steps slowed as the weight increased, and as the weight increased, so did my reluctance to be there.

I'm not letting this get to me. I straightened my back against the imaginary load and kept walking. Around one corner, then the next, with no augury in sight. Eventually I found myself at the center of the oracle, a place where four bookcases faced each other. In the dim light, their upper shelves, which nearly reached the ceiling, were indistinct.

"Something's wrong," I said, half statement, half question. "I don't understand what you're trying to tell me. Why can't you just speak? You've done it before, when that invader tried to destroy you. Is it that you don't want me to get lazy, expecting you to communicate clearly instead of using my intellect to figure you out? I guess that's your prerogative, but there really ought to be rules about this sort of thing. Unless there are rules, and I just don't know about them."

Silence. The weight had stopped increasing, but hadn't lessened at all. Air moved, brushing my cheeks and bringing with it a sour smell like rotten milk. I wrinkled my nose. "Okay, so something...not good? Is there something you want me to know that's not a part of this augury request?"

The room brightened, not by much, but enough for me to see that there really were clouds of particles filling the space. It was like being inside a snow globe, though one with dark sparkles instead of light. It was an apt metaphor, because I was beginning to feel shaken, light-headed from the weight pressing down on me.

The clouds of particles moved slightly with the air currents, filmy dark curtains that brushed my skin. It made it look like the books were shifting—except they *were* shifting, fidgeting on the shelves like a bunch of two-year-olds. I held my breath, afraid to disturb whatever was happening. Silently, books drifted from the shelves, spinning and tumbling and making me even dizzier than before. Traces of gold light sputtered along the edges of their covers and spines, sparks that left short trails wherever they ran, as if they wanted to kindle a fire but didn't have the strength. The flickers of light reminded me of Fourth of July sparklers, but dimmer. This felt more like a funeral than a celebration.

The books began to settle in an uneven stack on one of the shelves, at eye-height to me. My heart beat faster. I'd seen this once before, when the oracle had produced an augury choosing Ryan Parish as the next Ambrosite leader for the Pacific Northwest. It was going to communicate with me, after all. I waited for the books to stop moving, then read down the first letters of the titles.

SANTIAGO

It left me no more enlightened than before. Who was Santiago? Or...wasn't the capital of Chile called Santiago? And I thought there might be a Neutrality by that name as well, somewhere in South America. "Thank you," I called out, in case the oracle might feel I didn't appreciate its gift. "I don't know what it means, but...thanks."

The dark particles faded, then disappeared, and the light shone out red-tinged. "So it's no augury after all," I said, musing aloud. I opened the paper and read the question again. "Looks like Mr. Galarza will have to find his keys the old-fashioned way." So what was it about this augury that the oracle had chosen it to give me the weird message? Could it be a warning? What if—

My fingers went numb. What if this Galarza was one of the Mercy? I had no way of knowing whether the augury requests I received were from traitors, and the oracle had its own inscrutable ways of choosing who received auguries. It hadn't given Galarza an augury, but that could mean anything. I closed my eyes and cursed. Why couldn't the oracle be less cryptic?

A wind rushed past me, strong enough to rock me back on my heels. It smelled hot and dry and dusty, as if it had blown here from a distant desert. It snatched the paper out of my hand and carried it away. I turned to retrieve it and saw nothing. I searched around for a bit and came up empty. Odd. I shook out my fingers and sighed. One more strange thing for the books, or at least my custodian's diary. There was nothing I could do but pray the oracle was on the side of the Wardens.

The rest of the day passed busy but uneventful. I managed to finish all the mail-in auguries in time for Judy to take them to the post office, then chatted with a few Ambrosites who came in about an hour before closing time. They, too, wanted to talk about South America. It made me wonder about the Pondicherry Node and whether anyone had gotten through it. When the Ambrosites left, I called Lucia and left a brief message: "We heard from Argentina and Colombia today. Did Pondicherry ever respond?"

I set my phone on the counter and stretched, enjoying the heat radiating through the big plate glass window. It was such a pretty day…maybe we should go for a walk in that little park across from the apartment building after dinner. That reminded me that I'd committed to making dinner that night. I sighed and rested my elbows on the glass countertop. I wasn't sure I'd ever learn to love cooking, but I could at least learn to be competent at it.

My phone rang, buzzing against the glass. "Where in Argentina and Colombia?" Lucia said.

"The Covarrubias Node, and…I lost the address in Colombia, but it wasn't anything I recognized."

"There are no Neutralities in Colombia. It had to be a private individual. Did he give his name?"

"Diego Galarza."

"Ah. He's an old friend." Well, that answered that question. I guessed it wasn't beyond possibility that Lucia knew every important Warden in the world. "Was his augury about the Long War?"

"No. It seemed ordinary. But the oracle wouldn't give an augury, and it behaved strangely. It gave me the name Santiago."

"What do you mean, gave you the name?"

I recounted what had happened and ended with, "It wasn't more specific than that. Santiago's not exactly an uncommon name, though. I don't even know if it meant a surname or a first name."

"Or a Neutrality," Lucia said. "I'll try to reach Velez. As far as I know, that node hasn't been attacked. Yet."

"You don't think—"

"What?"

"You do *trust* Mr. Galarza, right?"

Lucia snorted. "I've trusted Galarza with my life, more than once. And he's free of the traitor's mark, if that's what you were getting at."

I flushed. "I just thought it was possible…never mind. Did you ever hear from the Pondicherry Node?"

Lucia snorted. "Everyone's going to hear about Pondicherry soon enough. They were attacked by the Mercy and drove them off, not without heavy casualties on both sides."

"But they defeated them! That's good, right?"

"Good that the Mercy didn't win. Better if we could use their victory to help South America. More nodes and Neutralities go dark every day. My map has a great gray blotch covering most of Mexico, Central America, and the northern part of South America. And I can't do a damn thing about it unless they call for assistance, or the Board overrides them."

"Why won't they ask for help?"

"Those are some powerful Neutralities down there. They probably don't believe they need help, certainly not from us *gringos*. North and South America haven't exactly been cordial neighbors in the last century. Too much pride on both sides." Lucia snorted again. "Prajapati said Pondicherry didn't see any unusual tactics or strange magics on the part of the Mercy, which is also a thing I wish we could do something about. I don't like mysteries."

"And I've just given you a new one."

"Not to be ungrateful, but it's a mystery with a low priority for me. I've got the Gunther Node preparing to move out the instant one of those Neutralities pushes the panic button. But keep me informed if you get any more communications from the south. Though if they are fighting the Mercy, they're likely not in a position to wait a week to receive an augury that might tell them what to do." She hung up, as usual without saying goodbye.

I put my phone away and went downstairs to get the broom. So Pondicherry was safe, if decimated—but how had they succeeded in driving the Mercy off when so many others presumably hadn't?

I let my mind wander as I pushed the broom along the narrow corridors formed by the bookcases. Maybe Pondicherry was stronger than the others. Maybe the Mercy hadn't sent a very big force against them. Or maybe those unusual tactics people had reported seeing in South America were more effective than anyone guessed. Maybe the Mercy had new magic no one knew anything about. But, then, how had they developed it, if they'd been hiding among the Wardens all these years? Someone would have noticed, surely?

It made me wonder how new magic was developed. Hitler's Nazis had created an entirely new aegis that produced the glass magi, but the Nazis had been nuts for research and development and had had extensive resources at their command. So a new kind of magus was probably out of the question. New techniques for existing magi, though...I had no idea how those were developed. Maybe Malcolm did. I knew he and his team were constantly practicing new ways of fighting in the hope that some of them might be effective in fighting invaders. The Mercy, infiltrating the Wardens' organization, could certainly have observed and stolen those sorts of techniques, then built on them.

My broom's head caught a jutting corner, jarring my arms and bringing me out of my reverie. I found I was at the center of where the oracle would be if it were active. I hadn't seen that slip of paper Galarza's augury request was written on anywhere. Maybe it was trapped in the oracle's timeless space. Why would the oracle care about keeping it? Another thing I had no way of knowing.

I swept my way back to the front of the store and leaned the broom's long handle against the wall near the counter. No new customers had come in, and Judy wasn't back, as I discovered when I checked the office. A dating service. My heart went out to Judy, and I slapped that sentimental notion down. She would hate it if I felt even the slightest approximation to pity for her. And how else was she supposed to meet guys? She was taking a brave, assertive step.

The rear office door swung open. "Everybody in Portland had something to mail today," Judy groused. "I almost just went home, but I...wanted to check my BeMatched email." Her cheeks were pinker than usual. "I'd rather not do it where there's any chance of Father finding out."

I leaned on the front of the desk and tapped my fingers, trying not to sound impatient. Judy glanced at me over the monitor. "You want to see this?"

"I don't want to intrude."

"Give me a second to log in to the site." She moved the mouse around, clicked, and said, "Okay. Here it is."

I hurried around the desk to stand behind her. "Oh, there's a lot!"

"Five possibilities." Judy's inbox had pictures of the five guys alongside little pocket descriptions and a short message from each. "This one looks interesting."

"I don't know. You're not really into sports and he says hiking is his favorite activity."

"True. How about this one? He likes the theater, reading, and... hmm, he's a lawyer."

"Nothing wrong with that."

"Specializes in litigation. He argues with people for a living."

"Well, don't count him out. He might be nice."

"True." Judy scrolled down the page. "Wait a minute. This one's a fashion designer."

I squealed. "Judy! Look, he's also into fine dining and art. That's good, right?"

"It's not bad," Judy said grudgingly, but her cheeks were pink again. "You think I should contact him?"

"Is that how it works?"

"It says I can communicate at my own pace. Helena, I have no idea what to say!"

"Just...that you're interested in fashion, and ask him what he designs? You can have a conversation about that for hours."

"I feel I should be insulted by that, but I'm not."

"I *meant* that you know a lot about it."

"I know. I was joking." Judy sighed. "All right." She typed at length into the Reply box on the screen, then hit Send. "And now I have to wait. I hate waiting."

"It's after six. Go home and do something fun." I straightened and took my purse from the bottom drawer of the desk. "*I* have to go home and cook my first dinner."

"I hope Malcolm has the number of a good pizzeria on hand."

I scowled at her. "Why is everyone so sure I can't cook?"

8

I slouched into the office the next morning and sagged against the desk. "Rough night?" Judy said, already industriously typing away at the keyboard.

"Bad dreams." Or so I assumed. All I could remember upon waking was a nebulous fear of things lurking in the shadows, not human or animal or invader, but always there at the edge of my vision. I shook my head like a dog rising out of a pool and felt the cobwebs fly away. "And too little coffee, probably." No coffee, actually. Malcolm had left before I got up this morning, and I didn't want to admit I didn't know how to work his coffeemaker, with its sleek black case and enough buttons to operate a commercial jet liner.

"I sorted the augury requests already." Judy nodded at the stack of envelopes on the corner of the desk. Her fingers flew across the keyboard. "One from South America. Argentina again, handwritten. I wrote the Google Translate version on it. It's the top one."

"Geez, you're efficient today." I eyed her typing. "Are you writing to Mr. Gucci again?"

"Please, Helena. Mr. Givenchy, maybe." She smiled. "He's interesting, if nothing else. We haven't talked about meeting yet, though."

I picked up the top envelope and read its contents. "Weavers again?"

"I know. Weird, right? I called Lucia and left her a message, but she hasn't called back."

"How do you find time to do all that *and* communicate with your new friend?"

"It's a matter of properly allocating your resources. Also, I might have come in early. Father left for the Mendoza Node last night and the house echoes when he's not there."

"You'd better have a date with this guy soon. Your work ethic is going to drive me crazy." I gathered up the stack of envelopes and retreated.

At a safe distance from Judy and her work ethic, I set the stack on the front counter and took out the Argentinian augury request. *Where do the weavers stay?* I was starting to think "schemers" might be a more accurate translation. "Weavers" just made no sense. Mulling it over, I took a few steps into the oracle and was met by a dim, reddish light. No augury. I read over the Spanish words, feeling my throat tighten up. It had to be my imagination that those quickly penned words, jagged and pointy, looked desperate. If only they'd called...it probably wouldn't have made a difference. I supposed it was just possible that the augury's recipient, Jimena Cortez, was still alive and this was just one of those auguries the oracle wouldn't fulfil, but in my heart I knew otherwise.

I folded this one and carefully stowed it in my pocket, not wanting the oracle to sweep it away the way it had Galarza's, but no hot sirocco came up. Between this and the lingering effects of my bad dreams, it was shaping up to be a horrible day.

I managed another handful of auguries before ten o'clock, which soothed my spirits somewhat, but I was still tired and irritable enough that I was barely civil to the customers who came sauntering in when I opened. I took comfort in the fact that none of them had brought their familiars along. What I didn't need was to be growled and lunged at by monsters keen on sucking the magic from my body. I thought about it idly as I searched for the next augury. Surely they couldn't actually touch me, right? Not with their harnesses in place. No matter how appetizing I smelled to them, or whatever it was about a custodian that was so appealing.

Judy, on the other hand, was sickeningly cheerful all morning, to the point that I almost snapped at her just for asking in a chipper voice how my dinner had gone. "Fine," I said. "The meatballs fell apart, but they tasted fine."

"So your first meal was a success. Good for you!"

"Is there any way I can get you to stop being cheerful?" I said, more angrily than I'd meant.

The smile dropped away from Judy's face. "Sorry."

"No, I—" I let out a huge sigh. "I'm just in a bad mood. I'm glad you're happy."

"I'm trying to be wary, but...he's funny, Helena, and we have a lot in common...but how likely is it that I got this lucky first time out of the gate?"

"Skeptical is good. It's easy to make yourself sound appealing online. You really ought to have coffee with him or something. Meet in person."

"I've been working up to asking him for something like that."

"So do it. Then you'll know."

Judy nodded. "I will."

My spaghetti and meatballs—or spaghetti and meat crumbs—tasted better reheated, to my surprise. I'd have to try it again sometime. Malcolm had been enthusiastic about the meal, maybe a little too enthusiastic...seriously, why was everyone around me so leery of my decision to learn to cook?

The afternoon wore on. More mail-in auguries, more walk-in requests. The Nicolliens were replaced by Ambrosites. This time, Pondicherry was all anyone wanted to talk about, specifically, how had that Neutrality managed to fight off the Mercy when so many others had failed? In between trips into the oracle, I learned a bit more about the Pondicherry Node. It had been founded at the end of the eighteenth century by the French, whose struggles to keep the node working had been hampered by the constant battles between the French and the English and their Indian allies (who were some-times their enemies).

"Technically it should be Puducherry now," one of my customers, Juliet Dawes, told me, "but Marya Prajapati is a Francophile and a history buff."

"And a canny fighter," Allie Sanford said. "If anyone could hold off the Mercy, it's Marya. I'd almost back her against Lucia, if I weren't afraid of Lucia tearing my head off and using it as a basketball."

"So you think that's what made the difference? Ms. Prajapati's leadership?"

"I don't know," Juliet said. "What about the reports that the Mercy used new techniques in South America?"

"Those are just rumors," Allie said. "We don't know what's going on down there."

"My father is in Colombia now, consulting with Isabela Albar-rán," Judy said. "He's trying to convince her to ask the Board to inter-vene, force the Neutralities to ask for help. It's not going well."

"I've heard Parish is going to assemble our teams in anticipation of going to South America's aid," said Juliet. "Has Malcolm said anything about that, Helena?"

"No, and I'm sure he'd tell me if he were leaving," I said. "That's $900, Juliet. Allie, I'll take yours now."

While I was searching for Allie's augury, I tried not to think about Malcolm leaving for the south. Ever since gaining his new aegis, he'd been a stronger fighter, or so his team had told me. He had greater control over metal and could withstand more direct attacks from invaders. Under the right conditions, he was actually bulletproof. None of that stopped me worrying about his safety when he went on the hunt. The idea of him going into the vast unknown South America had become frightened me. Not that I would ever try to stop him; I'd promised never to try to make him other than who he was. But I felt I had to keep my fears to myself, so as not to worry him, and it burdened me with cares I was used to sharing with him.

I pulled Allie's augury off the shelf—*The Joy of Sex*, and wouldn't that be fun to tease her about?—and headed back. If Malcolm's team ended up going south, I'd be supportive. And didn't I want the Wardens to defeat the Mercy? There was no reason to believe they'd been, well, merciful to the occupants of the nodes they captured. If Malcolm could prevent people from dying, that was something I wanted.

"I don't know. It feels anticlimactic, chasing invaders when who knows what is happening down there," Allie was saying as I emerged from the stacks. I handed her the augury and enjoyed the flicker of emotions that passed across her face: astonishment, chagrin, amusement. "Barker's going to *love* this," she said. Mikey Barker was her newest team member, an eighteen-year-old bone magus who blushed at absolutely everything.

"You sure this wasn't a personal augury?" Judy teased.

"Oh, believe me, I already know all about it," Allie said.

The door opened. Allie reflexively hugged the book to her chest so the cover was hidden. Caught midway to saying something suggestive, I closed my mouth. Then I registered who my newest customer was. "Madeleine," I said. "Um. Welcome to Abernathy's?"

"Good afternoon," Madeleine said. She wore a short black skirt and a matching sleeveless top that would have looked casual if she hadn't paired it with a circlet of pearls the size of quail eggs and a feathered hat straight out of a '50s Technicolor extravaganza. She took off her giant bug-eye *Breakfast at Tiffany's* sunglasses and glanced around at the shelves and the front counter with mild interest, like she'd never seen the inside of a bookstore before.

"$650," I told Allie, and took a few steps toward Madeleine as Judy opened the receipt ledger. "Can I help you with an augury, Madeleine?"

"I am not here for an augury," Madeleine said. "I wanted to see where you work."

"Oh. Um. This is it." I hoped she wasn't expecting me to take her on a tour of the entire store, because I wasn't feeling that friendly toward her.

"I see. But these cannot be auguries, yes? Otherwise anyone might take one for herself."

89

"No, you're right. Only I can retrieve auguries."

Allie, still clutching her book close to her chest, scurried out past us without saying goodbye. I had no idea if she and Madeleine knew each other, but guessed Madeleine was famous enough that Allie considered staying out of her way the better choice. I glanced over my shoulder and saw Judy leaning against the counter, flipping the pages of the purchase ledger. She looked so casual it was impossible not to see her poised to attack Madeleine if she tried anything funny.

"You are Judy Rasmussen, *non*? William Rasmussen's daughter?" Madeleine sounded way too neutral about that.

"I am," said Judy, but didn't elaborate further.

Madeleine nodded, then ignored her, to my relief. If she meant to start a fight, it would be with me. "I have been thinking," she said, "and I believe it would be good for you to host a party. To honor your new home."

Oh, you do, do you? No word of apology for what she'd said at dinner the other night. "That's a nice idea, but I'm not sure when I'd have time. I work every day except Sunday."

"I would be happy to arrange it. You need only mingle with your guests." Madeleine tapped her sunglasses against her other hand. "I wish only for Malcolm's happiness."

If I hadn't been so suspicious of her, I'd have been relieved at her words. As it was, I said, "Even if it's with me?"

Madeleine shrugged. It was a graceful gesture that conveyed both indifference and resignation. "It is as you said. He must make his own choices."

I figured that was the best I was going to get from her. And maybe this was a good way to normalize relations between us. Maybe I'd regret it later, but I didn't want any bad feeling between us to be on my part. "I'll check with Malcolm and let you know when would be a good time for us. Maybe this weekend?"

"Certainly. And you need do nothing else. I will arrange it all." Madeleine put her sunglasses back on and smiled. With her eyes made invisible by the big black lenses, she looked like a mannequin in an upscale department store, with her smile painted on. "Until then."

Once the door had swung shut behind her, Judy said, "Did she really just offer to run your life? And you agreed to it?"

"She was way more polite than at dinner Sunday. I figured I could accept her olive branch, however grudgingly offered. And it's just a party. Hardly my whole life."

"She has the look of someone who'd use a party as a crowbar to get into the rest of your life."

"Well, I won't let her. And Malcolm won't either." I sounded more certain than I felt.

"You don't have to be nice to her just because she's Malcolm's mother, you know."

"I know, but I think Malcolm doesn't want the relationship to disappear, or he wouldn't let her be part of his life. And I don't want to force him to choose between us."

"It sounds like he's already chosen." Judy scowled. "I just hope you don't regret this."

"Me too. So...what are you doing this weekend?"

Judy sighed. "Apparently I'm coming to see your new apartment. I've heard it's luxurious beyond the dreams of mortal men."

"It's not *that* nice. But it is pretty nice. I just wish..."

"Wish what?"

"Nothing." I felt bad complaining about the place when I had only lived there two days, but it still felt uncomfortable, alien. "I'm just not used to luxury, is all."

The phone rang, startling both of us. "I'll get it," I said, and hurried to the office.

A torrent of Spanish filled my ear before I could greet the caller. "Wait, slow down," I said. I could make out only a few words, he was speaking so rapidly: *a la vez, augurio,* and *más rápido.* "I don't understand you. Do you speak English?"

The speaker cut off. There was some muttered conversation in the background. Then a new voice came on the line. "I speak English," he said, his words thickly accented. "Not much."

"That's all right." I felt unexpectedly guilty at not speaking his language. "Do you need an augury?"

"Yes. And *un decodificador*. The *augurio*, it is...*cómo se dice*, needed much and now."

"Yes, sir. An augury and an interpreter. It will take at least an hour. Is that soon enough?" His urgency had infected me.

"*Sí, sí*, is enough. My name is Rodrigo Batista and my question is... I do not all the words know. 'How do we stop *los tejedores?*'"

Los tejedores. Weavers. "'How do we stop the weavers?'" I repeated back to him. "Who are—" I stopped myself. Much as I wanted to know more, I needed to find his augury and an interpreter as quickly as possible. Questions could wait. "Call this number again in one hour," I said, and having gotten his assent, I hung up and rushed out of the office.

"Judy, call Jefferson Fleischer and see if he can get down here immediately. We just got a call from...I don't know where, but someone who speaks Spanish, and they want an augury interpreter. He sounded desperate. It could be South America."

"Jeff never answers his phone before six o'clock," Judy said. "I'll see if I can reach Shona Khalaf. What's the question?"

"More about weavers," I said, and ran into the oracle.

I half expected, based on previous experience, to see the ruddy light of "no oracle." But the cool blue light relieved my mind. *Hurry, hurry,* I chanted, though my hurrying wouldn't matter so long as the interpreter wasn't there when I returned. We rarely made use of them directly, but among the Wardens were a handful of people who made a living interpreting auguries for others. If Batista was in the kind of tearing hurry I imagined, getting someone to interpret the augury for him would naturally be far faster than waiting for the postal service to deliver the book.

I found the augury wedged so tightly between a row of Ngaio Marsh paperbacks I had to pull almost the whole shelf out to free it. *Textiles of South America.* I'd seen it before, but couldn't remember who'd received it. I ran, the book tucked under my arm, and nearly bumped into Judy on my way out. "Shona's on her way," Judy said. "Are they on hold?"

"I told him to call back in an hour. That should give Shona enough time for at least a quick answer." I realized I was breathing heavily and calmed myself. "He must know about the weavers."

"You didn't ask him?"

"There wasn't time. I figure I can talk to him when he calls back. I hope they're not actually fighting right now. Imagine how awful if the augury was too late."

We looked at each other, horror dawning. I opened the front of the book. "*Rodrigo Batista, No Charge,*" I read aloud. The silver ink gleamed in the bright afternoon sunlight. "I'm afraid to look away," I said.

"And *No Charge*," Judy said. "This has to be important."

I laid the book, open, on the counter, and we stared at it. "You said Shona was coming?"

"She said she'd be here in fifteen minutes."

We fell back into silence. I couldn't stop hearing Batista's voice, the controlled tension of it, overlaying fear. *Hurry, hurry.*

"I talked to Dominic," Judy said.

"Who?"

"Mr. Givenchy. We talked on the phone for a bit."

"That's wonderful!" I might have sounded a little too enthusiastic, but the tension of waiting was getting to me.

"It's just talking. But...he has a nice voice."

"I'm excited for you. Are you going out soon?"

"Maybe in a day or two. I don't want to rush things."

"That makes sense."

More silence. I was starting to feel the need to pee, but I didn't want to leave the book until Shona got to it. I flipped up a few pages without turning over the title page with its silver ink. "This isn't the first time someone's received this one as an augury. I just can't remember who else got it."

"The one who died. Miguel something," Judy said. "From the Durango Node."

"Miguel Moreton. Right. That can't be a coincidence."

The door bells chimed, and we both startled. A short, dark woman, her hair entirely covered by a hijab, came toward us. "I was surprised to hear from you," Shona said, her voice gravelly and low.

"It's someone from South America," Judy said. "They want this augury interpreted immediately."

"Immediately, huh?" Shona took the book. "Where's the contract?"

"I forgot to ask. It's urgent," I said.

"You know I shouldn't work without the official authorization."

"*South America,* Shona," I said. "He sounded desperate. I'm sure he'll give you the authorization when he calls back."

Shona flipped through the pages. "It's legible, so the oracle doesn't object. I guess I can make an exception. What's the question?"

I handed it over. Shona read it, her lips pursed in thought. "How much time?"

"He's calling back in forty minutes."

Shona's laugh filled the store. "You're not asking much, are you?"

"If you can't do it, we need to know—" I said.

"I can do it. I'll need some privacy."

We ushered her into the office and shut the door. "I hate waiting," Judy said.

"Me too," I said, dashing for the toilet.

We waited. A few Ambrosites came in; I filled their augury requests absently, carrying on conversations with half my mind elsewhere. Judy got the broom and swept up nonexistent dirt. I dusted the shelves, which didn't need it. Every few minutes I checked my watch. Its hands were moving so slowly I poked at the stem, wondering if it had been joggled into stopping the watch. It was almost six, but neither of us felt like getting ready to leave.

The office phone rang.

I dropped my duster and ran for the office, beating Judy by virtue of having longer legs. When I opened the door, Shona was already on the phone, speaking rapidly in Spanish. *She's Muslim, how does she know Spanish?* I thought, wildly and irrelevantly. She held up her hand in a warning gesture when we entered, her words pausing for a moment. Then she shook her head and spoke again, more urgently. She flipped the augury open and ran her fingers along a line of text; she sounded like she was quoting something. Then she nodded, said "*Buena suerte,*" and hung up.

I gasped. "I wanted to talk to him!"

"You did? I'm sorry. Go ahead and call him back," Shona said. "I didn't think to ask him how he planned to pay."

"It was no charge," I said, "and I don't have his number."

"Sorry." Shona closed the augury and stood. "You know you're not entitled to hear someone else's augury."

"His augury could mean the secret for defeating the Mercy!"

"It's still private. If I'd known you cared, I'd have asked him to waive privacy. But he was in a hurry, so it didn't occur to me."

I resisted the urge to grab Shona by the ears and scream my frustration at her. "Isn't there—couldn't you tell Lucia? Anything?"

"I can't. No one would ever hire me again. But I can tell you there wasn't anything about fighting in it. So I doubt it would be useful to Lucia." She came out from around the desk. "That'll be $100."

Grumbling to myself, I paid Shona, then Judy and I walked her to the front door. After she left, Judy said, "I can't believe you didn't get his number."

"I didn't think I'd need it!"

"I'm not blaming you. I'm just saying, I can't believe we were this close to knowing what the weavers are. Stupid Shona and her stupid rules about privacy."

"You know those rules are to protect everyone."

"I do. I'm still irritated."

"Me too." I rubbed my eyes with the palms of my hands. "I give up. I'm ready to go home and take a long, hot bubble bath. I deserve one."

"I'm ready for dinner. And my father should call tonight. Maybe he'll know something more. You should probably let Lucia know what happened, even if we didn't get the information."

"She'll just yell at me for not getting Mr. Batista's number." But I dutifully called and left a message.

My phone rang as I was pulling into the parking garage at Malcolm's—at *our* apartment. "You got an augury through to Honduras?" Lucia demanded.

"I—what?"

"Batista works at the Velasquez Node in Honduras. I've been trying to reach them for the last half hour—no luck. But they did receive their augury?"

"It was another one about the weavers. I don't know—Shona wouldn't tell me what it meant."

"Khalaf is way too honorable for my tastes, but I can hardly fault her for not wanting to ruin her reputation and her livelihood. Besides, it doesn't matter. Velasquez Node was one of the lone hold-outs in Central America—damn it, I warned Rodriguez she needed help, and she wouldn't listen. If Velasquez not responding means the Mercy has taken it, that means all the Central American Neutralities are lost and it's only a matter of time before South America goes the same way."

The seat of my car still radiated warmth from soaking up the sun all day, but I felt cold, my fingers only barely gripping my phone. "And then what?"

"What you'd expect," Lucia said. "They're coming north."

9

I sat on the freezing cold chair next to the front door. The bookstore smelled of onion, wafting toward me on a chilly draft. The bookcases, not much more than unfinished yellow 2x8s nailed together, stood crammed like rickety ladders reaching up beyond my sight. Where was Mr. Briggs? Should I follow him? I stood and took a few steps. The bookcases rushed toward me, surrounding me. They cast shadows that moved and whispered. I turned on my heel and couldn't see the way out. I walked, following the sound of distant conversation, my heart beating rapidly. Something was following me, something that stalked the shadows. My steps grew faster until I was running. Smoke filled my vision. "Something is coming," Mr. Briggs said. Blood spread across the back of his blue and gray argyle sweater—

I gasped, coming out of the nightmare like a swimmer emerging from the depths. Tears filled my eyes, and I wept silently, afraid of waking Malcolm. I wanted to cling to him, bury my face in his neck, but I knew from experience Malcolm didn't respond well to being woken abruptly. Instead I rolled onto my side, facing away from him, and cried out the fear and horror the nightmare had filled me with. This one was the worst yet.

It's not real, it's just your imagination, I reminded myself, but I wasn't very convincing. This was the fourth night in a row I'd slept poorly, and every one of those nights had ended in a nightmare I barely remembered. This time, I'd been at Abernathy's, but it was the day I'd come for the job interview, and Mr. Briggs... I shuddered at the memory of his body lying face down on the basement floor, blood pooled around him. I'd had nightmares of it once or twice after it happened, but it had been a year and a half ago. So what was triggering these images now?

My crying jag wound down, and I wiped my eyes and checked my phone. 5:34 a.m. I should try to get back to sleep, but experience told me I'd just lie awake going over the memory of the nightmare until Malcolm's alarm went off at 6:30. I rolled out of bed and went into the bathroom to wash my face, sliding the door shut behind me.

I turned on the light and stared at myself in the mirror. I looked as haggard as you'd expect of someone who hadn't slept well in four days. Four days that should have been comfortable and relaxing, on the nice bed in the fabulous apartment...maybe that was it. Maybe I just hadn't adjusted to the new place yet. I splashed water on my face and toweled off. I needed to let go of my old place, if only because I felt in agreeing to move here, I'd promised Malcolm I'd make it my home. Even if I still didn't know how to work the coffeemaker.

Judy wasn't at Abernathy's when I arrived, for a wonder. I dropped my purse in the drawer and went to the front of the store to retrieve the mail. Plenty of payments, a lot of augury requests. Nothing from South America. I tried not to feel discouraged, and set about performing the mail-in auguries. At least the rest of the world was free from the Mercy's attacks. Though with the way my life was going, thinking that would make it untrue.

At ten o'clock, when I opened the door to admit the waiting Nicolliens, Judy still wasn't there. It worried me; even if she was sick, she always called to let me know. Maybe she was on a breakfast date with Mr. Givenchy. The thought cheered me. I took the first augury slip and entered the oracle, which hadn't succeeded in cheering me all morning. It was just one of those days...which appeared to be turning into one of those weeks. If it went on longer than that, I might go crazy.

When I emerged, carrying a Merriam-Webster dictionary that weighed at least ten pounds, Judy was there, leaning against the counter with a scowl on her face I hadn't seen in months. "$275," I told the waiting Warden. "Judy, will you write up his receipt?"

Judy's scowl deepened, but she took the ledger and receipt book and began writing. I didn't want to ask what was wrong in front of all the customers. If she'd been on a date...but surely it couldn't have gone *that* badly, right?

I accepted the next augury slip and made my escape. Time enough to grill Judy when I could do it privately.

It was nearly one o'clock when that time finally came. I waved goodbye to the final customer and let out a deep sigh. "I can't remember the last time the morning was so busy," I said. "Did you... want to talk about something?"

Judy closed her eyes and covered them with her hands. "I went for coffee with Dominic," she said. "He's very nice. We talked for a while and had a lot in common. Then we said goodbye and I came here."

"That...doesn't sound good."

"It wasn't good. We just didn't have a...a spark. I mean, I think we could be friends, but it's never going to be more than that. And I'm just so *mad* about it!"

"Are you sure? Sometimes people...grow on you?" It sounded stupid the second it left my lips.

Judy lowered her hands. "What, like a fungus?"

"I'm serious! I didn't fall in love with Malcolm until..." I remembered how practically from the first moment I'd seen him, I'd been attracted to him, and let that sentence die a merciful death.

"I'm never going to find anyone," Judy moaned.

"Don't get discouraged. You knew going into this that it might take a while."

"Yes, but he was so perfect!" Judy gazed at me, her black-fringed blue eyes filled with annoyance. "We *should* have connected. But we could both tell it wasn't going to work."

"Well, why don't we look at some of the other profiles? And maybe you can contact more than one at a time. Or is that bad form?"

"I don't know." Judy sighed. "I guess I should get back on the horse, huh?"

"If that's what you want to call it. That sounds sort of suggestive to me."

Judy smiled, a weary, cynical expression. "It's a little early for me to be desperate enough to date a horse, isn't it?"

We ate lunch at the computer, going over Judy's prospects and narrowing them down to three. Judy sent off messages to each, then took a bite of chow mein and said, "I had no idea this would be so exhausting. Or that it would make me so hungry."

I speared up a final shrimp from my carton. "It's just Chinese food that does it. Or is it that you're always hungry an hour afterward?"

"I can't remember." Judy carried her carton across the hall to the break room to throw it away. "I've regained my optimism, though. One of these guys has to be worth the effort."

"Or all of them will be, and you'll have to flip a coin."

"A three-sided coin."

The bells over the door jangled. "When you find one, I want to be there to see it," I said, dropping my own carton in the trash and heading for the front.

To my pleasure and surprise, Malcolm stood there, leaning against the front counter as relaxed as a jungle cat. I kissed him and exclaimed, "What are you doing here? It's not two o'clock yet."

"It is 2:01," Malcolm said, "and much as I'm happy to see you, I'm here for an augury."

I glanced around him. No one loitered outside the store. "Where is everyone?"

"Lucia has summoned all the team heads, Nicollien and Ambrosite, to a meeting at the Gunther Node. I deputized Quincy to go in my place, because I have a theory I'm pursuing." He held out an augury slip. "I imagine none of the teams wanted to waste money on an augury that might prove irrelevant, depending on what Lucia has to say."

I took the slip and opened it. "'Where will the weavers strike next?' Malcolm, what are the weavers? Do you know?"

"Our best guess is that they are a specially trained type of wood or steel magus. And that *is* a guess. Unfortunately, no one who has encountered them has been in a position to tell us more than that."

"You said last night at dinner they haven't taken all of South America. Did they fail, or have they just given up?"

"All but seven of the South American Neutralities have been taken. Two of those were attacked, but managed to repulse their attackers. The remaining ones all report not seeing anything out of the ordinary. They also believe that *they* won't be defeated because of greater numbers or weapons or...they have many reasons. But they won't call for help. I hope North America will be less stubborn."

I folded the slip and stuck it in my pocket. "I'll get this for you. Won't Lucia be mad about you ditching the meeting?"

"Not if I return with good news," Malcolm said with a smile.

His smile dispelled the tiredness and worry I'd been carrying around all day, and I walked into the oracle with a lightness of step that matched my heart. The blue-tinged light soothed me further. "Things are going well," I said to the air. "I'm getting used to the new apartment, and...is it wrong for me to think that with Lucia in charge, the resistance to the Mercy will be more effective? It could just be because I know her, and I don't know any of these other custodians, but she's smart, and tough, and I really feel we have a good chance."

I caught a glimpse of a brighter blue gleam and hurried around the next corner to find a book glowing brightly at me. *"Shadow Woman,"* I said, turning it over to look at the back cover of the brightly colored dust jacket. "I hope it's easy to understand."

"$500," I said when I returned to Malcolm's side. Judy, who'd joined him while I was in the oracle, opened the ledger to write his name inside. "Can I ask what theory you're pursuing?"

"Lucia has mapped the progress of the Mercy, and I believe, based on her map, I can tell where they will strike next," Malcolm said. "I further believe that they are sending these people called *los tejedores*, or weavers, as an elite strike force that disables a node or Neutrality's defenses before the rest of the attackers sweep in and capture it. This augury is to prove my theory by independently identifying the next point of attack."

"You don't look happy."

"I'm not happy. If I'm right, the next node they strike at will be Las Vegas."

I gasped. Judy shut the ledger with some force. "There are three nodes in that area besides the Holley Node," she said. "Will that be the first place they strike north of the border?"

"If I'm right, yes," Malcolm said.

"But the Holley Node is practically in downtown Las Vegas! How will they keep that a secret?"

"The Mercy doesn't care about concealing itself from ordinary men and women. It will be up to the Wardens to keep it from becoming a national disaster." Malcolm tucked the book under his arm and kissed me in farewell. "Lucia will likely be sending people over for auguries later. Be ready."

"We will," I said.

When the door shut behind him, Judy said, "I feel so helpless."

"What are the other nodes there?" I asked.

"Small ones. Two under Nicollien control, one Ambrosite. They won't have the personnel to defend themselves against the Mercy. I hope Father comes back soon. He's good friends with Antoine Lefebvre at one of those Nicollien nodes and I'm sure he can convince him to ask for help."

"I thought it was just the Neutralities that were so stubborn about not wanting help."

"Sort of. With the smaller nodes, it's the responsibility of the area faction leaders to step in when something goes wrong. It's just that Molly Tanner—she's the Nicollien head of the Southwest region—isn't very strong, and she tends to follow the prevailing opinion. If Father can *be* that opinion, everything will be fine." She didn't look as sure as she sounded.

"The only thing we can do is keep doing auguries, and hope Lucia has a plan." I sighed and rubbed the back of my neck, which felt stiff. "Which I'm sure she does."

———

Lucia herself came into the store at twenty minutes to four. "I notice your boyfriend thinks he's too valuable to waste his precious time on me," she said. Her assistant Dave Henry, following her closely with a large briefcase, rolled his eyes. I guessed he'd been hearing about Malcolm all afternoon.

"Did his augury help?" I asked.

Lucia snorted. "I'm not admitting anything." She thrust a handful of augury request slips at me.

"This is going to take a while."

"So get started. These are important, Davies."

I dropped all but one on the counter and escaped. *What are the weavers?* the first one read. I cursed; the light was red-tinged and once again felt heavy. "Why can't you answer this?" I said. "It would be really helpful." The air shifted, and I spun around, my heart pounding. Nothing. It was my imagination.

"No augury," I told Lucia, holding out the slip. She read the question and cursed, more eloquently than I had. I took the next one. If they were all "no augury," maybe this would take less time than I'd thought.

But none of the others were rejected, and Lucia ended up with a stack of mixed hardcover and paperback books. Dave set the briefcase on the counter, extracted a couple of bundles of cash from it, and handed the briefcase and the rest of its contents over to me. "I hope these are helpful," I said, dutifully counting the money even though I was sure Lucia wouldn't cheat me.

"So do I," Lucia said.

"So...is the Holley Node in danger?"

"We're all in danger, Davies. But...yes, I think Campbell is right about where the Mercy will go next."

"But they haven't occupied all of South America," Judy said. "Why are they coming here already?"

"We think they don't want to waste resources besieging places that have already thrown them off once," Lucia said. "Bad enough that they have to maintain their newly acquired territory. Between you and me, that's what frightens me most—that they have enough people to hold those captured Neutralities."

"Couldn't we try to retake some of them?" I asked.

"If South America weren't in turmoil, they would. But they still aren't asking for help. Mendoza Node might. Castañeda's not a complete idiot. But he's still trying to go it alone. So at this point, I've given up trying to make them see sense. We'll have enough trouble trying to prevent the Mercy from sweeping over North America the way they have the south."

She looked grimmer than usual. Dave's face was bland, the way it got when he was trying not to say anything Lucia wouldn't want him to. "But the North American Neutralities will cooperate, right?" I said.

Lucia looked away, like there was something interesting happening beyond the store windows. "Neutralities are meant to operate independently. We don't ask for help unless it's dire. The north isn't any different from the south in that respect. I've been talking to my counterparts and I hope I've convinced them that this isn't the time for rugged individualism. I guess we'll find out in the next few days how successful I was."

She shook her head, and for a moment she was just a tired, middle-aged woman in yoga pants. Then the moment passed, and she flashed a cynical smile. "Tell Campbell not to think he's won," she said, pushing open the door. She and Dave walked to a small white van parked in Abernathy's magically reserved parking space and drove off.

"I'm scared now," I said.

"Me too," said Judy. She hefted the briefcase off the counter. "I think I have time for a run to the bank, if I hurry. I hate leaving a lot of cash in the store overnight, no matter how good the security is. Especially now it's unoccupied at night."

I helped her count up the cash and prepare the deposit paperwork, then sat at the desk and fiddled with the mouse. There wasn't much left to do, and it was late enough in the day that people were unlikely to come in. The decision to divide the store's hours into Nicollien time and Ambrosite time had inadvertently caused the magi to come in as early as they could manage during their respective times, leading to what Judy called the morning and afternoon rushes. I missed the early days of my custodianship, when Nicolliens and Ambrosites had mingled freely in the store at all hours. I'd hoped the appearance of a common enemy in the Mercy would cause those old animosities to vanish, but so far, it hadn't happened.

The phone rang, startling me upright. "Hello, this is Abernathy's, how can I help you?" I said, juggling the receiver in my surprise.

"Ms. Davies. I have an augury request." It was the smooth-voiced man, Galarza. "Are you ready?"

"Just a minute, Mr. Galarza." I pulled pen and paper from the center drawer. "Go ahead."

"The question is, 'Who has possession of the keys?'"

"I'm sorry, sir, but the oracle won't answer any question beginning with 'who.' You can rephrase it."

There was a moment's silence, during which I heard a murmur like distant voices talking. "Very well," Galarza finally said. "Let us try 'What will the keys unlock?'"

I scribbled it down below his name. "Would you like to wait, or should I call you back?"

"I will wait."

The sun was lowering in the sky, casting its deep gold light over the bookcases closest to the door. Motes of dust cascaded through the beams, less beautiful when I considered they'd end up on the books and I'd have to clean them up. Clutching Galarza's augury slip tightly in memory of that hot, gusting wind, I walked into the oracle.

The light went blue-tinged, which was a relief. I walked through the corridors slowly, casting about for the blue-limned augury. The sounds from the street outside had vanished. Even my footsteps were swallowed up in the silence. Warm air touched my skin, and if not for

MELISSA MCSHANE

that, it might have been one of Portland's rare snowy days, muffling all sound.

Ahead, the light glowed stronger. I quickened my steps, which still made no sound on the ancient linoleum, and rounded a corner to find a book glowing high on one of the shelves. I stretched for it, but it was just out of my reach. *Viv* was tall enough she could have reached it. Probably would have waited until I was watching so I could appreciate her long arms, something she'd been doing since she hit her first growth spurt and I didn't. Tucking the augury request into my pocket, I clambered up on the two lowest shelves and snatched the book with my fingertips.

It slipped out of my fingers and fell hard to the floor. Cursing, I hopped down and picked it up. The augury, still glowing blue, had landed face down amid the pile of tatty old textbooks that looked like they'd come from a library somewhere. I picked it up and turned it over. The cover of the mass market paperback bore a picture of a man standing in front of a spaceship and the title *Santiago* in bold red letters. It was scuffed like someone had been using it to buff a fender, and the spine was cracked in several places. I opened the book—

—and the light went blood red, as if the sun had gone behind thick stained glass. No silver ink decorated the title page. I sucked in a horrified breath and ran, clutching the book in one hand. I took the turn out of the oracle at speed and dashed for the office, dropped the book on the desk and snatched the receiver. "Mr. Galarza? *Mr. Galarza!*"

"Yes?"

I sank down on the edge of the desk. "Are you all right?"

"Of course. You have my augury?"

I looked at *Santiago*, then at the receiver, as if I expected to be able to see down the line to Galarza's face. "Um...I'm sorry, no. It refuses to answer. But—look, I'm really sorry. Does the name Santiago mean anything to you?"

"Santiago? No. Why do you ask?"

"I..." I didn't want to make guesses about the oracle to a complete

106

stranger, even one Lucia vouched for. "It's nothing. Did you want to try a different question?"

"Not today, I think. Thank you, Ms. Davies." There was a click as Galarza hung up. The whine of a dead line echoed in my ears. I sat holding the phone for almost a minute before hanging up. What had that been about? What did Santiago mean, and why did the name keep coming up when Galarza called? Lucia had said the Santiago Node was fine, they hadn't seen so much as the shadow of the Mercy sniffing around, but what if things had changed? *Or what if someone named Santiago knows about Galarza's stupid keys?* There were just too many possibilities.

I trudged back to the shelves and put *Santiago* away in a different place. Then I sat behind the cash register and fiddled with the keys. The thing was older than the store and looked it, with the ornate brass trim and the antique Victorian valentine appliqued to its top. We never used it except when someone made an ordinary purchase, which happened rarely. But it was beautiful, and I'd never considered getting rid of it for something modern and computerized, which would only have looked out of place in the store.

Distantly, I heard the office door open. Judy, back from the bank. "I was just going to check my email one last time," she called out.

I slumped back to the office and looked over her shoulder, uninvited, but she didn't object. "I have to make dinner tonight," I said.

"You sound so enthusiastic."

"I just feel tired. Mr. Galarza called back. No augury again."

Judy turned and looked up at me. "That's weird. Same subject?"

"And the oracle gave me a book titled *Santiago*. I just don't get what it's trying to say."

Judy closed down her email and set the computer to hibernate. "You do look tired," she said. "Maybe you should do takeout instead of cooking."

"I'm not that bad at cooking."

"I didn't say you were. It's just that by the time you get home, and then cook, it's going to be 7:30. And you look in need of an early night."

I shrugged. "You might be right." But it was the idea of driving across town to Malcolm's apartment that wearied me. So much easier if I still lived here. I blinked away the fog and mentally slapped myself. It wasn't Malcolm's apartment, it was our apartment, and I loved being with Malcolm more than I loved the little apartment over the store.

But as I locked the back door and got into my car, I couldn't help glancing up at the curtained windows and wishing I hadn't given my word.

10

The setting sun filled the living room with golden light that warmed me to my core even as it blinded me. I twitched the gauzy drapes closed, diffusing the light without dimming it. The sunlight burnished the leather armchairs and made the sofas, with their oddly soft woven upholstery, look even creamier than usual. I thought about reclining on one, but I was wearing a summer dress with a short skirt that would no doubt hike up if I tried it. Instead I ran my fingers across the black metal of the cold fireplace and marveled at how clean it was. The cleaning service was really good. I suppressed a fleeting annoyance that I should have been the one to do the cleaning. It didn't matter who did it, so long as it got done.

Behind me, the bartender was setting up, glass bottles clinking musically in an octave of tones. He had very nearly been my breaking point. Madeleine had oh-so-reasonably pointed out that we'd want to mingle with our guests, not serve drinks, but my problem was I didn't necessarily want this to be the sort of party with fancy drinks. But I'd given Madeleine permission to run the show, and Madeleine wanted liquor. If I hadn't already seen that she limited her alcohol consumption to a martini before dinner and half a glass of wine during it, I'd have suspected her of being an alcoholic.

Wonderful smells came wafting in from the kitchen, where Madeleine's cook—I had no idea what the man's name was and I was afraid to enter his domain to ask him—had already been hard at work when I arrived half an hour ago. I hadn't had time for dinner, and my stomach growled at my omission. I guessed I could make a meal out of hors d'oeuvres if I had to, or at least curb my hunger until everyone was gone.

Footsteps on the hardwood floor announced Malcolm's arrival. He looked amazing in a dark blue button-up shirt, open at the neck, and a suit jacket and matching pants. I'd suggested he just wear a T-shirt and jeans, and he'd smiled and said, "I've been to any number of my mother's parties, love, and she makes everything feel formal. This is a compromise." So I'd changed into this dress and hoped it was fancy enough.

Malcolm crossed the living room to take my hand. "You look beautiful," he said in a voice low enough that the bartender couldn't hear, "and I can't help wishing we weren't about to be overrun by our friends."

I smiled and ran a hand over his freshly-shaved cheek. "They have to go home sometime."

"True." He kissed me, and said in a louder voice, "Have you sampled the food? It's excellent."

My stomach chose that moment to rumble again, making him laugh and lead me in the direction of the kitchen. The cook glanced up at us from where he was rapidly chopping vegetables. Malcolm addressed him in French, to which the cook replied in the same language, eyeing me. Malcolm laughed and said, "Luc says such a beautiful woman should never fear her own kitchen."

I blushed. "I'm not afraid of the kitchen. I *am* learning to cook, you know."

Malcolm spoke to Luc again. Luc nodded and wiped his hands on the very clean towel he wore tucked into his apron's strings. He picked up one of the platters and extended it to me with a smile. I took one of the morsels, a pastry triangle that smelled like seafood, and bit into it. The flavor of shrimp and crab and cayenne pepper exploded in my mouth. I chewed rapidly and stuffed the rest of it into my mouth, suddenly ravenous. "That's amazing," I said when I could speak again.

Luc smiled and nodded, saying something with a gesture over the platter and two others, one bearing rounds of sourdough with some kind of creamy spinach topping, the other holding the tiniest shepherd's pies I'd ever seen. I took one of those and ate it in two bites. "Wow. Now I want to learn to cook so I can make all this."

"I'm sure Luc would be happy to teach you," Malcolm said. He said a few words to Luc, who nodded and went back to chopping vegetables. Malcolm and I exited the kitchen, nearly bumping into some black-clad servants coming the other way. "He loves feeding people who appreciate food."

"I certainly do that. I think my mom should meet him. They'd have so much in common. Mom even speaks French, a little."

"We should arrange it."

A chime rang out through the dining area, where Madeleine's people had shoved the long table and its myriad chairs against one wall to make more room for mingling. "Um. Are we supposed to answer the door, or is there a servant for that?" It made me feel even more like a stranger than I already did.

"Let's find out," Malcolm said, leading me through the living room to the short hall that went to the front door. Viv and Jeremiah stood there, gazing around the room in wonder.

"I feel underdressed," Jeremiah said. He wore his usual Birkenstocks and shorts with a T-shirt bearing a picture of a tree with roots that curved in spirals—no, they were in squares. Square roots. That one, I got. Viv wore a bright orange miniskirt that clashed with her cerulean hair and a halter top printed in orange and magenta swirls.

"It's not that kind of party," I said, feeling awkward because I'd let Madeleine make it that kind of party. But I was damned if I'd let my friends feel out of place. "You want the private tour before the hordes show up?"

I left Malcolm waiting to greet our other guests and took Viv and Jeremiah through the living room to the master suite. They were both suitably impressed. "I've never seen a tub this size that didn't have the Olympic rings printed on it," Viv said, sitting on its edge. "Do you ever get lost in this place, Hel?"

"It's not *that* big."

"This shower is big enough for three," Jeremiah commented.

"Okay, it's big. But I'm getting used to it."

I showed them what I thought of as the public bathroom and the second bedroom, which Malcolm was using as a home gym. Jeremiah whistled in appreciation at the elaborate sets of free weights and the stationary bike. "I want one of these."

"We have to choose a new place first," Viv reminded him.

"It could be a new place with free weights."

"Or it could be a new place with a room for me to practice in."

"You two practically need a house, with all your extra things," I said.

Viv and Jeremiah exchanged glances. "We've considered that," Viv said, but the way she said it made me feel I should direct the conversation elsewhere. So I took them out to the kitchen, where we looked inside but didn't enter so as not to disturb Luc, and wound up near the bar. Madeleine, who'd been in the apartment when I arrived, had left to change her clothes and hadn't returned yet. So I felt safe asking for a beer instead of something elegant and refined.

"So where is Malcolm's mother?" Jeremiah said, sipping his wine. "I thought this was her party, so to speak."

"I don't know. I'm a little relieved, to be honest." The doorbell rang again. "I have to go. Have some hors d'oeuvres, they're really good."

A black-clad butler stood at the door to open it for guests, so Malcolm and I ended up standing at the far end of the little hall to greet people. Music, something classical I didn't recognize, began playing, so subtly it seemed to be coming out of the air itself. More guests arrived, mutual friends, Malcolm's Ambrosite colleagues and Nicollien friends of mine from the store, and several people who weren't Wardens at all and knew nothing of the Long War.

For the first half hour I felt tense, certain that someone would give the secret away, or some Nicollien would start a fight with an Ambrosite or vice versa. But no one did. Eventually I reminded myself that this wasn't a Harry Potter novel, and Wardens were used to being surrounded by non-Wardens, and began to relax and even mingle.

"This place is beautiful, sweetheart," my mother said in my ear, making me jump. She laughed and said, "You need to relax. Everyone's having a good time."

I hugged her, and then Dad. "I don't know why I'm nervous. I guess I'm just wondering where Madeleine is." *And what she has in mind for screwing with me next.* Madeleine had been nice all week since the disastrous dinner party, but I was still wary, since I didn't think she'd changed her fundamental nature or her attitude about me. It was going to be a long time before she accepted me into her family.

"We'd love to finally meet her," Dad said.

"I'll introduce you. She was just going to change her clothes—oh, there she is." Madeleine had changed from her casual pantsuit into an elegant white gown that, rather than making her look overdressed, made everyone around her look tawdry by comparison.

Madeleine saw me and made her way through the by-now-sizable crowd in the dining room. "Helena," she said, clasping my hand, "these must be your parents, you look so alike."

"Yes. Madeleine, this is Roman and Louise Davies. Mom, Dad, this is Malcolm's mother Madeleine Campbell."

"Pleasure to meet you," Dad said, shaking Madeleine's hand. A faint look of distaste crossed her features, but was gone so swiftly I couldn't call her on it. Even so, it irritated me. "We've enjoyed getting to know Malcolm. You must be very proud of his success."

"He is a credit to the family," Madeleine said. "Following in his father's footsteps."

That stopped the conversation in its tracks, as I could see my parents didn't know what to say about Alastair Campbell, dead these five years. I piped up, "Madeleine, thank you for arranging all this. It's a great party. Everyone seems to be having fun."

"It is the least I can do for my future daughter-in-law," Madeleine said.

My mother gasped. "Helena!"

"We're not engaged," I said quickly. "No, we're really not, I'd have told you! Madeleine, what made you believe—"

"Surely you would not live together without being engaged," Madeleine said, sounding not at all embarrassed. "I would think your parents would have taught you this. It is simply correct behavior."

"Excuse me?" Dad said, his voice dangerously edged.

"Of course it is not my place to criticize," Madeleine said, "but *I* have always taught my children the difference between right and wrong. Excuse me, I must have a word with Pierre." She sailed away without a backward glance.

"What the *hell* was that about?" Dad said. Mom put a hand on his arm and shushed him. "How dare she insinuate...I don't know what she was insinuating. She has no right to judge!"

"I don't know," I said. My face felt hot and I wished I dared go after Madeleine and pull her hair out by the roots. "I'm sorry. That was rude behavior even for her. I have no idea what she was thinking."

"Malcolm's nothing like her," Mom said. "Sweetheart, you shouldn't have to put up with that."

"I don't, and I won't," I said. "Look, I need—Viv's here with Jeremiah, you could say hello to her, I have to—"

I ran for the bedroom and shut the door behind me, willing my face to return to its normal color. I didn't care if it was bad manners; I needed some privacy. Damn Madeleine Campbell. How dare she?

The door opened quietly. "Are you all right?" Malcolm said.

I turned and put my arms around him, resting my hot cheek against his shoulder. "I'll be fine. Madeleine just insulted my parents."

Malcolm swore and put his arms around me, holding me close. "What did she say?"

"I'd rather not talk about it. No harm done, but I had to get away or I'd have started a fight."

"And here I thought Mother had changed her mind. I'm sorry." He sighed. "I'll have a talk with her. I don't know how much good it will do, but she has to understand that sort of behavior is unacceptable."

"I wish I'd never agreed to this party. I should have hosted one myself if that's what I wanted. I just thought…never mind."

"You thought you could be the bigger person. I know. I think we should limit our interactions with her until she's ready to be reasonable."

"And what if that day never comes?"

Malcolm sighed and held me tighter. "We'll figure something out. But you are far more important to me than she is."

We stood there holding each other, listening to the muffled sounds of the party and the music, which in contrast was as loud and clear as it was outside. "Where is that music coming from?" I finally asked, lifting my head.

"The apartment is fitted with a sound system that pipes into every room, or can do," Malcolm said. "I thought I showed it to you when I showed you the security features."

"You might have. It was a little overwhelming."

"You'll get used to it in no time. It's barely been a week."

An unexpected pang struck me at his words, but I didn't have time to examine it because his phone rang. Malcolm said, "Sorry," and pulled it out to check the number. His brow furrowed. "Campbell here," he said, answering it and taking a step away from me that made me feel abandoned. "I hadn't heard. No." A long pause. "If they haven't called for help—yes, you know I agree with you, but what can we do at this point?" Another long pause. Malcolm's expression went bitter. "I can work with Spinelli," he said, "but I'm not so sure the feeling is mutual. All right. Will half an hour make a difference?" A short pause, and this time I could hear a familiar voice speaking loudly in the distance. "I have guests, some of them non-Wardens— all right. Yes. We'll be there."

He disconnected and stood staring at the phone in his hand as if he wasn't sure what it was for. "What did Lucia want?" I said.

Malcolm let out a deep breath. "The Holley Node was captured by the Mercy twelve hours ago. The survivors made it to a safe location, but the Neutrality is gone. I suppose we should be grateful that there were survivors, given how few there have been to date, but…" He shook his head. "Lucia wants all the fighting teams gathered at the Gunther Node in half an hour, to go over strategies. I think she isn't going to wait for permission to go into the other Neutralities in the area."

"Well, it's about time! I don't understand why the Neutralities have been so stupid about not asking for help."

"It's a tradition with a long history behind it that boils down to how custodians work together, or not. The strength of a Neutrality is its independence. Asking other Neutralities for help in policing the factions or themselves risks masking larger problems. But I agree with Lucia that that tradition was never meant to stand against an outside enemy like the Mercy."

"So do we need to get everyone out of here?"

"I imagine most of the Wardens here received text messages summoning them. I'm afraid I'll have to leave you, love, to deal with the rest of our guests."

"They're going to want to know why you're leaving. And why you're dressed like a commando, since I assume you won't be going in that getup." I waved my hand at him.

Malcolm smiled and kissed me. "The day I can't sneak out of a room full of people is the day I will hang up my knives for good. Just…entertain them. I'm sorry to abandon you."

"I understand. It's all right. Will you be back tonight?"

"That depends on what Lucia has to say. But I promise to call as soon as I know."

I left him changing and went back to the party. No one seemed to have noticed my absence. I saw Judy, who must have come in while I was hiding in the bedroom, and ran toward her while trying not to look like I was running. "Thanks for coming."

"Like I said, I had to see your palace. Where's Malcolm?"

I quietly filled her in on Lucia's call. Judy's eyes widened. "All the teams?"

I glanced around. Sure enough, the crowd had thinned. My parents had disappeared, though I was sure they wouldn't leave without saying goodbye and were around someplace. Viv and Jeremiah were having a heated discussion near the empty fireplace. Madeleine stood in the door to the dining room, talking to a servant. "All the teams. But who knows what that means in practical terms?"

Viv's arms were flying in agitated gestures now. That meant nothing good. I nudged Judy and we drifted in their direction.

Jeremiah was saying something that cut off as soon as he became aware of our presence. He didn't look happy. Viv looked furious. "Tell him he's being stupid," she said to me as soon as we were close.

"Um...no. What's going on?"

"Lucia told him not to go to this meeting," Viv said. "He's going anyway."

"I'm not going to stand by while other Wardens are risking their lives," Jeremiah said. "I'm as good a fighter as any of them. And I know the Mercy better than they do."

"But Lucia told you *not to go*," Viv insisted.

"She's afraid of conflict between me and the Wardens." Jeremiah's jaw was rigid. "If we can't make common cause against this enemy—"

"Jeremiah, if Lucia told you not to go, shouldn't you listen?" I said.

"Yeah, because you know she's capable of ripping out your spine and using it as a xylophone," Judy said. "I wouldn't cross her."

Jeremiah looked away, out the window. The sun had set half an hour before, and someone, probably a servant, had drawn back the filmy drapes so we had an excellent view of downtown Portland, sparkling with light. "I refuse to be helpless," he growled.

"You're not helpless," Viv said. "She needs you. Just not right now."

"Call her later. Ask her what you can do," I said. "At the very least you can prepare for defending Portland, if it comes to that."

He sighed. "Viv—"

"Let's go home," Viv said. "Like Helena said, you can call her later.

She's not going to exclude you when she needs all the fighters she has."

Jeremiah nodded. "Thanks for inviting us, Helena," he said, smiling. It lacked its usual brilliance, and my heart went out to him. I remembered how Malcolm had felt when he'd lost his aegis and been sidelined as a fighter, and hoped Jeremiah wouldn't do anything stupid.

11

Judy and I said goodbye to Jeremiah and Viv at the door. I was sure Malcolm was already gone, which left me feeling bereft even though that was stupid. He'd be back, or he'd call, and either way I'd know what would happen next.

I wandered through the living room, picking up abandoned glasses and paper napkins. When I returned from disposing of them in the kitchen, I ran into my parents. "We're heading out," Dad said, "just wanted to say goodbye."

"Thanks for coming," I said, hugging them both.

"It's a very nice apartment," Mom said. "Though you look like you're bouncing around in it like a pea in a cup."

"It's only been a week. I'll get used to it."

"And, Helena?" Dad said. "You know we'd never criticize your choices, right? We like Malcolm, he makes you happy, and that's really all we care about."

"I know," I said. "I'm so glad I have you for parents, and not—" There wasn't any point finishing that sentence when we both knew who we were talking about.

I felt grateful Madeleine was nowhere to be seen when I'd seen my parents off, because I was increasingly filled with unfocused anger and she seemed like a good target to vent it on. Why on earth had she decided to attack me by attacking my parents? And how could anyone think so little of her own son that she wanted to choose his romantic relationships for him, whatever he might think to the contrary? Well, I wasn't going to be fooled again. Anything Madeleine Campbell offered me, I'd refuse, no matter how innocent it looked. Then I'd run the other way. Malcolm might believe she'd come around, but I wasn't going to count on it.

It felt like forever before the last guest left and the servants began clearing away the party detritus. Madeleine emerged from the dining room and approached me, smiling slightly. "It is a good party, *non*?" she said. "Everyone enjoys himself, and you, too, have fun?"

"Until you insulted my parents," I said. "How dare you speak to them that way?"

Madeleine raised one penciled-on eyebrow. "It is simply truth. Parents should teach their children right behavior. You should not live with someone you do not intend to marry."

"That's none of your business. Or is it just that I'm not Andria? Because I'm sure you weren't this nasty about it when *Andria* was living here."

Madeleine shrugged, a gesture that said *I am too polite to argue with you*. "That was different."

Anger once again bubbled to the top. "That's ridiculous. It's absolutely the same. You need to stop pushing your antiquated attitudes on other people, and don't you dare ever talk to my parents like that again."

"Perhaps if you were more ladylike, I would not need to criticize."

I sucked in a breath and managed not to slap her. "Get out. Now."

Madeleine turned and left without another word. Breathing heavily, I sank down on the ottoman in front of the fireplace and seethed. Unladylike, was I? I'd show her unladylike.

"I'd apologize for hearing that," Judy said from the hall leading to the bedroom, "but you probably need to vent about it."

I shot to my feet. "That—" I stopped as I realized the bartender was still there, putting everything away. How many of the help had heard that? "Later," I said. "Why are you still here?"

"Father told me he wouldn't be home tonight after all. He's going to see about the Nicollien node near Las Vegas. I didn't want to be alone. Plus, I wanted to tell you about the date I had."

"Oh, right! Dinner tonight. How did it go?"

Judy knelt on the nearest sofa and rested her arms across its back, facing me. "He tried too hard. Kept talking about all the people he knows, most of whom I'd never heard of, and expected me to be impressed. And then he wouldn't let me split the bill. I don't mind a man paying for dinner, but not when it makes me feel obligated to him like it did tonight. *And* he's a lousy tipper. Of course, *he* thought everything was going great. He actually looked surprised when I turned him down for a second date. It made me feel bad for him. Not bad enough to go out with him again, though."

"Of course not. Well, that's one down. When will you meet the second one?"

"Brunch tomorrow. He's the one I'm least certain of. The ex-football player."

"Oh, he was cute, though! And he's a dot-com millionaire. That's got to be good for some interesting stories."

Judy stretched and glanced over her shoulder at the bartender, who'd finished packing things away and was preparing to leave. I was pretty sure all those bottles were going back to Madeleine's apartment, where she could drink her disappointment in me away. "I'm still optimistic. There are plenty of nice guys out there." She sounded less optimistic than her words implied.

"What about bad boys? Don't girls fall for bad boys? I mean, I never did, but there must be something to the saying."

"I went through a rebellious phase in high school. I'm over it now. Bad boys are so tedious. They all rebel in exactly the same way."

I waved goodbye to Luc and wished I could speak French. "Well, you're the expert," I said, curling up on the ottoman. "We just need to find you the right nice guy."

"And if he's a Warden, so much the better," Judy said.

———

Judy stayed until eleven, by which time Malcolm hadn't called or returned home. When she left, I took a tub of caramel butter pecan ice cream to bed with me and sat up eating and watching *Topper* and marveling at the special effects. Okay, by today's standards they were nothing special, but back then they must have made that movie the *Rogue One* of 1937. It kept my thoughts from circling back around to wondering where Malcolm was and why he hadn't called yet. Surely he wouldn't have gone to Las Vegas without calling?

I heard the front door of the apartment open and shut. "Malcolm?" I said, abandoning the movie and the ice cream.

"It's me," Malcolm said, coming toward me down the short hall to the bedroom. He looked exhausted, though not as if he'd been in a fight. He put his arm around me and steered me back to the bedroom, where he sat on the bed and removed his left boot. "Nothing's been decided," he said, starting in on the second boot. "All we know is the Holley Node was taken, but the three small nodes nearby were left untouched. Lucia and the custodians of the five other Neutralities in the vicinity of Las Vegas—"

"I thought it was just the Holley Node that was close to Vegas."

"It is. 'In the vicinity' meaning the Neutralities on the West Coast and surrounding Nevada. Those custodians are all here, discussing plans. The good news is they're willing to work together. The bad news is they can't agree on the next step. Lucia wants to attack the Holley Node immediately, but some of the others want to figure out where the Mercy will strike next and increase the defenses there."

"Those both sound like reasonable plans. I can see how they'd have trouble deciding what to do."

Malcolm removed his fatigues and stood there in his boxers and T-shirt, looking as if he was having trouble deciding what to do, too. I put my arms around him and guided him to sit on the bed. "Let's sleep, and in the morning, they'll have decided on a plan."

"Very wise," Malcolm said. "Though you should probably put that ice cream away before it melts all over the bed."

I made a face at him and took the ice cream to the freezer. When I returned, Malcolm was asleep, half under the covers. I pushed and prodded until he moved into a more comfortable position, then turned off the lights and the movie and got into bed myself. It was so comfortable I drifted off almost before I knew I was sleepy.

———

My long, trailing nightgown swished around my bare feet as I walked, one measured pace at a time, between the bookcases. Something was in there with me, something whose breathing matched mine. Ahead, the deepening shadows twitched, disappearing when I turned quickly to look at them. The breathing grew louder, still matching mine. My vision grew dim.

Smoke. There was smoke in the bookstore.

I coughed, choked, and wheezed as smoke filled my lungs. The crackle of flames was louder than the breathing. Sunrise—no, not sunrise, but fire. It lit the shelves and filled my nose with the stink of burning lumber and melting lacquer. Tiny voices cried out from every direction, screaming for help, and I knew without knowing how that it was the books. I ran, but the corridors never ended, they twisted in every direction, and I was lost—

I sucked in a deep breath of cool, untainted air. My body shook with terror, and I wrapped my arms around my chest and struggled to control myself. I felt sticky with sweat. Something had been chasing me, and there was fire—

The store was on fire.

I rolled out of bed and nearly collapsed as my shaking legs wouldn't support me. I had to get to Abernathy's immediately. The dream had to be a warning, it had to be, not a vision of what was already happening. I wasn't too late. I fumbled around looking for my clothes before I remembered I'd actually put them away instead of leaving them on the floor like I usually did.

"Helena?" Malcolm never sounded groggy when he woke, just perfectly alert. "Are you all right?"

"Something's wrong with the store," I said, stumbling to my closet without turning on the light. "I have to go there *now*."

"Did someone call? Helena, what's wrong with Abernathy's?"

I shook my head, forgetting he couldn't see me in the dark, and found the pants I'd worn to work the day before. "I don't know. I dreamed—there was fire—"

"You had a bad dream?" Malcolm turned on his bedside lamp, making my eyes water at the sudden brightness. "Nothing's wrong with the store. You just dreamed it."

I shook my head and pulled a shirt at random from the closet, buttoning it hastily. "It was real. A warning. I have to get there now."

"But how do you know?"

"I just know, Malcolm, and I have to stop it."

"I'll go with you," Malcolm said, sitting up. "If something's wrong, you might need help."

Malcolm's Mustang cruised through the midnight streets at higher speeds than were strictly safe. I pulled my legs up and wrapped my arms around them, trying to forget the horrible memory of the stinking smoke, the yellow flames, the tiny voices crying out for help. I leaned my face against the window, chilly despite the warm night, and closed my eyes. We'd be in time. We'd be in time.

The Mustang took another left at speed, pressing me into the door further. I sat up and strained to see to the end of the street. If there were flames, they'd be visible from a distance, throwing up clouds of smoke and sparks. Nothing. The street was dark and silent except for the roar of Malcolm's engine. Malcolm slowed to pass the quiet, unlit buildings. "I don't see anything."

"Around back, please?" I said. Malcolm drove around to the rear of the store and parked next to Abernathy's back door. I jumped out and ran inside, through the office and into the heart of the store. It smelled of paper and unvarnished wood and, more faintly, the woody scent of Malcolm's aftershave. No fire, no char, no smoke and sparks. I walked slowly through the corridors, touching books here and there to reassure myself that they were undamaged. Peace, tentative like a sprouting blade of grass, wound itself into my heart. It had been a long time since I'd felt this good.

"Helena?" Malcolm called out. I retraced my steps and found him standing by the cash register, examining the counter. "I checked the front door and the lock and alarm are still set. No one's been here since you locked up yesterday. And I see no signs of arson or even attempted arson. Everything's fine."

"I'm not crazy, Malcolm," I said. "I know it was a warning."

"I believe you. I'm just not sure what it was a warning of. There's nothing to say the store is going to burn down."

"It still reminds me that we have no sprinkler system, just that single fire extinguisher in the break room." I looked around. If a store could look innocent, this one did. "I want to stay here tonight."

"You what?"

"I need to sleep here. To make sure nothing bad will happen."

"Helena—"

"Just for one night."

Malcolm's lips thinned into a tight line. "No."

It was my turn to be shocked. "No?"

"Don't think I haven't noticed that you're doing your best not to get attached to the new apartment. This dream of yours is your mind's way of convincing you that you belong here."

"What do you mean, I haven't gotten attached? I've been trying my best, even though—"

"Even though what?"

Anger and exhaustion won the day. "Even though it really isn't my kind of place."

"You haven't given it a chance."

"I have so. It's not working."

"Well, I'm not moving back here."

"Nobody's asking you to."

Too late I realized how that sounded. I'd meant only that I didn't want this to be our permanent home, but Malcolm's expression had gone flat, the way it did when he was struggling with his anger. "I see," he said. "I didn't realize that's how you felt."

"Malcolm, that's not what I meant."

"Then what did you mean? Because it certainly sounded like living with me is no longer something you care about."

My sleep-deprived brain was shouting at me to say something, anything that would turn this situation around. "You know that's not true."

"Do I?" Malcolm brushed past me, and after a fuddled moment, I followed him through the shelves to the office. "I'm going home," he said. "Are you coming?"

I ached with weariness and with the remembered terror of the nightmare. It had been so real, but what if it was nothing more than a dream? And what if it was? I couldn't take the chance. "I can't," I said.

Malcolm turned and left without another word. I heard the car engine roar, and then he was gone.

I locked the back door and set the alarm, then trudged up the stairs and into my old apartment. Without undressing, I kicked off my shoes and fell into bed. My own quilt, not fancy enough for Malcolm's apartment, still covered the bed, and I crawled underneath and was asleep in seconds.

12

I woke to the golden summer sun shining through my window, feeling more rested than I had all week. No nightmare images plagued me, just the memory—

I closed my eyes and cursed. I'd fought with Malcolm, and he'd left. And I hadn't gone with him. How stupid had I just been? Pretty stupid, I concluded. In the bright light of morning, the nightmare that had propelled me out of his apartment and across town became what it was: not a warning of trouble, but a meaningless bad dream.

Outside, the muffled sound of car engines filled the street. I checked my watch, or at least looked at my wrist—I hadn't put my watch on when I left in such a hurry early this morning. And I'd left my phone behind as well. I groaned. I'd been so far beyond stupid they'd need to invent a new word for what I was.

I trudged downstairs in my bare feet and picked up the office phone, but sat staring at the buttons, wondering who to call. Malcolm was my first impulse, but if he was still angry—and I really couldn't blame him for that—he might not answer. He might also be busy with whatever plan Lucia had come up with. I refused to consider that I was being a coward and punched in Viv's number instead.

It picked up after three rings. "Hello?" Viv said, sounding curious. Of course, I wasn't using my own phone.

"It's Helena," I said. "I'm at the store and I forgot my phone."

"Oh. I thought you didn't work on Sunday."

"It's a long story. Can you come get me? My car is at the apartment."

There was a pause. "You're at the store with no car and no phone. This had better be a fantastic story." She hung up.

I set the receiver down and went back upstairs to use the bathroom. I was starving, but we'd cleaned out the kitchen and the refrigerator, which wasn't even plugged in right now. I checked the break room mini-fridge and came up with a Diet Dr. Pepper (Judy's) and half a carton of shrimp lo mein (mine). Breakfast of champions. I thought once again about calling Malcolm and again decided not to, much as I wanted to fling myself at him and beg him to forgive me. That was better done in person.

The phone rang. I raced to answer it, not knowing where my haste came from. It was Sunday, and the store was closed on Sunday; this was probably a wrong number. Or could it be Malcolm, calling to make up? "Abernathy's," I panted into the receiver.

"Ms. Davies."

"Mr. Galarza! How are you?"

"Very well. I have an augury request for you."

"Oh, uh, the store's closed right now, I just happened to be here..." *Screw this.* "But I guess as long as I *am* here, I could...what's your question?"

"The question is, 'Where should we travel next?'"

"All right. Um, is everything all right? In Colombia, I mean? Because of the Mercy?"

"We have seen nothing of them. But I am not in Colombia now. I am, how do you say it? On the road."

He sounded polite, but distant, as if he was waiting for me to stop yammering so I could fetch his augury already. "Sorry," I said, "just... I'll be right back."

I set the receiver down gently and hurried into the oracle,

hunched against whatever weird effect it might have for me this time. But the light was blue-tinged, and a hot breeze blew against my face, bringing with it the smell of the ocean, briny and damp. "I hope that's not going to persist," I said. "Dampness would spoil the books."

Silence, and the sound of the wind rushing past somewhere in the distance. I looked around and saw no augury immediately visible, so I started walking, keeping my pace slow despite my impatience. I couldn't help feeling Galarza's repeated failed auguries were in some way my fault, which was stupid and no doubt a product of my overdeveloped instinct for helpfulness. Lucia always said I had a tendency to dive into things armed with nothing but my sense of justice. I thought it was one of my better qualities, thank you very much.

The hot wind was growing stronger, and I tucked the augury request away in my pocket, in case the wind grew strong enough to blow it away as it had the first one. "Is Mr. Galarza just bad at choosing augury questions?" I asked, pitching my voice to carry over the noise of the wind. "Because I can't remember anyone being rejected so many times. Maybe I need to tell him to stop asking about his keys."

The wind died away to nothing. Silence echoed in my ears, so profound it pressed on my eardrums with a terrible aching pressure. Then it was back, but ten times as strong, whipping hair into my eyes and face so fast it stung, fluttering my clothes like it wanted to undress me. I clapped a hand over my pocket to protect the augury slip and shouted, "What is *wrong* with you? Is there some reason you're making me work for this augury? If you don't want Mr. Galarza to have it—"

The wind died again, leaving behind a profound silence. I pushed hair out of my face—I probably looked like a nightmare—and took a few deep breaths free of hot air. On the shelf ahead of me, a book began glowing. I'd never seen an augury come to life before, so to speak. Its outlines began as pale blue, but brightened gradually, as if it were connected to a dial someone was turning up a little at a time. Before it could reach its usual blazing peak, I took it off the shelf and opened it. *Rafael Santiago, $700,000.* My mouth fell open. $700,000?

Then I registered the name. Not Diego Galarza. Rafael Santiago. *Santiago*.

I put the augury slip inside the front cover and closed the book. "You aren't getting confused again, are you?" I said. Silence. The oracle might be under the influence of magic again, and that might explain all the weird effects, but I didn't think that was the case. The hairs on the back of my neck were standing up, and I felt an uneasiness that went all the way to my bones. If the oracle was working properly, and I had no reason to believe it wasn't...well, the oracle always knew the true name of anyone asking for an augury, as I'd learned in dealing with the murderer Mitch Hallstrom. And if someone calling himself Diego Galarza was asking for an augury, and the oracle gave it for Rafael Santiago...

I walked back to the office with the book tucked under my arm, thinking furiously. He'd claimed to be Diego Galarza, but I had no way of knowing whether that was true—I'd never met Galarza in person, never heard him speak. Anyone could call the store claiming to be anyone and I'd only find out the truth if the oracle revealed it. And those other auguries...I'd assumed the oracle had just been using Galarza's questions to tell me something, as I couldn't get into the oracle without an augury request to open the way, but it had been so insistent on the name Santiago. Something was wrong, only I didn't know what, or why it mattered.

I just knew it would be a very bad idea to give Galarza this augury. But I had no choice.

"Mr. Galarza?" I said, setting the book beside the phone. "I'm afraid the augury is going to cost $700,000. That's in US dollars."

"That is no problem," Galarza said.

Damn. I'd hoped that would be enough to dissuade him. "And... Abernathy's policy is that payment for an augury costing over $100,000 must be made in advance," I lied, and prayed I was right about this and that Abernathy's wouldn't reject me out of hand for a lie told on its behalf. Besides, it sounded like a policy I ought to implement.

"I can arrange a wire transfer immediately," Galarza said.

Damn again. "It will have to be tomorrow, when the banks are open. Can you call back then? I apologize for the inconvenience."

"It is no trouble. But what is the title of the augury?"

"I—I don't think—"

"Surely you will not begrudge me a little taste of the knowledge I will pay greatly for?"

I glanced at the title of the book. I couldn't falsify an augury, even if I hoped the oracle would allow it. "*The Rational Optimist,*" I said. "Can you give me your address?"

"Of course," Galarza said, and I wrote it down. "Thank you, Ms. Davies," he added, and the line went dead. I sat there staring at the paper, the receiver still pressed to my ear so the high-pitched whine drilled into my skull.

Las Vegas.

And he wouldn't give his real name.

My hand shook so much I couldn't hold the receiver. I set it into the cradle and tried to convince myself I was being stupid. There was probably a perfectly legitimate reason for him not to give his real name. Maybe this was an *aug. fam.*; those were always in the name of the person receiving them, not the one purchasing them. Though *aug. fam.* had to be declared before asking the question...even so, it was possible. And there were plenty of Wardens in Las Vegas who weren't associated with the Neutrality. Those smaller nodes, for example. This was all plausible.

Except all my instincts, and the actions of the oracle, were telling me this wasn't an innocent request. I'd been talking to a member of the Mercy. And the oracle had given him an augury.

"Why," I said, realized I was talking to an empty room, and dropped the pen on the desk. How could the oracle possibly choose to help the enemy of the Wardens? And I couldn't do anything about it. I was bound by my oath; I had to receive auguries for those who asked, without fear or favor. I shuddered. At least it would take a few days to ship this augury to Las Vegas. I hadn't helped the traitors yet.

Or...had I helped him without knowing it? I flipped open the cover and checked the copyright date. It was only a few years old.

What if...what if Galarza—if Santiago could find his own copy of the book? I'd never learned whether a specific book was the augury, or if any copy of the selected book would do. My hands shook again, and I dropped the book on the desk. Apparently I wasn't done being stupid. But the oracle had given him an augury; didn't it care about the survival of magery? Especially after resisting Santiago's requests for so long?

I took a deep, calming breath, then shrieked as someone pounded hard on the back door. In the next instant I collected myself and remembered that the Mercy weren't here in Portland. *Not yet*, a little voice deep inside me whispered. I ignored it and opened the door for Viv. "So why are you stranded here on a Sunday?" she said. "And why didn't you call Malcolm for a ride? Not that I mind."

I shook my head and climbed into the passenger seat of her old Econoline van. "I've been really stupid," I said, "and I hope Malcolm can forgive me."

The story took us across town to the freeway. "But you didn't have nightmares last night," Viv said.

"I had a hell of a nightmare last night! Weren't you listening?"

"I mean once you slept above the store, the nightmares stopped. Don't you think that's weird?"

"I—" I frowned. "Huh. I hadn't realized. You're right, that *is* weird. Do you think I've been subconsciously refusing to make Malcolm's apartment my home?"

"Maybe. Or maybe the oracle's trying to communicate with you."

"What, through my dreams? I don't think that's how it works."

"It's not like you know everything about it. Maybe there's some danger coming you have to avert. Or maybe there's going to be a fire and you have to be there to put it out."

"I think I'd be more likely to die in a fire there. It's not exactly equipped for fire safety."

"I guess a sprinkler system could do as much damage as a fire, with books."

"Right. There's a fire extinguisher in the break room and one in my—the kitchen upstairs. Malcolm seems to think that's plenty."

Viv pulled up in front of the Cheltenham. "I just think you should give the matter some consideration. If the oracle is trying to speak to you, you ought to listen."

"Thanks, Viv. For the ride, too. How's Jeremiah doing?"

Viv made a face. "He's still pissed because Lucia won't let him in on the plan. He's going out to the Gunther Node today. I made him promise to take me because he's less likely to start a fight if I'm around."

"You're such a good influence."

"You might want to ask your mom what she thinks about that." She drove off, leaving me standing in front of the apartment building, my clothes and hair disheveled and my head beginning to ache.

I waved at Mr. Clark, on duty at the front desk, on my way into the elevator. As I rode up, I ran through conversational gambits I might try:

Malcolm, I didn't mean to suggest—no.

Malcolm, I'm sorry I rejected you—too needy, and untrue.

Malcolm...I love you. Always a good start.

I ran down the hall and inserted my key in the lock. I'd found it in my pocket where I'd left it when I'd changed the night before. Good thing, too, because if Malcolm was gone, I didn't relish the idea of explaining to Mr. Clark why I couldn't get in.

"Malcolm?" I called out when I entered. No response. "Malcolm!" I ran through the apartment to our bedroom and found the door to the bathroom shut and the shower running. It was nearly nine o'clock, late for Malcolm to just be rising even on a Sunday. I slid the door open. "Malcolm."

"I heard you," Malcolm said, and my heart sank, because the sarcasm hung heavy in the waterlogged air. "Sleep well?"

That turned my heartache into anger. "Yes, actually," I snapped. "You?"

"The woman I love abandoned me, so no, not really." The water shut off, and Malcolm reached out for a towel. I took it off the nearby rack and handed it to him.

"That's harsh! I didn't abandon you. I just had to...I can't explain."

Malcolm stepped out of the shower, toweling his hair dry. "I apologize. I shouldn't have said that. I'm afraid I'm not in the best mood this morning, and I...anyway. It hurt, when you wouldn't come home with me."

"I know. I'm sorry. Can't you try to understand my position?"

"I don't think it's about your dream. Helena, I want to make you happy. I would give you the world if you'd let me. I want you to love this place, and I've done everything I can to make it appealing to you. I can't go back to that little apartment."

"I don't want you to!"

"That's not what you implied last night."

"I didn't mean we should go back to living above the store. I was just—it wasn't the first time I've dreamed of something bad happening to Abernathy's, and I thought it meant something. But I was wrong. It was just a bad dream."

Malcolm wrapped the towel around his waist. "That's symptomatic of the real problem. You don't want to live here."

I shook my head. "I don't feel like I fit here. It's so luxurious, Malcolm, and it just doesn't feel like me."

"If you'd give it a chance—"

"I'm not sure that's going to change. But I want to be with you, and if that means—look, maybe you're right. It's only been a week."

Malcolm sighed. "Come here," he said, and drew me into his arms. I put my arms around his shoulders, damp with condensation, and sighed happily. "I'm sorry I spoke so harshly to you. I know it's been a difficult transition. And it was wrong of me to suggest your dream wasn't a warning from the oracle. That was my selfishness talking."

"So what do we do?"

"I wish we could work this out now, but there's no time. My team has been called up."

"In the middle of the day?"

"Not for hunting invaders," Malcolm said. "We're going to retake the Holley Node."

13

"But what about the Mercy moving on? Shouldn't you be protecting whichever node they're going after next?" I stood aside as Malcolm left the bathroom.

"Not after Lucia received new information." Malcolm went into his closet and got out fresh underwear and a set of black fatigues. "You know Lucia's map of the Mercy's progress helped us identify their next targets. What we have learned is that the Mercy changed tactics five days ago. Up until then they were consolidating territory, claiming nodes of all sizes and murdering the Wardens staffing them. But then..." He pulled his T-shirt over his head, ruffling his damp hair. "Yesterday a team of magi secretly infiltrated the Rojas Node in Uruguay, which was captured five days ago. They reported that the Neutrality was empty. Not a single living person remained, just the bodies of the dead Wardens, piled up like...you don't need the details."

"Thanks." The partial image made me wish he hadn't said anything. "So why did they capture it if they weren't going to keep it?"

"They stripped the node of its *sanguinis sapiens*," Malcolm said grimly. "Milked every last drop from the source and took it with them. The Rojas Node might as well not be a Neutrality anymore. It will take most of a year for it to produce raw magic again."

"A *year?*" I sat on the bed, my knees wobbling. "I guess at least it will recover, right?"

"That's a very positive way of looking at what may be the worst disaster magery has ever faced." Malcolm pulled on his pants and strapped his gun to his right thigh. "Rojas is not the only Neutrality the Mercy has drained. There may be as many as six. And Holley Node is almost certainly on its way to being number seven."

"So you're going to attack it and stop them doing it."

"Exactly. We've had to divide our forces. Half of us are going to the Krebbitz Node, outside Fresno, which will be their next target. The other half will attack the Holley Node. My team is going with the latter group."

My heart pounded harder. "I see," I said.

Malcolm paused in his dressing to kiss me. "I know how hard it must be for you to wait, and wonder. I can't even promise to come back to you. I *can* promise that we will fight our best, and that I will not take stupid risks. Though I'm not sure I should even promise the latter, what with Lucia's strategy."

"What strategy?"

Malcolm sheathed his knives and sat to put on his boots. "Lucia wants information about the weavers. She's sending a handful of glass magi to take readings and see what they can learn about them. And she's assigned my team to protect them. It could be extremely dangerous, or it could be extremely boring, if the weavers have all left. We won't know until we're there."

I realized I'd clasped my hands tightly in my lap, so tightly the bone showed white, and made myself relax my grip. "Is that because you are what you are?"

"Thanks to Darius Wallach's efforts, I'm no longer the only magus with the tungsten steel alloy aegis, but I am the most experienced of our small group. So yes, Lucia thinks my extra abilities will be an advantage, and she *really* wants those glass magi protected. I can't blame her. Glass magi don't have offensive capabilities beyond what any magus can do. These four are brave to take the risk in the hope we'll learn something we can use."

"Is it anyone I know?"

"I don't know yet who Lucia chose. But I'll give them your best wishes regardless."

Malcolm stood and took my hand, pulling me up to stand beside him. "I'm glad you came home," he said. "I didn't want to leave with such bad feelings between us."

I stepped into the circle of his arms and rested my cheek against his shoulder, breathing him in. "I'm sorry I didn't come home with you. Though I wouldn't have—" Shock ran through me, turning my heart into a timpani. "Malcolm, someone from the Mercy called the store."

Malcolm's gentle grip on me went rigid. "How do you know it was the Mercy?"

"A lot of little things that added up. The oracle did an augury for him. I'm afraid I told him the title."

"Why should that matter?"

"If the augury isn't for a specific, physical book, but for any old copy—"

"They can find their own copy and read the augury." Malcolm swore, and held me tighter. "But you don't know if that's the case."

"No. And I don't know why the oracle didn't reject this question when it wouldn't give him the others. Unless..."

"I shouldn't ask you what the question was."

"I don't think the Mercy deserves to have its questions kept confidential. He wanted to know where they should travel next." I gasped. "Malcolm, suppose the oracle is steering them where the Wardens will be best able to fight?"

"That's a lot of supposition."

"I'm just reaching for an explanation that doesn't have the oracle a traitor to magery."

"I understand your desire, but I think jumping to conclusions is a bad idea."

I sighed. "You're right. I just feel I have more questions than answers these days."

Malcolm put two fingers under my chin and tilted my head so I was looking at him. "Something you can address while I'm gone."

"How long?"

He shook his head. "Long enough for me to miss you already." Then he was kissing me, his lips warm and soft on mine, and I leaned into his kiss, twining my fingers through his hair and wishing it could go on forever. He slid his hands down my back to rest just above my hips and pulled me closer, a gentle but insistent movement that made me go warm all over. "This can't go where I want it to go," he murmured against my mouth.

I kissed him a final time, then pulled away, smiling. "I'll be here when you get back, and then it can go wherever you like."

"I'll hold you to that." Malcolm kissed my forehead, lightly, and gave my hand a final squeeze. I followed him to the front door, where we shared one last kiss, then I watched him walk away down the corridor to the elevator and waved goodbye as its doors shut. I closed the apartment door and sagged against it. I felt too numb to cry—numb from encountering the Mercy, from having to say goodbye to Malcolm before we'd completely made things right, from not knowing what to do next.

I trudged into the living room and looked around. It was just too fancy—no. I wasn't going to think like that anymore, it would just make things harder. Yes, it was way more luxurious than I was used to, but maybe that could change. Malcolm loved this place. What could I do to make it mine?

I sat on one of the sofas and bounced for a minute. It was too warm to turn on the fireplace, not that I knew how, or I'd see how it felt to cuddle up in front of it. I could turn on some music, something I liked...assuming I could figure out how to work the music system. Well, I was damn well going to try.

It took a few minutes' poking around to discover the console that controlled the music. It looked like it was connected to some kind of satellite radio service, because there were a gazillion stations. Music by decade. Music by genre. Music by artist. And a dozen buttons and sliders, all neatly labeled. This was harder than I'd thought. I poked a button labeled *Bedroom* and heard, drifting from the bedroom, the sounds of something classical and upbeat. I didn't think I'd chosen classical and upbeat. What about...Broadway Musicals? I hated watching musicals because in most of them, the songs stopped the story dead, but I loved listening to the soundtracks. I tuned into that station and the classical music in the bedroom turned into Idina Menzel belting out "Defying Gravity."

I whooped and pushed every button there was. The apartment suddenly filled with music, loud enough that the windows thrummed with the sound. I quickly turned down the volume, but not by much, and stood with my eyes closed. I might easily have been in a Broadway theater, the sound quality was that good. This...was actually a lot of fun.

I ran to the bedroom and stripped off my clothes, turned the shower up to full, and scrubbed myself clean to the sound of "Agony" from *Into the Woods* and then something from the *Matilda* soundtrack. Bathed and clad in clean clothes, I danced my way back to the living room and flung myself on a sofa. The music had moved on to *Hamilton*, which I'd never seen—was there a way to get it to play the entire soundtrack? I rolled off the couch and went back to pushing buttons.

An off-key tone rang dissonant through the melody. Weird. It sounded again, and this time I recognized it as the doorbell. Oops. I must have disturbed the neighbors. Flushing crimson, I swiftly turned the volume down to a barely audible hum and ran for the door. "I'm sorry, I didn't mean—"

Madeleine stood there, an irritated look on her face. "I dislike waiting," she said.

"I didn't think about how loud the music was. I'll turn it down."

She made a waving motion with her hand, dismissing my words. "I did not come about your music. These apartments are sound-proofed, and ours have been treated with a permanent sound-cancelling illusion." She walked past me without waiting for an invitation that I absolutely was not inclined to give.

"Then…" I couldn't think of a way to ask her her business without sounding rude. Much as I disliked her, I certainly wasn't going to take the low road.

"I have just returned from conveying many magi to the Krebbitz Node. I know Malcolm is gone and I thought to provide you with some company."

I'd almost forgotten Madeleine was a stone magus. Could I get away with shoving her bodily out the door? "That's nice of you, but I don't mind being alone," I said. "I am curious about how a stone magus ward-steps. That is what you did, right?"

"It is a form of ward-stepping, yes. Different when one does it oneself as opposed to conveying another." Madeleine sank into one of the leather chairs with the air of someone who planned to make it her new home. "Most comfortable for you and the other is to work with a second stone magus to carry the person across, but it is also slowest. Today I altered the stone wards to have identical… pattern, it is in English. It confuses reality enough that a person may step onto one ward and be instantly transported to a different one."

"That's amazing."

"It is sick-making, unfortunately. But speed is of the essence now, in defending the Krebbitz Node and retaking the Holley Node." Madeleine, I now noticed, looked drawn and tense, her skin pasty and her eyes dark-circled.

"It must take a lot out of you," I said. Madeleine waved that away, too.

"It is how we serve, as Wardens," she said. "I as stone magus and you as custodian of Abernathy's."

That sounded like a leading statement, but I wasn't sure where she thought she was going with it. "Wardens all do different jobs, that's true."

"Andria is not a magus. She is a capable administrator of Campbell Security." Madeleine's voice sharpened. "Perhaps too capable."

"I...don't see how that's possible. Shouldn't Campbell Security have the very best?"

Madeleine regarded me narrowly. "She threatens Malcolm," she said. "He does not like strong women. He likes mousy, quiet ones." She waved her hand in my direction.

I sucked in a furious breath. "Excuse me?"

"Then how else do you explain his rejection of Andria?"

Words filled my mouth, stilling my tongue. "Maybe because she's manipulative, scheming, two-faced, and selfish?" I finally sputtered. "Which explains why *you* think she's such a kindred spirit!"

Madeleine's lips thinned in anger, and for a single wild instant I thought *She looks just like Malcolm.* "You do not speak so of a woman you barely know," she said.

"I've seen enough of her to know I'm right. Give up, Madeleine. You've lost."

"I will not give up on my son seeing the truth."

"The truth?" I laughed. "That's not truth, that's just you being delusional."

Madeleine said something in French that I didn't think was complimentary. She added, "A Campbell deserves better than someone like you."

"I wish I understood your warped logic. No, wait, I forgot—I don't care. But I think most people would say the custodian of one of the most powerful named Neutralities in the world is plenty good enough for anyone. Even a Campbell."

Madeleine's expression shifted. She said, "I will make it worth your while to release my son."

"What?"

"I can pay you a million dollars. From me to you. You just have to tell him goodbye."

I stared at her in disbelief. A million dollars? "You have got to be kidding."

"One and a half million. You will never get this chance again."

"Madeleine—" My throat was dry. I swallowed so hard it hurt. "Don't you care even a little bit about what Malcolm wants?"

"He does not know what he wants. It was his father's wish to see him happy with Andria." The corners of her mouth turned down in a frown. "Please."

"There's no amount of money in the world that could make me give Malcolm up. And, Madeleine? If I were you, I'd never try to use his father to convince him to do what you want. I think it would go badly for both of you." I took a step backward, toward the door. "I think you should leave now."

Madeleine rose. She was shaking all over, though I couldn't read her face to know what emotion held her in its grasp: anger, disappointment, fury? Maybe all three. "You will wish you had taken my offer," she said.

"I really won't. Goodbye, Madeleine."

I followed her to the door and saw her safely out, then leaned against it for the second time that day and concentrated on breathing in and out until my heart calmed down. *Imagine having her for a mother-in-law,* I thought, *for the grandmother of your children.* She was terrible, and would be a terrible influence on our children, and I didn't think Malcolm appreciated just how bad she was.

Our children. I hadn't thought in terms of having children with Malcolm before, but the idea felt good. Natural. For the first time, I looked into the future and could easily see myself with Malcolm for the rest of our lives. Married. How funny, that my encounter with Madeleine would get me thinking about marriage—or maybe it was just her mention of engagement at the party that had done it. Malcolm hadn't proposed to me before because I wasn't ready. Maybe that had changed.

I looked up at the curving brass rods of the light fixture. One of the bulbs had burned out, and I didn't know where we kept spares. Or if spares were something the building maintenance took care of. That was a level of so-called comfort I was not going to get used to, depending on other people to change a damn light bulb. I let out my breath in a high, thin stream. I couldn't marry Malcolm if his mother was still an immediate part of his life. She wasn't a minor problem, she was a full-on disaster. And I couldn't go on living in this apartment if Madeleine was in a position to attack me whenever she felt like it.

I sighed and scrubbed my eyes with the heels of my palms. Malcolm would be home soon, and we would figure all of this out— the apartment, his mother, our future together.

Maybe.

14

My earlier good mood had evaporated, and now the music still playing quietly in every room felt inappropriate. I turned it off and lay down on one of the sofas again. I was starting to feel hungry—well, I had only had half a box of lo mein and a Diet Dr. Pepper. Maybe I could make something, not just throw food together, but actually cook. Getting used to the intimidating kitchen was part of learning to love the apartment. And it would keep me from thinking about where Malcolm might be right now and what he might be doing.

I sat at the center island and flipped the pages of my cookbook. Chicken soft tacos, that sounded easy. I didn't think I was ready to tackle steak, though the book made it sound simple. Pork stir fry. I could do that. I started making a list to take downstairs to Mr. Clark. Maybe he could get all this stuff before lunch.

I heard my phone ringing in the bedroom and dashed for it. Viv. "What's up?"

"Jeremiah went to the Krebbitz Node," Viv said. She was crying. "Against orders."

"*What?*"

"I told him not to—I don't know how he convinced someone to take him."

"Viv, he'll be all right. He can take care of himself."

"Surrounded by hundreds of Wardens who all hold grudges? He can't protect himself and fight too."

"They don't all hold grudges. Evanna Nicholes supports him."

"Evanna's just one person. And she went to the Holley Node. Hel, I'm so scared for him."

"Why don't you come over? You shouldn't be alone." I figured neither should I. "You can help me cook."

"Are you sure you want to tempt the apocalypse by cooking at a time like this?" It was weak, but at least it sounded like her.

I went for faux outrage. "Why does everyone think I can't cook? I haven't ruined a single meal since I started."

"You've only cooked three meals since you moved in. I think it's a little early for celebration."

We traded a few more friendly jabs, then I hung up and went downstairs with my list and to warn Mr. Clark that Viv was coming over. I didn't know him well yet, and I was afraid he might think Viv, with her blue hair and unusual fashion sense, might be the sort of undesirable it was his job to keep out. But he was perfectly polite and professional and promised my groceries would arrive before noon.

I rode the elevator back upstairs and shut the front door behind me. The silence of the apartment echoed, and melancholy settled back over me. They might be fighting already. What would the glass magi do? Could Malcolm and his team protect them? I shook away a tear and went to the music console to turn on something to drown out my fears. '70s arena rock, Malcolm's favorite. I cranked it up and pretended it was playing because he was here. He'd told me his father had gotten him into this kind of music. I wondered if he ever listened to it and pretended his father was there, as I was pretending now.

The system had gone through a number of songs I wasn't familiar with, plus "Tom Sawyer," before Viv rang the bell. She had a six-pack of Diet Coke bottles and a bemused expression. "I didn't know you liked Rush."

"I don't. That is, I don't *not* like Rush, it's just…"

"You need to turn on something that doesn't remind you of Malcolm, sweetie." Viv brushed past me and found the music console. "Wow, you could use this to launch the space shuttle." Neil Peart's drumming cut off mid-stroke, and Regina Spektor's melodious voice filled the air. "I have never been jealous of anything you have until right this moment. I covet this system."

I laughed, and it didn't sound forced. "Thanks for coming over."

"Thanks for inviting me. I'm trying not to think about Jeremiah. He was so angry with Lucia, I thought he might actually take a swing at her. So did Dave. He didn't look like he was confident he could take Jeremiah. Maybe that ought to be reassuring."

"Dave's not a magus. Anything he did to Jeremiah would be lethal. And it's not like Lucia can't handle herself."

"I know." Viv plonked down on one of the leather chairs and put her face in her hands. "Helena, what if he doesn't come back?"

"He'll come back. He'll fight the Mercy and prove himself and everyone will know where his loyalties lie."

"I hope you're right." She didn't sound certain. I took a Coke from the six-pack. It was warm, but I swigged it down anyway and let the caffeine have its way with me. I put the other bottles in the fridge and offered one to Viv, who shook her head. I sat across from her, closed my eyes, and listened to the music. It was sweet and sad all at once, and it made my heart ache with longing. I jumped up and turned it off. "Hey!" Viv exclaimed.

"I'm sorry. It was either that or burst into tears. Let's watch a movie. Something really silly. Like—something we loved when we were kids."

"*Bring It On?*"

"Perfect."

Figuring out how to work the streaming service took a while, and we didn't have any microwave popcorn, but after about fifteen minutes, we were settled in to watch. Just as the opening credits came to an end, the doorbell rang. "That's my groceries," I said, hopping up.

"You have a personal shopper?"

"I guess it's all part of the concierge service."

But it wasn't the groceries. It was Judy. "Please tell me you have hard liquor," she snarled, pushing her way past me.

"I, um...no, not really—what's wrong?"

Judy came to a stop in the middle of the living room, ignoring the movie playing on the giant screen behind her. "I'll tell you what's wrong," she said furiously. "Men are what's wrong. They're lying, lecherous, selfish, arrogant sacks of crap, and if I never see another man again, I can die happy."

Light dawned. "You had that brunch date with the millionaire today. I take it it didn't go well."

Judy flung herself into one of the leather armchairs. "I wondered why someone like him would be on an online dating site. You'd think he could find plenty of women interested in dating him." She crossed her arms over her chest and scowled at nothing.

"So what happened?" Viv prompted.

Judy rolled her eyes. "The brunch date was at his house. His mansion, actually. You think *this* place is nice, you should—it's got to be six thousand square feet, easy, and that's just the parts you can see. He told me there's an Olympic-sized pool in the basement, and there's a tower you could lock Rapunzel into. It practically smelled like money. But in a tasteful way. I was impressed."

"So he went overboard to impress you," I said.

Judy waved me to silence. "A butler answered the door. An actual butler."

"Judy, *you* have a butler."

"Only for parties. Not for all the time. Anyway, he showed me in, and I stood there taking it all in. Then Aldo—his name's Aldo, sounds like a dog's name—came down the stairs. And he was dressed to impress, I can tell you that. Michael Bastian all the way."

"Oooh, I love his clothes. Was it the casual collection or a suit?"

"His clothes don't matter, Viv."

Viv whistled. "You must be seriously pissed off to say that."

Judy threw herself out of the chair and paced below the TV

screen. "So Aldo comes in, and he's charming and friendly, compliments my dress, asks if the drive wasn't too long. Small talk. And I think, hey, this is pretty nice, I like him so far. And *then*—" Judy stopped pacing and turned to face us—"he says, 'So, do you want to have sex before the meal, or after?'"

The room went silent. After a few seconds, I said, "What?"

"I'm totally serious. And so was he. Completely straight face, like he'd asked if I wanted my eggs scrambled or poached. So I laughed—I thought it had to be a joke—and said something like 'wouldn't want to have sex on a full stomach.' And he said 'Okay' and took my hand and led me up the stairs. We were most of the way to his bedroom before I realized he meant it."

"Judy! What did you do?"

"Once I figured it out, I yanked my hand away and shouted at him. Called him some names I won't repeat. But he didn't get mad or anything, just said that most girls like having sex with a millionaire and we could wait until after brunch if I wanted. So I called him a few more names and I came straight here." She started pacing again. "It's just so surreal I'm starting to wonder if I imagined the whole thing, but the look on his face...I couldn't make that up."

The doorbell rang again. "Wait," I said, and ran to answer it. This time it was the groceries. I accepted the paper bags from the man in the black suit, realized I didn't have any way to tip him, realized further I didn't know if I *should* tip him, and ended up just smiling and thanking him. I could ask Malcolm later, when he got back.

If he got back.

I set the bags on the kitchen's center aisle and put away the meat and other perishables, calling out, "Judy, how can someone like that not have all kinds of warning notices on his profile? Or get banned?"

"*I* don't know." Judy shrugged. "Maybe he's right, and some women get off on the smell of money. He hasn't been with the site long, so maybe he just hasn't been reported yet. I sure intend to report him first thing tomorrow morning."

"I'm so sorry," I said. "I thought he looked nice."

"Apparently looks aren't everything. Who knew?" Judy said. "I need a drink. It can be a Coke. I just have a bad taste in my mouth."

Viv got up and got a Diet Coke from the fridge. As she handed it to Judy, she said, "At least I'm not thinking about Jeremiah anymore."

"Why wouldn't you think of Jeremiah?"

Viv and I exchanged glances. "Do you know what happened with the Holley Node today?" I asked.

Judy's face went grim. "Father's out at one of the Nicollien nodes near Holley today. He was hoping to persuade them to join in the attack on the Holley Node. I think they turned him down. They're concerned about protecting themselves, as if the Mercy cared anything about these tiny little specks of nothing. Did Malcolm and Jeremiah go?"

"Malcolm is part of the attack on the Holley Node. Jeremiah went with the other teams to the Krebbitz Node."

"Against orders," Viv said. "And now I'm thinking about him again." She collapsed face-first on the sofa and drummed her fists on the cushions. Judy took her seat again and sipped her Coke.

"And we just have to sit here and wait," she said. "How long has it been since they left?"

"Malcolm left here almost two hours ago. I don't know when the attack began."

Judy stood. "That's it," she said. "We are *not* going to sit around waiting for the menfolk to get back from the war. We are empowered, modern women who don't have sex with random millionaires, and we're going to do something about it."

"About...not having sex?" Viv said, raising her face from the sofa cushion.

"About not knowing what the hell is going on. Bring your drinks. We're going to see the Kellers."

———

HARRY AND HARRIET KELLER LIVED ON THE WEST SIDE OF TOWN, IN A blocky house that had been ultramodern fifty years before and was still very attractive in a modernist sort of way. I ended my call as Judy threaded her way up the winding streets choked with greenery. "She says she was expecting us," I said in some confusion. "But she wouldn't say why."

"Probably because she knows we're empowered modern women," Viv said. "I'm still not sure why we're coming here."

"Because Harriet will know what's going on. She used to fight in the Long War before she and Harry went into business for themselves and started raising a family." Judy took the turn into the Kellers' long driveway. At this time of year, it was lined with blooming rosebushes of a dozen different colors, all leaning forward to kiss the sides of Judy's Nissan. When we parked and got out, I fingered the petals of a rose so dark red it was nearly black. The sweet scent of blooming summer mingled with the rich greenness of the arborvitae lining the backyard. It was almost enough to calm my troubled spirits.

"Girls, come in," Harriet said when the door opened. She hugged each of us, and her smile was so pleasant it did what the roses hadn't achieved. "I thought I'd see you earlier."

"Why were you expecting us?" I said.

Harriet's smile broadened. "Because you'll want to know what's going on with the attacks. Come in, come in, Harry will get you some ice water. It's a hot day, isn't it?"

"Hot enough to fry the ticks off a coon hound," Harry said, shuffling in with a tray of glasses and a metal pitcher that clinked. He'd never fully recovered physically from the invader attack that had damaged his aegis and made him not a magus anymore, but his voice was as strong as ever.

"I think you made that one up," Viv said.

Harry winked. "I'll never tell."

"So you didn't know I'm one of the glass magi receiving field reports?" Harriet said. We settled in on her pale gray sofas around the oddly-shaped glass coffee table Harriet used in her magic.

"Lucia didn't tell us *anything*," Viv said, "and I'm worried. Can you watch the attacks? Like on TV?"

"I'm afraid not. That requires a much bigger setup than this room would hold."

"Why aren't you doing it at the Gunther Node, then? They've got room."

"Because I work most comfortably and efficiently at home, not surrounded by any number of magi doing their own magic. So no, we can't see. But we'll be able to hear what happens when they attack the Holley Node."

"So it hasn't started yet?" I said.

"Not the Krebbitz Node?" Viv exclaimed.

"No, and no," Harriet said, looking closely at Viv. "Is your young man there?"

Viv nodded.

"I wouldn't worry. He's a strong magus and the Krebbitz Node is well defended by men and women like him," Harriet said. Viv said nothing. It wasn't the enemy Viv was worried about.

"Malcolm said his team will be defending the glass magi who are supposed to...I'm not exactly sure what they'll be doing," I said.

Harriet nodded. "The glass magi will be looking for traces of anything unusual, trying to work out what exactly these so-called weavers are. I don't anticipate they will meet much resistance, if the Mercy has moved on. I'm told in the other nodes, they left only technicians to extract the *sanguinis sapiens* and a few wood and steel magi to protect them." She stood and went to the drinks cupboard at the far end of the room. "But I and five other glass magi will be taking their reports as they come. Just in case we're wrong, and they don't make it back."

Her matter-of-fact tone chilled me. "But they'll come back."

"Don't worry, dear, Malcolm and Brittany will bring everyone back safely." She removed a black lacquered box twice the size of a shoebox from the cupboard, which I now saw was empty of drinks, and returned with it to her seat. She handed the box to Harry, who settled it on his knees. It had no lid, and overflowed with glassware in myriad colors and shapes. Harry picked through it, choosing a few objects and setting them on the small round table next to him: a blue pyramid the color of a midnight sky, a delicate golden lily, a crimson orb the size of a basketball, flattened on one side so it didn't roll. Harriet nodded and picked up the lily.

"Are you sure about this one?" she asked.

"Best tone and volume," Harry said. "And the seashell broke, remember?"

"Ah, true." Harriet set the lily aside and withdrew a reflex hammer from the pocket of her slacks. She tapped the surface of the table three times, lightly, then gave a much harder tap the fourth time. The glass began rippling like water someone had thrown a stone into, lapping against the brass frame encircling the table's top. With precise care, Harriet lifted the blue pyramid, which was about the size of her fist, and set it in the center of the table.

The shape of the waves changed. Where before they'd flowed wildly in all directions, now they spent themselves on the sides of the pyramid, which despite being small remained immovably in place. Harriet gently laid the lily atop the pyramid with the mouth of the flower pointed toward her, balancing it carefully so it wouldn't fall. The waves subsided slightly. They'd turned a faint bluish color, too, and from the table came a faintly acrid scent, like bleach. Viv sneezed, a tiny explosion in the silent room, but Harriet didn't seem disturbed by it.

Without a word, Harry picked up the orb and handed it to Harriet. She set it in her lap with the flat side up, then said, "I forgot the pen."

Harry took a fine point Sharpie from his vest pocket and handed it over with a smile that said *I'm still your partner, even now* and made me blush at how intimate it was. Harriet uncapped the pen and drew a few swift lines across the flat surface, then she said, "Are you receiving?"

A chorus of voices tangled in the air above the table. They sounded exactly as if they were in the room with us. Viv gasped in surprise. *"Sounds like our linkage is good,"* said a man's voice. *"Test the connection to alpha squad."*

Harriet put her hand over the mouth of the lily. "Walter's a good boy, but he does like to put things in military terms," she whispered. Removing her hand, she said aloud, "Testing now."

A faint whine pitched high enough to be painful filled the room. I automatically put my hands over my ears, but then it was gone, and I heard nothing but the ringing of tinnitus. I swallowed to try to unplug my ears, but Harriet said, "It will pass on its own in a few seconds—there." Sure enough, the ringing vanished. "Testing complete," she announced. "Alpha squad, send transmission."

The blue pyramid glowed with a light like that of an augury, radiant and clear. It flashed a couple of times and then went dark. Harriet put a finger on the base of the pyramid, seeming unfazed by the sharp, glassy waves still striking it. She closed her eyes, and her lips moved as if she were reading something. "All right, everyone, did you get that?"

The voices spoke again. I couldn't make out any one individual response, but Harriet didn't have any troubles. "Ansible silence now," Harriet said. The voices trailed off. "You can talk, but in a whisper so the ansible doesn't pick it up," she told us.

"Is this what an ansible is?" I asked, gesturing at the table and its contents.

"Ansible is a word for any instantaneous communication at a distance," Harry said. "Darius Wallach is working on a more portable version—it's what alpha squad is carrying, with all their other gear. They probably clink when they walk."

"We're doing it this way so the records of the team in the field— Walter's 'alpha squad'—will be instantly transmitted from their devices to ours," Harriet said, leaning back in her seat. "We should be able to hear some of what they say, too."

"Phones are generally more reliable," Judy said, "unless you're sending data and you want it to be completely secure. An ansible can't be hacked."

"That is so cool," Viv said. "I want one."

"Talk to Darius and see if he needs a guinea pig," Harry said. "He usually does."

I was still intent on the ansible. "When will they...move in?"

"I was told the assault would begin at noon." Harriet checked her watch. "Twenty minutes ago."

A shock ran through me. "It doesn't sound like there's fighting."

"Alpha squad is supposed to wait for the area to be secured," said Harriet. "That could take a while. And Malcolm has military training. They won't break radio silence, as it were, unless something happens."

I realized I still held my glass of ice water and little beads of sweat were rolling off it, as comfortable as the Kellers' house was. I took a drink and savored the coolness. Glass magic was so beautiful, all those colors and shapes. How had someone come up with the idea for glass magi in the first place? Well, they were Nazis, they'd probably just wanted a better way to spy on people. But all these other things glass magi did, those had to have been invented by someone. It occurred to me that Harry and Harriet, as old as they were, had to have been among the first glass magi. What had they witnessed in their long lives?

The whine returned, higher and sharper than before. "...stay together," I heard Malcolm say, as clearly as if he were standing next to me, and I jumped, startled. "Quincy, keep us covered."

The noise now sounded like the kind of feedback you get from electronics placed too close to a microphone. Harriet fiddled with the blue pyramid, and it stopped, winding down until it was nothing but a faint hum. I heard footsteps, several of them, then a woman saying, "Go left—no, right."

A hand took mine. Viv's eyes were fixed on the ansible, but her hand clutched mine tightly, and I gripped hers in return, hoping desperately to hear Malcolm's voice again. "There's nothing here," said the same voice, then Malcolm said, "Don't count on it. Keep moving."

The pyramid's blue light flashed again in an erratic pattern. "They're transmitting," Harriet whispered, but she didn't touch the glass. I wondered if the pyramid was making an actual recording, and if it was, what medium it would use. Something you could plug into a computer? Or did it take a glass magus to read what was saved there?

"Stop," Malcolm said, and such was the authority in his voice I clenched Viv's hand tight. "Something…over there…move…" His voice kept cutting out, not fading like the static between radio stations, but as if he'd just stopped speaking for a moment and didn't bother to repeat the words that fell into the silences.

"I don't…there…" It was the other speaker, her voice cutting out the same way. Then there was silence, a terrible, waiting silence that reminded me of the pause in a movie soundtrack just before the killer leaps out to attack. I was just about to say something, anything to break the silence, when the woman said, "What the hell is that?" She sounded terrified.

There was a rattling sound. Gunfire. Malcolm shouted, "*Fall back!*"

15

I clutched Viv's hand so tightly she cried out and pulled away from me. The air was full of screams and gunfire, making me wish I could find the volume control and turn the fighting down, anything to make it less terrible. The pyramid flashed and flickered as if it were on fire. Harriet leaned forward and put her fingertips on opposite sides of the base. Her eyes had rolled up in her head, showing nothing but white, but her grip was firm and her breathing steady.

Her lips began moving rapidly, again as if she were reading under her breath. Harry muttered something irritably, but waved me away when I looked at him in inquiry. I closed my eyes and strained to hear Malcolm's voice. He was alive, I was sure of it, and he'd get them all out safely.

More shouting, and a high-pitched fuzzy whine that seemed to come from the orb, which perched precariously on Harriet's lap. Then someone shouted, "I can't see them!" in a terrified voice, and Malcolm said, "Stop looking for them. Quincy—"

"Not an illusion," Olivia Quincy said. Her voice sounded tense, the way it did when she was concentrating on several illusions at once. "Something else."

A couple of explosive gunshots went off practically in my ear, and I jumped and covered my ears with my hands. Someone cried out in pain. Then there was a crash, and something shattered with the tinkling sound of broken glass. The blue light went out like someone had flipped a switch, and the room went silent.

"*No!*" I screamed. "No, it can't—"

"Calm down, Helena. It just means their half of the ansible shattered," Harriet said, her eyes still rolled up and her fingers firmly resting on the pyramid. I caught a glimpse of Harry's grim expression. It didn't fill me with confidence. "Walter, are you there?"

"*Walter went offline,*" a woman said. "*So did Diantha and Rich.*"

Harriet swore, startling me—she rarely said anything worse than 'darn'. "Did they get the information?"

"*No idea. Regroup?*"

"Regroup," Harriet said, removing her hands from the pyramid and taking the golden lily off its peak. The temperature in the room, which had been cool and air-conditioned, surged upward several degrees, enough to make me grateful my water was still icy. I took a drink, my hand shaking so the water splashed up the glass's sides, and watched the waves of glass on the table settle back into a smooth sheet. Malcolm had to be all right.

"Let's go," said Harriet.

"Where?" Judy asked.

"To the Gunther Node. I need to decant this information into something that can make sense of it. Nothing they were receiving is like anything I've ever seen before. Not illusion, not magic—at least, not magic we know...these weavers seem almost inhuman."

"Could they be invaders in human form?" I asked, remembering the one that had worn a human as a suit.

Harriet shook her head. "Invaders give off a very distinct signal. No glass magus would ever mistake an invader for anything else." She stood, wobbled, and put her hand on Harry's shoulder to balance. "The teams will all retreat to the Gunther Node as well."

I stood and set my glass on the tray. "We need to go *now*."

Judy, Viv and I rode in silence to the Gunther Node, which was a long enough ride that I had plenty of time to work myself into a panic over Malcolm. If something had shattered their device, it might have been close enough to kill. Malcolm would have no trouble putting himself between the glass magi and harm. I clenched my fists in my lap and said a formless prayer. Prayer was something I was getting better at. Surely God didn't want the invaders to overrun the world? He might send a little influence our way, protect the Wardens from the Mercy...or maybe He expected us to work it all out ourselves. Either way, I didn't think prayer was a bad idea.

Judy skidded through the turn into the entrance to the Gunther Node and had the car in Park practically before it had stopped moving. A lot of cars and white vans clustered around the airplane hangar that served as the entry point. Crowds gathered in knots here and there, pressing forward to the white painted circle on the concrete floor that smelled cold and damp even in the summer. We tumbled out of the car and ran toward the hangar, crunching across the gravel to the soft springiness of the blacktop. The air, moist with the humidity of a coming storm, pressed down on me like a wet towel. I looked at the crowds, all eager to get in, and despaired.

"Come on," Judy said, dodging people and shoving through places where she couldn't dodge. Viv and I followed her, apologizing, for her if not for ourselves. We caught up to Judy where she was arguing with one of Lucia's people, a steel magus named Kerianne. "We just want to go now," she was saying. "It's not hard."

"Wait your turn," a buxom redhead standing beside them said.

"The custodian of Abernathy's doesn't wait," Judy said, not looking at the redhead and leaning in on Kerianne as if the woman weren't half a foot taller than she. "And you're holding up the line."

Kerianne rolled her eyes and gestured. "Next twenty," she said, indicating that I should stand next to her. More people shuffled their way into the circle. Kerianne dropped to one knee and pulled out a card on a long lanyard around her neck. She dipped the card into a crack in the concrete and pulled it out swiftly, like swiping a credit card. "Twenty-one," she said, and the world blinked, and we were in the giant concrete chamber that was the transit hub of the Gunther Node.

I hurried to step out of the circle so Kerianne could bring another group through. The chamber, always loud and busy, now smelled of blood and fear. The floor was covered with wounded Wardens who either moaned steadily or lay in unnatural stillness. Magi moved among them, some applying first aid, others, bone magi, performing healing on the wounded. And there were dozens of wounded, maybe more than a hundred. I couldn't count that high without my eyes filling with tears.

"Come on," Judy said again.

"Where are we going?" I asked.

"I don't know, but we can't just stand here and do nothing."

"Maybe we should have waited for Harriet and Harry," Viv said.

I glanced around the chamber. "I feel so helpless."

"Helena!"

I spun around. It wasn't the voice I most wanted to hear, but it came a close second. "Olivia!"

Olivia Quincy picked her way across the crowded floor toward us. She looked disheveled but unharmed. "Everything's all right. Campbell will be fine."

A chill went through me. Her words had been reassuring, but her tone of voice was anything but. "'Will be' fine? What happened to him?"

"He went toe to toe with a weaver. I've never seen anything like it. The woman moved like she was only partly there, like an aegis. And her weapon...I don't know what it was made of, but it looked like sharpened shadow...I just don't know. Campbell took her out, but she nicked his lung and it collapsed. Tinsley's with him now. I promise, Helena, it will be all right. He's a survivor."

"Can I see him?"

"Sure. Follow the orange line through the orange door, then take the second right after it's joined by the teal line. I have to collect the glass magi for their report." With a wave, she darted away.

I searched for the orange line under all those bodies. "It's over here," Viv called out, and I ran, hopping around injured Wardens and distracted bone magi, thinking only of Malcolm and what he'd felt, facing the weaver down. Derrick Tinsley was a talented bone magus, and he'd save Malcolm's life, I was sure. Mostly sure. I ran harder, hearing Viv and Judy on my heels.

The second right was a locked door. I pounded on it, not caring what anyone else thought. Eventually, the lock clicked open, and a woman I recognized peered out. She had dark skin and dark hair pulled into a pouf at the back of her head. Darius Wallach's assistant, the one I thought might be his granddaughter. Bloody vinyl gloves covered her hands. "People are trying to work," she said irritably.

"Malcolm Campbell. Where is he?" I demanded.

A flicker of recognition touched her eyes. "This way," she said, including Viv and Judy in her invitation. I hurried after her, not waiting for my friends.

The dimly-lit room beyond looked like my high school science lab, complete with crazy blown glass in shapes Nature never thought of, though it lacked the chemical smell I remembered. Whiteboards covered in mathematical equations and Calvin and Hobbes cartoons hung from every wall. I bumped into a table as I took my first steps into the room, and it rolled slightly, forcing me to catch hold of its edge before it struck another one.

A door in the opposite wall stood ajar, white light coming from around its sides. I made for it as swiftly as I dared in the dimness and pushed it open fully. There were several people inside, but I had eyes only for Malcolm, who sat with his eyes closed, leaning back in a wooden chair that looked like a relic from *Little House on the Prairie*. His fatigues were torn and stained with dark blood on his left shoulder. I gasped, and his eyes opened. For a moment, he didn't seem to recognize me. Then he smiled and reached out his hand. "Helena," he said.

I crossed the room, which wasn't small, in two steps and dropped to my knees beside him, out of the way of Derrick, who stood with one hand on Malcolm's uninjured shoulder. I took Malcolm's hand and squeezed it. "You're all right."

"He is now," Derrick said, releasing Malcolm. "He *should* be resting. Some people don't know when to take a hint."

"I depend on your competence to keep me upright," Malcolm said. He stood, stretched, and beckoned to me. I threw my arms around him, not caring that he smelled of soot and blood, or that the blood drying on his shirt was still tacky. His heart beat was slow and steady, his breathing was even, and I didn't care about anything else.

"Do you have it?" Malcolm said. I was about to respond when another voice said, "Don't be impatient. This is the most difficult thing I've done all day, and I built an ansible out of glass chips and a couple of bootlaces three hours ago."

I recognized the voice as belonging to Darius Wallach, self-styled mad scientist of Gunther Node. I lifted my head from Malcolm's shoulder to see what he was doing, and wished I hadn't, because what he was doing was an autopsy.

The woman stretched out half-naked on the operating table a few paces away was darkly tanned, with black hair falling loose around her face. Her eyes appeared sunken in dark hollows, as if someone had pressed on them with a sooty thumb. It was impossible to tell if she was pretty or not, because her features were contorted like she'd been sculpted of soft clay and the maker had grabbed her face when he was finished, and twisted.

Her chest...I swallowed nausea and had to look away. Wallach had sliced lengthwise down the middle of her chest and opened her sides up and away from each other, revealing lungs and a heart he was in the process of slicing open. Behind me, the door opened wider, and running footsteps and the sound of vomiting told me somebody's stomach had revolted. I swallowed again and breathed deeply, which was a mistake: to the soot and blood smell of Malcolm's clothing was added a stink of human waste and some kind of bitter chemical. I buried my face in his chest and felt him stroke my hair, which calmed me somewhat.

"There it is," Wallach said. A moment later I heard a tiny click, like something hard striking metal. Cloth rustled, a sheet being pulled up. "Your guess was right, Mr. Campbell," he added. "This isn't an ordinary aegis."

I lifted my head. Wallach had covered the corpse, for which I was grateful. He held a small steel bowl in the bottom of which rolled... something. It was about the length of the first joint of my pinky, but only half that in diameter, spindle-shaped, pointed at the ends and bulging slightly in the middle, and it was covered in blood. Wallach picked it up with a fat pair of tweezers and carried it to a sink, where he rinsed it off. It was still stained red, but now looked grainy, like wood.

"A new kind of wood aegis?" Malcolm said, examining it. He was moving a little stiffly, but otherwise seemed completely back to normal after the healing.

"Maybe," Wallach said. He set the bowl down and, humming to himself, searched the nearby shelves. I recognized the song; it was "Macarena." I stepped away from Malcolm, still keeping hold of his hand, and saw Judy's expression. Viv was gone—apparently she was the one who'd lost the battle with her gag reflex. Judy looked like she wished she had. I'd seen dead bodies before, just not one cut up so... clinically. I had to swallow again and focus on what Wallach was doing.

Finally he grunted in satisfaction and held up a scalpel. Using the tweezers to hold the aegis in place in the little bowl, he pressed down with the blade lengthwise along it, parallel to the grain. For a moment, nothing happened. Then the surface of the aegis cracked like a thin layer of ice, and the blade made a long, narrow slice that blossomed into layer after layer of color, frayed at the edges. "Well, I'll be damned," Wallach said, poking at the layers. "It's made of cloth."

"Cloth," Malcolm said.

"Weavers," I said. "They've invented a new kind of magus."

"Developed," Judy corrected me. "My father needs to know about this."

"Everyone needs to know about this," Wallach said. "Whatever those glass magi learned is going to be crucial to defeating them."

"They got a lot of information," Judy said, "as far as we could tell, anyway. Harriet Keller was bringing it in for analysis."

"I'll go find her, then," Wallach said, then realized he was still wearing gory gloves and stripped them off. Malcolm squeezed my hand and released me.

"And I will report to Lucia," he said, "as will the others who survived."

That made me feel sick again. "It...wasn't many, was it?"

Malcolm shook his head and led the way out the door, passing Viv, who looked paler than usual. "It was a trap. The weavers concealed themselves and were waiting for us. We stopped the harvesting and had regained control of the node when they struck. Partly there, partly not...there was far more luck involved than I'd like in my killing of that woman. I think..." We reached the concrete corridors, and Malcolm turned right, opposite to the way we'd come. "I think I can see potential for adapting our fighting techniques. It was foolish of them to engage me directly without killing me."

"They couldn't have known one of the new steel magi would be there," I said, skipping to keep up with him and his long legs.

"They know we are somewhere, and it's possible they're reaching the limits of their resources, stretching themselves thin."

Malcolm pushed open a door and I recognized the short hallway beyond; it was the one off Lucia's office. We hadn't gone any of the ways I recognized, which made me suspect there was some kind of magic to reaching Lucia's lair. Malcolm crossed to Lucia's door and rapped sharply on it. After a moment, the door swung open, and Dave Henry said, "Come in."

Lucia was bent over some of the milk crates containing hanging file folders behind her desk. "Glad you're not dead," she said, straightening. She swung her rolling office chair out and dropped into it. "Spill."

"Darius Wallach confirmed the Mercy has developed a new aegis. One made of cloth." Malcolm paused for Lucia's reaction, but she did little more than narrow her eyes in thought. "The glass magi no doubt perceived more than the rest of us, but what I observed is that the cloth magi, the weavers, slip in and out of ordinary space in much the way an aegis does. Timing is essential in fighting them. They seem to operate by a rhythm that is unique to each magus."

"Timing," Lucia said. "But you have to figure that timing out quickly because they're trying to stab you while you do."

"Precisely. As I told Helena, there was an element of luck to my defeating the weaver whose body we returned with."

"I'll take luck." Lucia drummed her fingers idly on the desk. "The glass magi are decanting their information right now. We'll know soon if they learned anything else we can use."

"What about the Krebbitz Node?" Viv burst out.

"Your boyfriend is in serious trouble when he gets back," Lucia said. "Doesn't he have any sense of self-preservation? The Krebbitz Node came under attack half an hour ago. They're holding their own."

"He's a magus, Lucia," Viv said. "He fights the invaders. You can't expect him to just sit quietly in a corner while other people do the fighting?"

"And how much good will he do any of us if he's been knifed in the back?" Lucia stood explosively and slammed one fist down on the desk. "I have plans for Washburn. Plans that don't include him getting himself uselessly killed. Plans that are plenty dangerous, since he seems to live for danger. If he comes back, I'll share those plans with him."

"Maybe you should have done that sooner," Viv said.

Lucia's eyes narrowed again, this time in anger. "Don't think because you're now a Warden, however irregular, that I'm interested in your opinions. Jeremiah Washburn is one of the many, many cogs in the machine I run. That machine is bigger than you can imagine, and I don't have time to explain its workings to every single cog therein. Now—all of you, out." She sighed, and added, "Stratemeyer is in Red 17, receiving reports on the defense of the Krebbitz Node. If you're interested."

We filed out of Lucia's office and the door shut firmly behind us. "Where's Red 17?" Viv demanded.

"I'll take you," Judy said. "I'm guessing you two are going to learn what the glass magi discovered."

"I am, certainly," Malcolm said.

I grabbed Viv's hand and squeezed it. "It's going to be all right, I know it is."

Viv's eyes were red-rimmed with tears she wouldn't shed. "It has to be."

16

We followed the lines until we came to a place where red and blue diverged, and took separate paths. "Where are we going?" I asked.

"The glass magi—the ones belonging to the Neutrality—have a... room," Malcolm said, "though you'll see 'room' describes it poorly. The node was built during an era when fears of outside interference in magery were high. As you can probably tell."

"So it really was built as a bomb shelter."

"Though they were as concerned about invader attacks. The defenses against a large invader and a nuclear bomb are remarkably similar. At any rate, you've seen pictures of the computers of that era."

"The ones that are the size of a room, with all those tape reels and punch cards."

"The Gunther Node experimented with computerization before the true potential of the glass magi was known. After it became clear glass magi could process information through magic that it would have taken a contemporary computer twice as long to analyze, the node removed the old computers and turned their space over to the glass magi."

"But I know the Gunther Node uses computers. I've never seen this glass magic."

"Microminiaturization made computers useful to us again. They handle the day to day work. The glass magi process information relating to invaders, the space they come from—what little we know of it—and magic itself. Things a computer can't be made to comprehend."

We'd been following the red line as we talked, and now it joined a white line that was...ragged was the best word I could find to describe the way its edges were fuzzy, unlike the sharp precision of the red line. It wavered slightly, too, probably nothing that would be noticeable if it weren't running parallel to the red line.

Eventually, the red line came to an end, and we proceeded along the white line alone. The hall, made of cinder blocks painted gray, was lit by fluorescent tubes in pairs running down the exact center of the ceiling. It made Malcolm's skin look sallow. I didn't want to know how it transformed me.

We'd long ago left behind the noise and commotion of the transit hub, and now we walked in eerie silence, my sandaled feet slapping the concrete floor, Malcolm moving silent as a cat, as usual. "How do you do that?" I asked, more to break the silence than because I cared. Though I was curious.

"Do what?" Malcolm said.

"Walk so quietly."

"I didn't realize I was. Habit, I suppose." For a few steps, Malcolm's boots trod heavily along the corridor, then reverted to their usual stillness. "It seems I can't not do it. Funny." He gestured. "This is it."

He held the door for me in the casual way he always did, and I stepped inside—into what sounded like a wind chime factory. My next thought was that it was a party, with hundreds of glasses tinkling against each other. But no, there were dozens of men and women dressed in ordinary clothes from business suits to shorts and Hawaiian shirts, carrying flat trays and shallow baskets filled with the kind of glassware I'd seen Harry Keller pick through at his house. A warm, weak yellow light filtered over the scene, dulling the glassware and turning the men and women sepia or orange or plum.

Malcolm had been right about not calling it a room. It was more like a tunnel, with a ribbed roof of olive-painted steel that gave the place the appearance of a duct in a military base. And the walls...I let out a breath in astonishment. The walls were a mosaic of glass tiles in every conceivable color, made dull by the yellow light but no less beautiful for that. The mosaic wasn't a picture, but a pattern, or really a series of patterns. Men and women removed tiles about two inches on a side and replaced them with others so the patterns constantly changed. It was so beautiful I took a few steps toward the nearest wall and Malcolm brought me up short with a hand on my elbow.

"Don't," he said. "This magic is more complex than you or I could imagine. Those magi train for years to be able to read the Pattern."

"I wouldn't touch it," I protested, but I stayed where I was. "What is it?"

"A global analysis of the incursion," Malcolm said. "It tracks the places where invaders threaten to break through and shares that information with every other Neutrality instantaneously."

"So, it predicts the future? Like the oracle?"

"No, it perceives alterations to our reality that signal an invader attack. The details are far, far beyond me."

"What does all this have to do with what your glass magi learned?"

"The Pattern doesn't," Malcolm said. He steered me further into the room, toward a group of three mismatched tables. I noticed there were many of these groupings, no more than four in a group, throughout the tunnel, and all of them held boxes or baskets of glassware. Harriet stood near this one, watching Harry, who sat at one of the tables messing with the contents of a basket. At least, it looked like messing around to me; he was matching pieces, discarding some, connecting others. I remembered Martin Maxwell doing the same last year when he investigated the oracle for signs it was being tampered with. That wasn't a happy memory. Martin had turned out to be one of the Mercy.

"It's going to take a while, Walter," Harriet was saying to a tall, plump man standing next to her. He was one of the ones in Hawaiian shirt and cargo shorts, shod in flip-flops and wearing a giant diver's watch. His hair was thinning on top, his scalp and cheeks freckled.

"This operation cannot be compromised," Walter said, his commanding tone of voice at odds with his appearance. "We need information ASAP."

"If you'd quit yammering, I might finish this more quickly," Harry said in a distant tone of voice that said he was only partially listening to the conversation. He screwed two pieces of glass rod together and set them to one side. "This isn't exactly easy."

"Mr. Keller, sir," Walter said. If a voice could snap to attention, his did. "My apologies."

Harry snorted and screwed two more pieces, these shorter and fatter, together. "But Harry's not a magus," I whispered to Malcolm.

"Don't need to be a magus to do this," Harry said, making me flush with embarrassment. "You do need more than half a century's worth of practice." He hooked the two threaded rods together into a weird crystal matrix that gleamed dull orange in the yellow light and handed it to Harriet. "That should do. But you'll need a flat surface for the projection."

"Thank you, dear," Harriet said. "Malcolm, find me an unused table. A long one."

I looked at the bits of glass covering the table where Harry sat. "What did you do, if it wasn't magic?"

"Built a translator for the pyramid receiver," Harry said. "Somebody else has to activate it, but it will convert the information the glass magi sent into a format we can see and hear. Used to be a specialty of mine, back in the day."

"So you were never a member of a fighting team?"

"No. Not that I wasn't trained to fight. We all are. But I always wanted to fight the Long War on my own terms." Harry pushed himself out of his chair, his joints popping. "I left the physical fighting to Harriet."

"Don't let him fool you, dear, he was one of the first Wardens to learn kung fu," Harriet said, "and he taught it for years." She drew Harry's arm through hers and patted his hand. "It was one of the things I found most attractive about him."

"Your mother never liked it, though," Harry said. "Told me I should learn to box like a red-blooded American."

"She came around eventually," Harriet said. "Malcolm, will you turn it on its side? The long way."

Malcolm had returned with a long, lightweight plastic table he now upended, so it stood on its side like a small door. Walter helped him orient it, then accepted the glass matrix from Harriet. Harriet removed the blue pyramid from a Neiman-Marcus bag on the table and inserted it into the matrix with a click. It pulsed once with that blue light, then lay dormant.

"Step back," Walter said, turning to face the upright table. He gripped the matrix with what I realized were handles on either side, held it tight to his chest—and a brilliant blue light shot from the tip of the pyramid to strike the table's flat white surface.

Lines of blue light crawled like capillaries across the table, humping and rolling over one another until the table was covered by a fine, irregular blue mesh. I became aware we had an audience. All the men and women except those engaged in tending to the mosaic came to stand nearby, watching in silence. It made me uncomfortable, knowing I probably didn't belong there and didn't understand what was going on. I edged closer to Malcolm.

The mesh was turning dark brown and...I could only call it withering, though the mesh didn't look alive in any sense. Bits of it broke away, sifting like ash to the floor. As quickly as it had appeared, it was gone, leaving only a faint brown residue that shone where the lights struck it. The pyramid still glowed, though, pulsing like a heartbeat, *thrum-THRUM, thrum-THRUM*. And a new light arose, one white and clear. I couldn't tell where it was coming from. Certainly not the pyramid, and the light from the ceiling hadn't changed. It swept over the table's surface like a faint spotlight, back and forth, searching for something.

Shadows rose up on the table, as faint gray as the light was white.

I'd done a digital arts class in community college, and they'd taught us to create images in layers, background, foreground, and everything in between. This looked like that, like a series of layers building on one another until a three-dimensional figure appeared on the "screen" of the table's surface. It was a human—mostly. The face was concealed by a mask, or maybe a veil, though the rest of it was dressed in olive drab fatigues similar to what Malcolm wore. Its hair was concealed by a tightly-fitted hood, and I couldn't tell if it was male or female.

But what disturbed me most, what made me hesitate to call it fully human, was how parts of it—just weren't there. Whole sections of its arms and torso were simply gone, the remaining parts of its body sunken in as if trying to fill the gaps. And yet it didn't seem disturbed by this, like it was the natural one and the rest of us who couldn't phase in and out of things were abnormal. Without thinking, I took a step closer, thinking I might be able to see through the veil. As if that would diminish its power, if its face were visible.

"Moving to the next ring," Walter called out, and the figure turned to dust and scattered across the floor. Again, the layers built up until we saw another figure, this one armed with a couple of long knives. Malcolm. He stood ready on the balls of his feet, waiting. Then he swung and connected with someone who came at him out of nowhere. His antagonist also bore knives, and the two of them went at it so fast I found myself holding my breath, even though I knew this was a recording.

Beside me, Malcolm made a funny grunting sound. "What?" I asked.

"I rarely get to evaluate my own performance from the outside. It's fascinating. I can see ways in which I might improve."

"All I see is a terrifying dance of death," I said, which made him chuckle.

"Mr. Campbell, do you want to see that again?" Walter said, again so formally I wanted to laugh.

"Once more," Malcolm said, and the sequence of motions started again. It was easier to watch the second time, but still frightening, especially when the weaver connected solidly with Malcolm's chest, making him stagger back a few steps before recovering. It ended with Malcolm smashing the weaver's knives aside and pulling her into a deadly embrace, thrusting his knife deep into her belly and dragging it up toward her ribs.

"Moving on," Walter said, before I had time to be truly horrified. This time, the shadow layers formed a lot of tiny print laid out like a book I couldn't read. The glass magi, however, had no trouble, because they all started murmuring to each other. The "book" turned a page, and now there were diagrams along with the print. That happened two more times before the pages faded and disappeared. The murmuring turned into actual conversations that grew louder as more people tried to be heard over others.

"Quiet," Walter said. "Harriet?"

"The other receivers will have to confirm the information the glass magi sent," Harriet said. "But I think we have enough to be going on with. Will some of you inform the bone magi what we've learned? I don't mean to disparage the front line fighters—" she nodded at Malcolm, who inclined his head in acknowledgement—"but I think, based on this, our bone magi are best equipped to neutralize the weavers. Or at any rate make them susceptible to traditional fighting techniques."

"Is that what all those words were, at the end?" I asked Harriet as the rest of the magi dispersed.

"Information on vital statistics, body alterations—though unfortunately not the secret of *how* they phase," Harriet said. "That will take time to analyze—and speaking of analyzing, there's Darius. How are you?"

"It would be nice if I had a few more bodies," Wallach said grumpily. "Just one aegis isn't enough for me to reverse engineer it. But everyone's too busy trying not to get killed."

"Can't blame 'em for that," Harry said.

"Can't I?" said Wallach. "Oh, fine, be that way. I spoke to Ms. Orme—did you get the facts about the weavers' bodies?"

"We did," Harriet said. "I'm not sure if it will be soon enough to make a difference."

"Not soon enough for the Krebbitz Node, that's for sure," Wallach said. "They've called for reinforcements."

Malcolm's hand closed painfully hard on my shoulder. "I have to go," he said, leaning down to kiss me. "My team is needed."

"Go," I said, though I didn't think he was waiting for my permission. Malcolm dashed back the way we'd come, shutting the door loudly behind him. I stood staring after him, feeling lost.

"Come along, dear, we'll take you to the transit hub," Harriet said, patting my hand.

"It's hard, waiting for them to come back," Harry said, his voice uncharacteristically gentle.

"Mr. Campbell is harder to kill than a cockroach," Wallach said, "and God knows enough invaders have tried. Don't worry."

I smiled at the image of Malcolm scurrying along like a cockroach, but it was half-hearted. Even so, what else could I do but wait?

Harry and Harriet and I walked in silence back along the white line. I thought about asking why it was so wobbly—surely they were old enough to remember the building of the Gunther Node?—but decided I didn't care. "I should find Viv and Judy. They went to, um, Red...17. For updates on the Krebbitz Node."

"That's just around the corner," Harry said.

The door to Red 17 was one of those enormous garage-door sized units, outlined in red with a big red 17 painted on its front. Unlike a typical garage door, it opened from side to side and was heavy enough it took all three of us to slide it open. Beyond lay an eerily quiet room, with people wearing glass headsets and speaking into little glass microphone buds that lay along their cheeks. One wall was taken up by square monitors about six inches on a side, each displaying a different black and white scene, or in a few cases, static.

Viv and Judy stood a few paces away, hovering over a magus who held an oddly shaped box with two knobs protruding from it. Everything else in the room was glass, metal, or plastic, but this was made of wood, had seven sides, and looked as primitive as the magus's headset looked futuristic. The magus twiddled the knobs, then said, "That's better. Go two-four-three and wait for my signal."

"He's talking to Jeremiah," Viv whispered. "He's alive!"

"I'm so glad," I whispered. "What's he doing?"

"Everett is directing him to the heart of the Krebbitz Node," Judy said. "Jeremiah's going to disable the harvester so the Mercy can't drain the node."

"That sounds dangerous."

"It sounds heroic!" Viv's eyes were alight with excitement and pride, but her hands were clenched on the back of the magus's chair.

The magus, Everett, swore. "Back! Back! They're almost on top—no, damn it!" He ripped the headset off and looked like he wanted to throw it. "I've lost him."

"No!" Viv shouted, making every head in the room turn. "Get him back!"

"I'll try." Everett put the headset back on and went back to fiddling with the knobs. "Washburn. Washburn! If you can hear me, it's the third door after the stairs."

Viv was whiter than usual. "Jeremiah's not stupid. He'll do this," I said.

"At least no one's stabbed him in the back," Judy said.

"That is not an image I needed to have, thanks."

"I was trying to be positive."

"You three." It was Lucia, standing in the door. "Time to go."

"But—" Viv said.

"We're evacuating the Krebbitz Node. There's nothing more you can do here."

"But Jeremiah doesn't know! He's in the heart of the node, trying to disable it!" Viv shouted. "You can't just leave him there."

Lucia's face went grim. "That damned fool—what does he think he's doing?"

"His *job*," Viv said.

Lucia let out a long, thin stream of breath. "Give me that," she said, snatching the box from Everett's hands. She slapped its top a couple of times, then wrenched both knobs full to the left. A high, shrill squeal stabbed my ears, and I gasped and flung my hands up to protect them as Viv and Judy did the same. A chorus of swearing went up that diminished when people registered who was there. None of the noise bothered Lucia at all. She repeated the process twice more, then handed the box back to Everett. "Emergency evacuation protocol," she said to my dumbfounded face. "Washburn will know what it means. Whether he's wise enough to heed it is beyond my capacity to guess. If he's on a mission..." She swore in exasperation, then turned to go. "I suppose it's too much to expect the three of you to go quietly home."

"My father went to the Krebbitz Node when the Holley Node turned into a rout," Judy said. "I'm not leaving him."

"And Malcolm went too," I said.

Viv just glared at Lucia, who surveyed us with another exasperated stare. "Don't get in the way," Lucia said, and strode off in the direction of the transit hub.

"Well, that was very forthright of us," Judy said, "but I'm not sure where to go now."

"Back to the transit hub, and find a place to wait. Maybe we can help with first aid," Viv said.

We hurried after Lucia, each of us absorbed in our own thoughts. It bothered me that all I could do was sit around and wait for Malcolm. The oracle couldn't help them now, and I was no fighter. I didn't even know much first aid. But I didn't like being helpless. *Judo,* I thought, *Lucia could teach me. And how hard it is to knife fight?*

The great chamber had been noisy the first time we'd passed through it. Now it was a nightmare of screaming and shouting and the stink of blood and gunpowder. We stood to one side, caught in the horror of the...it wasn't an evacuation, that implied a degree of order. It was a rout. It was a disaster. But they'd been prepared at the Krebbitz Node; how could things have gone so wrong?

More people flashed into being, not at the white circle but elsewhere in the room. One of them fell to her knees and threw up. I recalled what Madeleine had said about ward-stepping and wondered if she was here somewhere. I probably should hope she was, since we needed every resource we had, but the thought of fighting with her again made me want to lie down in the fetal position and wait for everything to be over.

Judy gasped and said, "Father." She ran across the room to where William Rasmussen, dressed not in his usual suit but in filthy fatigues, was stepping away from a newly transported group of Wardens. I watched her take his hand, briefly, and turned away. The Rasmussens weren't emotionally demonstrative people, but I'd have thought they could at least unbend enough for a hug. None of my business.

"Helena, Viv. Take these and follow me," the bone magus, Sue, said. She thrust a pile of rolled bandages at me and jerked her chin in emphasis. Startled, I hurried after her. The nightmare was achieving some kind of order, as Wardens directed the new arrivals to bring their wounded for care. It looked like Sue had been designated triage nurse, because she moved purposefully through the rows of wounded, identifying the ones who needed healing and those who could be bandaged and left to wait for a while.

"We're about to the limits of our magic," Sue said. "We can regenerate, but our supplies of *sanguinis sapiens* are running low as well. So it's the cold equations for us."

I wasn't sure what that meant, but Viv and I helped to bandage some of the survivors. Between the two of us, we did a decent job, though it confirmed to me that my decision not to become a medical professional was a good one. At some point, I was collared by a different Warden, not one I knew, to take cups of water to the injured. My world shrank down to endless paper cups of water, to endless rolls of bandage, to pinched, anguished faces, until I couldn't remember a time when I was anything but a pair of bloodstained hands.

Hands. I was the oracle's hands. And the oracle had given the Mercy an augury.

I'd almost forgotten about that, what with everything else that had happened, but surely the oracle wouldn't collaborate with the enemy? The idea I'd had, that the oracle had directed the Mercy to where they could be defeated by the Wardens, seemed foolish now. And it wasn't as if I could prove it, not having the augury with me. Or...could I?

I lifted a woman's head so she could drink. I still had the book the oracle had chosen for Santiago. What if I had a professional reader interpret it based on Santiago's question? Was that even possible? Well, yes, it was possible—the question I was looking for was, was it ethical? The oracle wouldn't have given the augury if it wasn't a legitimate one, and I couldn't interfere with a legitimate augury no matter whose it was. I didn't want to risk losing my position as custodian on so slim a hope as that one.

"Helena," someone said. I looked up. It took my exhausted brain a moment to realize it was Malcolm. I stood carefully and stepped around the fallen Warden to put my arms around him, too tired to do more than that. Malcolm held me up. He didn't seem injured at all, but his body trembled as if he were at the limit of his reserves.

"I'm so glad you're here," I whispered. "Can we go home?"

"Helena," Malcolm said, "Olivia Quincy is dead."

17

I looked up at him, my mouth slack with confusion. "But I just saw her a minute ago," I said, realizing as I did so that it had been much longer than a minute since Olivia had sent me after Malcolm. "She can't be dead."

"Shot in the head while we were helping another team escape," Malcolm said. His voice was steady, but distant. "We retrieved her body, but there was nothing Tinsley could do for her."

"Malcolm. *No.*"

"She saved six lives at the cost of her own. She wouldn't regret the sacrifice."

My chest hurt with a breathless ache. I leaned into Malcolm and sobbed, felt him stroke my hair, and wished he'd let himself mourn. He'd known her for years; I should be comforting *him*. But I couldn't stop thinking of how cheerful Olivia had been, reassuring me that Malcolm was well. Not even imagining that her death was only hours away.

I wasn't sure how long it was before my crying wound down. I wiped my eyes and reached for Malcolm's hand. "Malcolm, I'm so sorry."

"I don't have time to mourn," he said, his face so impassive it made my heart ache for him. "I must report to Lucia. I just...needed a moment alone."

"I understand. Do you...have you seen Jeremiah?"

"No. But he must be here somewhere."

"Maybe. Viv said he was trying to shut down the harvesting equipment so the Mercy couldn't drain the node."

Malcolm cursed. "That's insanity. The fighting was worst there at the heart of the Neutrality."

"Don't tell Viv that. She doesn't need any more of a burden."

"I won't." Malcolm released me. "I'll go to Lucia, and...will you wait for me? I find I need the comfort of your presence."

"Of course. Besides, I'm helping. I couldn't leave before it's all over."

Malcolm kissed me, a long, sweet kiss that made me forget where I was for a moment, and then he was gone. I watched his tall, retreating form until he disappeared through one of the doors, then went back to bringing water for the wounded. Olivia. It didn't seem real. It was going to be a long time before I stopped expecting to see her walk through Abernathy's door.

Someone shouted, an angry rather than terrified sound. I looked across the room to see a group of new arrivals backing away from Viv, who had her hands full of bandages and was holding them like weapons. "What do you mean, he's still there?" she demanded. "He destroyed the harvester and you just *left him there*?"

The Wardens glanced at each other, clearly not sure what to make of Viv in a rage. "It was an evacuation. We had to leave, and—"

"So go back! Hasn't he proved himself enough for you?"

"We can't—" said one of the Wardens.

"You can," Viv said. "And you'd better do it now."

"The node is all but destroyed," another Warden said. "Washburn's probably dead."

"Then bring me his body and we'll have a hero's funeral, but damn it, you bring him back!" Viv was shaking. I picked my way across the floor toward her, though I had no idea what I was going to say that she hadn't already.

"Look, Ms. Haley, it's impossible," said the first Warden, and I groaned inwardly, because she was using a soothing tone of voice that was guaranteed to make Viv incandescent with rage.

Sure enough, Viv interrupted her with, "Do *not* tell me what's impossible, and don't you dare talk down to me, you stupid cow! If you don't go, I will, and then—"

"Enough," Lucia said. I turned to look over my shoulder. Lucia stood at the green-painted exit from the transit hub, with Malcolm by her side. She looked exhausted, but totally in control. "Parganas. Theodore. Get back there and retrieve Washburn. In one piece. If he comes back dead, I'm going to look very carefully at anyone who might have made him that way. Get."

Parganas and Theodore nodded sharply, joined hands, and their bodies collapsed in on a point near their navels and vanished. I winced. That had looked painful. I hoped they were enough afraid of Lucia to make a serious search for Jeremiah and not just hide somewhere for half an hour before coming back empty-handed.

Viv's shoulders were heaving, she was breathing so heavily. "People are so *stupid*," she said.

"I know," I said. "We have to keep working. They'll bring him back."

A snapping sound, like a sackful of joints popping, and a new batch of Wardens came through, bloody and battered. "I hope it's soon," Viv whispered.

It wasn't soon. I served my last cup of water more than an hour after Theodore and Parganas had left, then found a chair and stretched out my aching legs and back. I was so *tired*, all I could think of was my nice soft bed. *That's good, I'm thinking of it as mine now.* Malcolm hadn't reappeared, Judy was gone, which was a problem because she was my ride...though Malcolm's car was around somewhere, probably. I blinked through sleep-fogged eyes around the cavernous room. Viv was gone, too. I didn't see a single person I knew well enough to talk to. The last group of evacuees had come through twenty minutes earlier. Now only Jeremiah, Parganas, and Theodore were still unaccounted for. Everyone else was either returned or dead.

Something flickered in the corner of my eye. I turned my head, which felt like it weighed a ton, and blinked again. Three figures, one of them supported by the other two. I leapt out of the chair. *"Jeremiah!"*

All three of them were bloody, Parganas from a shallow scalp wound, Theodore from a mangled and probably broken shoulder. But Jeremiah looked like he'd been worked over hard. Both his eyes were swollen, he couldn't stand unsupported, and his hands... "What happened to him?" I said, helping Parganas lower him to a reclining position on the floor.

"The Mercy did," Parganas said, mopping blood out of her eyes. "That was just the opening act. We had to kill four of their wood magi to free him. Lucky most of them were trying to reverse whatever he did to the harvester, or we'd have all died there."

"What about the weavers?"

"Didn't see 'em. You want to chat, or do you want your buddy healed?"

"Sorry." I helped Jeremiah into what I hoped was a more comfortable position. "Find Sue, or someone, please? And...thank you."

"Didn't do it for thanks," Theodore said, then bit back a pained groan.

When they were gone, I leaned over and said, "Are you awake?"

"Wish I wasn't," Jeremiah mumbled. "Did it work?"

"I don't know. Sounds like it did."

I heard running footsteps behind me, and Viv dropped to her knees beside us. She looked like she wanted to touch him, but was afraid to. "You idiot," she said. "What were you thinking?"

"There wasn't much thought to it," Jeremiah whispered, and grimaced. "I ended up near the center of the node, and I figured, why not go for broke?"

"Because it's insanity?" Viv gently touched his hands. "They caught you, didn't they?"

"I'd rather forget about it, all right?" Jeremiah managed to smile on one side, a pale mimicry of his usual brilliant expression. "You don't want to know and I don't want to tell you. I'm never watching 'War Stories' again."

"What?" I asked.

"He means *Firefly*," Viv said, which enlightened me not at all. Tears rolled down her cheeks. "It's all right. It will be all right."

"Good," Jeremiah said, and fell unconscious.

We knelt beside him in silence for a few minutes before Sue came bustling up with a couple of burly Wardens. "This is going to need something better than a concrete floor," she said, indicating that her helpers should carry Jeremiah. Viv stood and followed her. I took a few steps after them before realizing Malcolm would need to be able to find me, and besides, there wasn't anything I could do for Jeremiah. So I went back to my chair and, despite the awkwardness of my position, fell asleep.

I woke to Malcolm's hand shaking me gently. "Can we go home now?" I said.

"Lucia ordered me to take you home," Malcolm said. "It didn't take much to convince me. You did a lot today."

"Not as much as you did. Or Jeremiah. They tortured him, did you know that? I hope he succeeded. How awful if he didn't."

"We won't know how well he succeeded until we retake the Krebbitz Node. But based on his report, he was successful."

"His report?" I sat up straight. "He's awake?"

"Awake and well, but weakened. He and Viv are staying here tonight." Malcolm ushered me toward one of the smaller white circles, where a black-clad tech waited. "And you and I are going home."

The world blinked, and we were back at the airplane hangar. I followed Malcolm outside to where his car was parked, the cherry-red Mustang looking totally out of place in this rural setting. It was nearly sunset, and I settled into the sun-warmed leather and closed my eyes. "I'm hungry. I missed lunch."

"Cheeseburgers, and then a shower, and bed," Malcolm said, putting the car in gear.

"You have the best plans."

We were too tired for sex, and with Olivia dead, it felt wrong somehow. Not that she would have appreciated us mourning her in that fashion. I'd be ready for it sometime soon, just...not now. But as I set my alarm, I found it impossible to remember everything that had happened that day. Not just Olivia, but the defeat at the Holley and Krebbitz Nodes, Jeremiah's terrible sacrifice, even the augury for Santiago, who was probably of the Mercy. Had that really been today?

I curled up next to Malcolm and said, as a thought occurred to me, "Your mother offered me one and a half million dollars to break up with you."

Malcolm stiffened. "She did *what?*"

"She has the weirdest ideas about what kind of relationship is right for a Campbell."

"Does she." Malcolm got out of bed and began dressing.

I propped myself on my elbows. "What are you doing?"

"I'm going to have it out with Mother. That she *dared* come here and make such a foul offer—"

"Malcolm, don't." I took his hand and made him sit beside me. "What do you think will happen if you burst into her apartment at this hour?"

"She has to stop. This is unacceptable."

"Don't you think you've made it clear how you feel? And it hasn't stopped her. I doubt anything you say will change her mind."

"Helena, you shouldn't be subject to that sort of attack."

"Why, are you afraid she'll figure out something I want more than you?"

"*Helena*—"

"I'm just teasing. I'm trying not to think about how angry she made me. She can't be part of our lives anymore, Malcolm. It's just going to get worse. But you can't fix it by storming in there at this time of night." I put my arms around him. "Come to bed. We'll figure it out in the morning."

Malcolm scowled, but took off his clothes and got back into bed beside me. "I love you," he said, drawing me into the circle of his arms. "I'm so glad you're with me. You give me strength."

"I'm glad, because you give *me* strength." I snuggled in closer. "I wish I didn't have to work tomorrow. It's going to be a long day."

"For me as well. With Holley and Krebbitz lost, the Mercy will almost certainly attack the Gunther Node next. We will have to make a stand here."

"How will they even get inside? Don't you have to teleport, or ward-step?"

"Remember that many of them are familiar with the Gunther Node and its protocols. They will find a way in. And we will have to assign guards to Abernathy's. It's unlikely the Mercy will have the resources to fight two battles at once, but no sense leaving you unprotected."

"It feels odd, keeping the store open when things are so uncertain."

"We need the oracle more than ever now. And magi everywhere need something to remind them that all is not lost. The Mercy will lose. It's just a matter of time."

"You're not just saying that to comfort me, are you?"

"They are already stretched thin, trying to maintain the territory they've taken. Now that we know the secret of the cloth aegis, their advantage shrinks to nothing. And Lucia is bringing in even more magi for the Gunther Node's defense. We will push the Mercy back, and then we will begin retaking territory. I wouldn't tell you to be hopeful if there weren't a reason to be."

"No, you wouldn't." I sighed and kissed him, then snuggled closer. "Then I suppose I just have to keep doing my job."

"For all our sakes," Malcolm said.

———

THE BASEMENT WAS COOL AND DRY. I STEPPED AROUND THE PUDDLE OF *blood that glistened, red and oily, in the fluorescent light. The stairs creaked underfoot like the wails of the damned. Somewhere nearby I smelled something acrid and stinging.*

Smoke. Abernathy's was on fire.

I raced into the stacks, looking for the source, and found myself within the oracle instead. The haze turned the blue light purple. I could feel the heat, but saw no flames. Let me out! *I shouted, or thought I did; I couldn't hear my own words. I ran through the narrow, terrible corridors, trapped inside as the heat rose, stinging my cheeks and hands. Smoke filled the air, choking me, blinding me. I tripped, landed hard on my hands—*

I woke gasping, tears streaming down my face, my whole body rigid with terror. The stench of smoke still filled my nostrils. I tried to still my rapid breathing, but the memory of the dream stayed with me, and my hands and wrists hurt as if I'd actually fallen on them. Against my will, sobs tore through me, shaking me to my core.

Hands touched my shoulders, rolling me over to my other side. "Shh, shh," Malcolm said, gathering me into his arms. "It's over. Don't be afraid."

I shook my head vigorously. "This can't not be real. The store is going to burn."

"I would like to tell you that's impossible. But I just don't know."

He held me close while I cried it out, and even in my misery my heart swelled with love for him. Finally, my sobs turned into shaky, deep breaths, and I wiped my eyes and said, "The dreams just keep getting worse. But I don't understand what they mean."

"How long has this been going on?"

"A week. Since we moved in."

"That...seems like a very big coincidence. If coincidence it is."

"And I didn't have a nightmare last night—I mean, when I slept at the store."

Malcolm pushed damp strands of hair back from my face and propped himself on one elbow so he could look at me. "Do you think the oracle needs you on the premises?"

"I don't see how it could. Mr. Briggs didn't live above the store. I was custodian for a week before moving in and I didn't have any nightmares."

"Unless it got used to having you there."

"I...don't know. Doesn't it make more sense that it's warning of a fire in the future?"

"Probably. I just like the idea of the store throwing a fit because you moved out."

I laughed. It eased some of the tension in my shoulders and stomach. "I don't know how self-aware it is, but it does seem to have desires. Maybe not desires on a level we can understand. If it knows there will be a fire, and it's capable of giving me visions of warning... maybe I—" I shut my mouth on the rest of that sentence.

It didn't matter. Malcolm knew what I'd been about to say. "I thought you were going to give it a real chance."

"I did. And I am. It's just...being custodian of Abernathy's isn't just a job, it's a calling. A serious responsibility. And if the store knows disaster is coming, I'm the only one it can tell. I don't want to move back to that apartment, Malcolm. But I don't want to ignore the warning."

Malcolm rolled onto his back, one arm still trapped beneath me. After a moment in which all I could hear was the sound of our twinned breathing, he said, "Why don't I ask for an augury about it tomorrow?"

"Like what?"

"Oh, possibly 'What danger do you face in the immediate future?' If it really is trying to communicate, that should be an easy response to interpret."

"That's a good idea. I wish I could get auguries for myself."

"If we're right, the oracle doesn't have to bother with auguries for you."

"True." It was an uncomfortable thought, that a supernatural creature, or whatever the oracle was, could access my mind whenever it wanted. That it was only in my dreams so far wasn't much comfort.

Malcolm once again put his arms around me. "Try to sleep."

"What if the dream comes back?"

"I have no solution for you. I would fight your demons for you if I could. This is beyond me. But maybe the oracle will content itself with one communication in a night."

"Let's hope so." I yawned and closed my eyes, trying not to remember smoke and the sound of flames. Malcolm's breathing continued slow and even, his heartbeat a calming rhythm, and eventually the two sounds helped me fall asleep.

18

Malcolm drove me to work that morning and promised to return at six to pick me up. At the counter, he wrote out his augury question and handed it to me. "What if it can't answer?" I said, scanning the words *What immediate danger does the oracle face?*

"Better not go borrowing trouble," Malcolm said. "One problem at a time."

I took three steps and was enveloped in the timeless peace of the oracle. Despite my lingering fears about fire, I couldn't help feeling calmer just by being in its presence. The blue-tinged light was brighter today, as if the oracle felt cheerful and was passing that feeling along.

I found the augury almost immediately. *Jane Austen's England*, the title read, and the cover bore a picture of a pastoral scene with white buildings in the distance. "I was hoping for something a little more obvious," I said. "Maybe something with fire on the cover." I held the book to my chest, enjoying the tingling sensation that spread through my body, and returned to Malcolm. "$900."

"That seems unusually cheap. I wonder if it means the oracle has chosen to be cooperative." He looked at it as skeptically as I had, turning it over to read the blocks of text on the back. "I'll have to turn this over to a professional. I don't have time to analyze it myself."

His coat buzzed, and he set the book down and removed his phone from an inside pocket. "Lucia has summoned the team heads to plan for the defense of the Gunther Node. She anticipates the Mercy will be here as early as midnight tonight."

That made me shiver. "That's fast."

"They have no choice. If they can't strike while we're still recovering from the blows dealt us at the Holley and Krebbitz Nodes, they are unlikely to succeed in taking the Gunther Node. I had thought we might attack Krebbitz again, on the same principle of attacking when they are in disarray, but Lucia says her intelligence indicates they have fortified it well."

"And you need a decisive victory to begin to break their attacks."

"Precisely." Malcolm tapped out a response to whatever text he'd received and put his phone away. "I'll give whoever interprets the augury permission to tell you what they learn. It should be sometime this afternoon."

"Thanks. It might even be better to have a neutral party read the augury, someone who doesn't have any preconceptions about what they'll find."

"Good point." We kissed, and Malcolm said, "I'll return at six, whatever happens at the Gunther Node today. I anticipate a long day of teaching magi to defeat the phasing ability of the weavers."

"Can you do that?" I asked as we walked back to the office.

"I will certainly try," Malcolm said, but he didn't sound very confident. I hoped for all our sakes his pessimism was unfounded.

When he was gone, I returned to the front, turned the sign in the window to OPEN, and leaned against the counter, letting my mind wander. No Nicolliens waited outside today. I guessed most of the magi were hunkering down against the oncoming fight. Which reminded me... I took out my phone and texted Lucia: SHOULD I BE WORRIED ABOUT MERCY ATTACK HERE? Maybe that's what the warning dreams were about—though it made no sense for the Mercy to want to destroy Abernathy's. Santiago's repeated requests for auguries said they wanted the benefit of the oracle as much as anyone. Still, if they were taking territory, the oracle was as valid a target as the Gunther Node.

I sniffed the air, which was fragrant with the same jasmine my sheets at the apartment were scented with. No acrid burning odors, but maybe I should invest in a few more fire extinguishers. It would make me feel better.

My phone stayed silent in my pocket. No response. No phone call. Well, Lucia was busy. I pushed away my formless fears and went to the office. Where was Judy? I didn't think she had another date, certainly not in the morning.

The back door banged open. "Sorry I'm late," Judy said, dropping her purse on the desk. "Traffic was really bad on the freeway. Even worse going the other way, though, so small blessings." She was dressed up even for her, in a powder blue miniskirt, stacked heel sandals that added two inches to her height, and a pair of sunglasses with giant lenses that looked like Madeleine's.

"Are you going somewhere special?" I asked.

"I have another date. A lunch date. You don't mind me taking off in the middle of the day?"

"Not if you aren't gone for three hours or anything crazy like that. You sure seem optimistic about this one."

"This is sort of a second date. And he's a Warden. From the Krebbitz Node."

"A Warden? Aren't they all busy getting ready for the next attack?"

"They can't stay keyed up for hours, and the Mercy won't be here until late tonight. And everybody has to eat sometime."

"That's true. So—tell me about him!"

"We met while we were both helping with the evacuation. We got to talking after the last patients were treated—he's a bone magus—and he asked if I wanted to get lunch with him today." Judy bounced on her toes. "I have a good feeling about this one."

"That's so great! I hope it works out."

"So do I. His name is Jensen and he's a veterinarian in his

mundane life. He's got two dogs named Remedy and Butch. And... that's pretty much all I know about him."

"That's enough to start with." I heard the front door open with a chime of bells. "Time to get to work."

Very few people came in that morning, and none of them wanted to chat, staying just long enough to receive their auguries and scuttle out into the sunshine like so many beetles. Lucia didn't respond to my text, but around 10:30 the door opened and admitted, not a customer, but a pair of enforcers I recognized. "Helena," Elmo Testaverde said. "Lucia sent us to keep an eye on things."

"Will I sound ungrateful if I ask why there's only you and Sammy LoBrutto?"

Sammy smiled and winked at me. "The rest of our unit is scattered around the neighborhood, watching for trouble," she said. "The real push is going to be at the node, but no sense being careless."

"Thanks. I appreciate it. Do you want coffee, or something?"

"No eating or drinking on duty," Elmo said, scratching his thick, black curls. "But thanks."

The bells jingled again. "Don't worry, we'll stay out of your way," Sammy said. She retreated to a position behind the counter, her back to the wall so she had a full view of the street through the plate glass window. Elmo crossed to the other side of the store. My new customer eyed them both nervously and handed me her augury slip in silence. Grinning, I made my escape.

Judy left at 11:30. "I promise not to take more than an hour," she said.

"An hour and a half would be fine," I said. "Just have fun."

"Here's hoping."

"Does Judy Rasmussen have a *date*?" Sammy said when Judy was gone. "I didn't think she ever relaxed enough for a social life."

"She does too relax," I retorted, irritated on Judy's behalf.

"With a father like that, it's amazing she ever meets anyone," Elmo said.

"I have to admit William Rasmussen intimidates me, or I might have asked her out myself," Sammy said. "Though I don't think she's a lesbian."

"She isn't," I said. "I'm going to have my lunch now. When do you get to eat?"

"When our replacements show up around two." Elmo stretched. "Though I'm not hungry."

"*I'm* hungry," said Sammy.

"You're always hungry."

"I have a healthy metabolism. Nothing wrong with that."

"My ravioli is calling me," I said.

I slid the plastic container full of leftover ravioli—frozen, not homemade, but if I wasn't up to making steak I *definitely* wasn't up to ravioli—into the microwave and watched it go around on the little turntable. I helped myself to a Diet Coke from the mini-fridge and took a long drink. I wish I'd thought to ask Malcolm who he was going to get to interpret the augury. Then I could...all right, it was probably a bad idea to harass the interpreter. If nothing less, it would slow them down, and I wanted results as quickly as possible. I could be patient. The interpreter would call this afternoon, and then maybe I could address the oracle's problem directly.

Something thumped, faintly, in the direction of the front door. It sounded like a book falling, a heavy book. I took the ravioli out of the microwave and listened. Another thump, this one louder—or maybe it was just that I could hear better now the microwave had stopped running. "Elmo? Sammy? Don't mess around with the books," I called out.

A crash, like a stool being knocked over. My blood went ice cold. Not books falling. That sounded like a fight. I tossed my ravioli on the counter and ran for the office. If there was fighting, I needed to get away before whoever it was had attacked Elmo and Sammy came after me. Except—I had no car, no weapon, nothing but my own two legs and a desire to get far away from here.

Something flickered at the edge of my vision. I turned quickly and saw nothing. The office was empty. I took a rapid step toward the back door and saw the flickering again, closer this time. Trying to still my panicked breathing, I put a hand on the doorknob, and shrieked as cold fingers went around my wrist. A figure clad in dark, tightly-fitting clothing popped into existence beside me. He wore soft-soled shoes that would be quiet on any surface and a belt like Batman's but without the hideous buckle. A veil like a soft, flexible fencing mask covered his face, but I could see his eyes gleaming. It was impossible to read his expression. His bare-handed grip on my wrist was firm without being painful.

He said something in beautifully fluid Spanish of which I caught only "*hablar con usted.*" Speak with you. "Let go of me," I said, yanking my wrist away, or trying to; my captor had a grip like a bench vise. He pulled me, gently but inexorably, toward the office door. I fought him, dragging my heels and hitting him with my free hand, and he stopped and hit me so hard in the face I nearly passed out. Only his grip on my wrist kept me from falling. He said something I didn't understand at all, but sounded like a warning, then picked me up and slung me over his shoulder and walked on.

Blood streamed from my nose, which throbbed sharply with every step he took. I tried to hit him again, but my arms and legs wouldn't respond. I closed my eyes against the sickening bobbing movement so I wouldn't vomit and tried to collect my wits. Someone wanted to speak with me. I wasn't dead yet. My nose felt broken and my head hurt so badly I wished I had passed out. Everything about this situation terrified me.

Abruptly, my captor stopped and swung me down, then supported me when my legs buckled under me. Through eyes swimming with pained tears, I saw that we were at the front of the store. Elmo lay slumped beneath one of the windows, a huge smear of blood staining the glass where he'd struck it and then slid down. A pair of trendily-dressed young women walked past outside, oblivious. Sammy was collapsed on the linoleum beneath the cash register, her eyes blank and staring, her chest a mess of blood and shredded cloth. More men and women dressed like my captor filled the store, none of them apparently armed, but Elmo and Sammy's condition told me that wasn't the case.

Wobbling, I put a hand to my nose to stanch the blood and hissed at how painful it was. I pushed the hair out of my face with my other hand and took a deep, ragged breath. "I don't—"

"Do not challenge me," said a smooth, cultured voice I recognized immediately. "Your death is still a possible outcome of this meeting."

Galarza—no, Santiago—stood beside the cash register, running a finger along its brass curlicues. He was probably in his mid-thirties, clean shaven, with sun-burnished tan skin and black hair cut short in a crew cut that looked in need of a trim. He wore olive green fatigues and leather boots like Malcolm's, though his were brown instead of black. My eyes were drawn to his hands, which were well-shaped with evenly trimmed nails on every finger except his right pinky, which was missing. He saw me staring and smiled. "Power comes with a price, Ms. Davies. As I am sure you are aware."

"What do you want, Mr. Santiago?" My voice was shaking, and I sounded less than brave. I couldn't stop looking at the bodies of my friends, bloody and crumpled like nothing living.

"What I have always wanted. An augury. And since you have been so unhelpful over the phone, I thought to come in person and be more...persuasive."

"The oracle rejected those auguries, not me. And I won't help you no matter how...persuasive...you get." I was sure he could hear my heart beating as loudly and rapidly as Viv's best jazz riff. How had they gotten past all the enforcers? And Sammy and Elmo were good fighters, so if they'd been killed... Fear bubbled up inside me.

Santiago lowered his hand to his waist, where it rested on the hilt of a knife the size of a small sword. "You claim you did not lie to me?"

"I don't lie about auguries. The oracle rejected the first two. And the third one, I told you the title of."

"That augury tells us nothing."

"That's not my problem."

Santiago drew his knife and brought it to rest against my throat. It was freezing cold, startling on a warm day like this one, and I went perfectly still. "I make it your problem," he said, "and I think now you will take me seriously."

I said nothing. I was afraid even to nod my head. But Santiago's beautiful brown eyes met mine, and he could see my acquiescence there. He lowered the knife and smiled. Even his smile was attractive. I hated his smile.

"I have a great need," he said, "to locate something of importance. You will take this augury, and you will bring me an answer. And then I will leave."

"Just like that?"

"Just like that." He smiled again. I itched to slap the smile off his face. I was sure the chances of him telling the truth were about the same as Madeleine and I going for facials together. He'd get what he wanted, and then he'd need to deprive the Wardens of the oracle's services. And I'd be dead.

"Do you have the augury request?" I held out my hand. The smile broadened, and Santiago handed me a folded piece of paper. *Where are the missing keys hidden?* I turned and began to walk away only to be stopped by Santiago's maimed right hand on my arm.

"I will go with you," he said. "To remove any chance of mistakes."

"That's impossible. I'm the only one who can enter the oracle." This was not strictly true. I'd been able to bring Malcolm into the oracle with me once, to fight an enormous invader trying to destroy it, but it hadn't been easy. And there was no way I was putting myself out to help this man.

"That is a convenient lie."

"Fine. Come with me." I took his arm, praying I was right about this.

After three steps, we were between the bookcases, and I had to turn slightly to keep hold of Santiago. He dragged at my arm, holding me back. When I looked at him, his smile was gone, and his gaze darted in every direction. "Where is the augury?"

"We're not inside the oracle. I told you, I'm the only one who can enter it. See?"

I released him, and he vanished. The stillness of the oracle rose up around me.

19

I let out a long breath and wrapped my arms around myself to still my shaking. Then I shoved the augury slip into my pocket, afraid of dropping it and invalidating the request. I had no intention of filling it, but I was afraid of losing the oracle and finding myself back in the store with all those terrifying, silent figures.

I snatched my phone with shaking fingers and tried texting Malcolm. The screen was silvery gray, with no cheerful little icons, and when I pressed and held the power button, thinking to reboot, nothing happened. Apparently there were no bars inside the oracle. "Okay. So what do I do now?"

It was half addressed to the oracle, half me thinking out loud, but it got no response. Out of habit, I paced through the corridors, looking for the augury. The light was clear and blue-tinted, with dust motes floating through the sunbeams passing through the distant, unseen windows. I thought of Elmo and had to stop, holding onto the nearest bookcase, while I cried—for him, for Sammy, for all the other no-doubt-dead enforcers. But I stopped before I could cry for myself. I wasn't dead yet, and I had resources I hadn't tapped.

I just didn't know what they were.

No blue glowing outlines heralded Santiago's augury. "I wish I knew how much you cared about your individual custodians," I said. "I mean, there's Judy, so if Santiago kills me, you'll still have a custodian." I hoped Judy's date would go so well she'd lose track of time. I couldn't bear the thought of her walking into this mess. Maybe we were lucky, and Santiago didn't know Judy existed. "I can't stay in here forever."

I came around the corner into the heart of the oracle, and stopped. Floating at the center of the space was a book outlined in blue, the size of an ordinary hardcover novel. I plucked it out of the air and its weight settled into my hands. *The Name of the Rose*. I'd read it several times, though I'd skimmed some of the overly-descriptive chapters. I opened it to the title page, and gasped.

Helena Davies, No Charge.

"But I can't have an augury for myself," I said. The Accords were very clear on this: no custodian could use her Neutrality for her own benefit. But...what it actually said was that I couldn't *ask* for an augury for myself. Nowhere did it say the oracle couldn't decide to give me one.

"There's no time," I began, then bit my lip in thought. What did I already know about this book? Translated by William Weaver, okay, that was an unsubtle hint. A library with a strange organizational system. A library you couldn't get into without knowing the secret. People dying to keep the secret—all right, a few dying just by accident. A book so important it was worth killing over. I started flipping the pages the way I would the Abernathy's catalogue, closing my eyes and stabbing the page with my index finger, but nothing jumped out at me that would make my situation suddenly survivable.

A bright blue light shone to my left. Another augury? I took this one from the shelf. *The Storied Life of A.J. Fikry*. I glanced over the cover copy. Another book about books. And there was my name on the title page again. "I don't—"

More blue lights shone, book after book. I dashed through the oracle, plucking books from the shelves. *The Eyre Affair. Howards End is On the Landing. The House of Twenty Thousand Books.* Finally, my arms full, I returned to the center and set the teetering pile on the floor. "So, the books are the key," I said. "But key to what?"

Distantly I heard the rush of the wind, and had my arms over my face when the hot sirocco blasted me, strongly enough to knock the pile of books over. They cascaded around my feet, anchoring me to the ancient linoleum floor. "What now?" I shouted.

books, a tiny voice within the wind said. *voices.*

"I was your hands once, but I don't think that's what I need now. Please. Tell me what to do!"

The wind scoured my arms and my bare legs, blowing my skirt around me like Marilyn Monroe in *The Seven Year Itch*. The tiny voice echoed—or were there many of them? *...books...weapons...hands...*

"I don't understand!"

The pressure of the wind grew, battering me, forcing me backward out of the pile of books until I fetched up against the shelf behind me. *...books...hands...*

Golden light rose up all around me. The books glowed, not the sharp electric blue of an augury, but a soft sunlight gold, the kind of light you only ever see at sunset when the clouds hang low above the horizon. My head and back tingled where they pressed against the books behind me. I stepped away from the tingling and turned around. This close, the light was distinguishable as millions, maybe billions, of tiny glowing letters, spelling out words I felt I should understand, but in no language I recognized. I took one of the books, a big, flat atlas with crisp, unworn edges, and tried to open it. It felt, not glued shut, but as if it wasn't meant to open. My hands tingled pleasantly, like carbonation bubbling against my skin.

Something flickered, just at the limits of my vision, and remembering the weaver who'd punched me I ducked, bringing up the book as a shield. I felt a pinch, as if someone had grabbed the fleshy inside of my elbow and twisted. I flinched away from the feeling only to have it repeated somewhere else. It stung, and instinctively I swatted it the way I'd slap a biting insect. For the briefest moment, the book connected with...something. It smelled of damp earth and bitter lacquer, and for a second I saw a human figure, black-clad and wearing a semi-rigid veil. Then it was gone.

I crouched, still holding the book in front of me. So the weavers could enter the oracle's space, if only briefly. And the books could touch them. But what was *I* supposed to do? I couldn't batter them to death with the thin atlas.

Another flicker, this one in front of me. Right in the heart of the oracle. The sight of it swept away my fear and filled me with anger. How *dare* these monsters enter *my* oracle? Before I could reflect on how stupid it was, I stepped forward and swung the book edge-on at the flickering shape.

It caught something. Briefly the flickering stilled, became a solid form, and then the corner of the atlas snagged the hem of the mask and flipped it off the weaver's head. The weaver's eyes met mine. They were wide and brown and utterly horrified. The stench of fresh lacquer filled the space between us. The weaver dropped her enormous hunting knife and clutched her throat, making gurgling, choking noises. She flickered again, fell to the ground, and convulsed, her breath coming in burbling gasps. I watched, my mind a blank, until she lay still. Then she flickered again, and was gone.

I lowered the atlas and stared at the place where the weaver had been. What was *that*? I'd only ever seen three dead bodies before, but I was certain she was dead, wherever she was. Numbness crept over me, blocking out any other emotion—fear, horror, disgust. Later I was sure I'd have nightmares, but for now I couldn't believe what I'd seen, what I'd done.

More flickering, and the scent of earth, was my only warning. I shrieked and swung the book wildly, connecting with the second weaver's stomach. It wasn't a heavy book, but the figure, flickering madly like bad stop-motion animation, bent double as if I'd swung a wrecking ball at his belly. Golden letters flowed from the spine of the atlas across the weaver's body, spiraling around him until he was coated with them.

The Book of Havoc

I slammed the atlas against his skull, making him drop to his knees. Then the letters found their way under the seam where the veil met the man's chest and poured through the gap like a stream of ants on the trail of sugar. The weaver screamed and clawed at his face, tearing the veil loose and flinging it at one of the bookcases. His eyes bulged, and he, too, groped at his throat like he was choking. I stood over him, breathing heavily, the atlas held at the ready, until he disappeared.

The book no longer glowed. I dropped it and picked up the mask. It still crawled with the insect-like letters, which lit up its interior. A thick layer of copper circuitry covered the inside of the hood, dense and tightly woven like the most intricate needlework design I'd ever seen. Flat copper rivets secured the veil, which was made of a flexible wire mesh, all around the face hole. I gingerly touched the circuitry, but felt nothing. Maybe Darius Wallach could make something of it. If I managed to reach him. If the weavers didn't find a way to kill me.

Arms went around me from behind. I screamed in pure terror and smashed my head backward, connecting solidly with my captor's face and making him grunt with pain. I hoped his nose was broken. I wriggled, but couldn't break free. The best I could do was turn around in the weaver's arms and get my arms up to claw at his face.

My nails caught in the mesh, and I yanked hard, trying to dislodge the mask. The weaver chuckled and released me, drawing his hunting knife. It was broader than Malcolm's slim blades, with a serrated edge opposite the honed steel sharpness of the other, and I shuddered at the dark stain tingeing the serration. The weaver advanced, still flickering, but more slowly now, spending more time solidly within the oracle. I backed away, keeping my eye on the knife, which is why I stumbled and fell over a stack of books some idiot had left on the floor.

I snatched up the first book that came to hand, a heavy textbook of some kind—I couldn't read the title through the golden letters coursing over it—and blocked his knife's blow. It struck the book dully, in a funny way, and I stepped back to find the knife was embedded in the textbook's cover. My movement jerked the knife out of his hands. I couldn't see his expression, but the way he took a step backward told me he was as startled as I was. I flung the book and its grisly burden aside and dove at the weaver before he could regain his composure.

It was pure insanity. He was taller than me by a few inches and outweighed me by forty pounds. But I caught him off-balance and bore him to the ground, desperately tearing at his mask. He grabbed my wrists and forced my hands away. Feeling my advantage slip away, I slammed my forehead into where I thought his nose probably was. He grunted with pain, and his grip on my wrists slackened. I jerked free, snatched the bottom edge of his veil, and ripped the mask off his head.

His convulsions knocked me to the ground, and I lay there, dragging huge breaths into my lungs, until the sounds of thrashing and convulsing were gone. Then I rolled over and pushed myself up. He, too, was gone, though his knife was still stuck through the cover of the textbook. I made a small effort to free it, then realized I wouldn't use his filthy blade even if I knew how and abandoned it.

I leaned against the nearest bookcase, letting it prop me up. I felt like I'd gone ten rounds with the heavyweight champ and was ready to be done. How many weavers were there? I'd seen six in the front of the store, not counting Santiago, but there had to be more if they'd disposed of all the enforcers Lucia had sent. I thought of attacking another three or more weavers and wanted to cry. This wasn't anything I was trained to do!

The golden glow intensified until the bookcases were nothing more than shining bars of light. Their radiance filled the air, dusting my skin with gold. I could almost imagine I could see through the shelves—and as I thought this, I noticed a creeping human figure passing just feet from where I stood. It was a shadowy blotch against the light, its knife raised to the ready. Distantly, I heard voices shouting, and Santiago yelling, "*es una mujer! ¡Necesitamos—*" and the passage of cars and trucks on the road outside. Then silence descended, and the shadow of the weaver vanished.

I took a few steps in the direction the figure had gone, then thought better of it. Instead, I chose a book from the shelves, something thick and wide and rich with golden letters. Half a dozen other books slid when I removed that one and toppled to the floor. For a brief, wild moment, I thought *I'm never going to get this mess cleaned up* and laughed, somewhat hysterically. Then I sneaked after my prey.

I searched through the oracle, book held high in preparation to swat someone, and found—nothing. Nothing flickered at the corner of my vision, nothing lurched out of thin air to attack me. My hands were shaking from holding the heavy book. Eventually I made my way back to the oracle's heart and lowered the book. "Are they gone?"

In response, the golden letters dimmed, then vanished. The book slipped from my nerveless fingers and fell face down and open on the linoleum. Breathing heavily, I picked it up and set it on a shelf, not paying attention to where, then sank to the floor, unable to stand on legs that felt like overcooked pasta. The fight had left the oracle a mess, with books scattered everywhere and scuff marks on the floor. I was too shaken to care. I might have fought off the weavers, but that didn't mean Santiago wasn't still out there, waiting for me to emerge so he could kill me. I couldn't stay in the oracle forever, not least because I couldn't warn anyone, beginning with Judy, who would walk into this completely unknowing. I had to find a way out of the oracle that would still leave me concealed within the maze of bookcases, free to call Malcolm and Lucia and Judy.

I struggled to my feet, using the bookcase to support me, and listened. Nothing. Maybe they'd run. The weavers must have reappeared in the real world, stone dead—how terrifying must that have been?

I moved quietly, though, finding my way back out of the oracle. Terrifying my attacks might have been, but Helena Davies without the power of the oracle wasn't anything to be afraid of. Still I saw and heard nothing. My heart beat faster. Was Santiago waiting just outside to snatch me?

I sniffed. Abernathy's hadn't smelled like anything when Santiago and the weavers had arrived. Possibly it felt the situation was too dire for the scent of fresh chocolate. Now there was a new scent, something hot and acrid. Something—

Smoke. It was smoke.

Abernathy's was on fire.

20

I ran, fear lending my feet greater speed, and burst out from between the bookcases. Panting, I dashed for the front door and flung it open—or tried to. It wouldn't budge. I worked the deadbolt and tried again. Still nothing. It might as well have been painted on the wall and not a door at all. I pulled on it, putting all my weight into it. The knob slipped through my fingers, and I stumbled backward, catching myself before I could fall.

Cursing, I grabbed the flimsy metal chair that still stood beside the door despite its being the least comfortable chair ever built, and swung it at the glass of the door. It rebounded into my face, smacking the bridge of my damaged nose and making me scream. I dropped the chair and clutched my nose, tears leaking from my eyes. The smell of smoke was worse now, and the flames audible, their crackling a witch's cackle to my ears.

I darted through the maze of bookcases, looking for the source of the fire, praying it hadn't spread far yet. Maybe I could put it out. The smoke grew thicker the closer I came to the fire, and I dropped to the ground and crawled, coughing and wheezing.

I felt the heat of the fire before I saw it. The entire back wall was in flames, the books curling in on themselves like flowers shriveling under a fierce sun. I thought I heard tiny voices crying out, but it was my imagination—no one could hear anything over the roar and crackle of the fire. My throat and eyes burned, and I backed up until the heat was too distant to feel. Then I ran.

Smoke curled down the short hall that led to the break room, not enough to blind or choke me. The fire extinguisher was gone, its brackets wrenched out of shape. I cursed Santiago and his damned weavers and raced upstairs to the kitchen. Maybe he—but that extinguisher was gone, too. Probably they'd have been too small to fight a fire that large, but the faint hope that had blossomed inside me shriveled up and faded away. I drew in a deep, focusing breath. It was too soon to give up.

I yanked the quilt off my bed, threw it in the tub and turned the faucet to full. It soaked the quilt, so slowly. Impatiently I pulled it out without turning off the water and ran downstairs again, through the smoke, trailing a stream of water. Covering my face with the wet quilt, I sidled rapidly between the bookcases and flung it over the flames. A huge hiss went up, drowning out the sound of the flames, and my heart lifted.

I twitched the edge of the quilt aside. Fire roared up again, undeterred by the wet fabric. High above where I could reach, the fire licked along the edges of the shelves and leaped the gap between one and another. It laughed at me and my pathetic attempts to extinguish it. My arms ached from holding the quilt over the shelves. Shaking, I let it fall, and the fire sprang up again, less powerful, more smoky, but every bit as persistent. I couldn't stop it. I couldn't do anything but get out, and call for help.

I ran for the back door. The heavy rear door was sealed as tightly as the front. I returned to the front and tried breaking the glass again, this time with the heavier stool behind the cash register. Nothing happened. I smashed it against the plate glass window and got nothing but a deep *doooiiiing* sound like a church bell. An elderly couple wearing track suits passed; I banged with my fists on the glass and shouted, but they continued on as if they saw nothing. Santiago had thought of everything.

I was trapped.

Trembling, trying to control my fear, I pulled out my phone and texted Malcolm. STORE ON FIRE CAN'T GET OUT COME NOW. I sent the message to Lucia as well, then, after a moment's thought, to Judy. Then I ran back upstairs to my old living room and pried at the windows. They, too, wouldn't budge. I leaned against them, pressing my head against the sun-heated glass, and tried to calm myself. Malcolm would come, and we'd save the oracle. Panicking wouldn't solve anything.

The room was growing smoky and hot. I ran back downstairs and tried my apartment key against the back door lock plate. Maybe setting the alarm off would get help here faster. But nothing happened. The last time I'd done it, it had blasted me twenty feet across the parking lot. Of course, last time I'd been outside... I leaned against the door, which was cool by comparison to the upstairs windows. That wouldn't last long.

No one responded to my texts. I sent them again, wishing I knew how to set off an alert or something, maybe a whistle or a klaxon, anything that would draw Malcolm's attention. If he was in the heat of battle, he might not notice it at all. Then I ran back into the store. The fire was spreading slowly, unnaturally slowly given how closely packed the books were. Clouds of smoke rolled across the ceiling. *That's going to take some cleaning*, I thought, then shook my head. The smoke was making me dizzy and stupid. I had to find a way out of here, and fast.

Stupid. I pulled out my phone again and dialed 9-1-1.

"9-1-1. What's the nature of your emergency?"

"Fire," I said, my voice raspy, and choked on a whiff of smoke. "Fire—the store's on fire—"

The man asked for my address, and I gave it. "Are you out of the building?"

"I'm trapped inside. The doors won't open and I can't break any windows."

He gave me more instructions, but my lightheadedness was coming back, and I only heard half of what he said. "I'll do that," I said, and hung up. *Stupid. They want you to stay on the line.* It had occurred to me that Santiago's illusion would probably prevent the firefighters from seeing the fire, and the nice 9-1-1 operator would think it was all a prank. I didn't want to be on the line with him when that happened. Besides, Malcolm might call.

I retreated as far as I could from the fire, which was the front door. "I don't know what else to do," I said. "I'm sorry. Fine custodian I turned out to be, huh?"

Voices whispered behind me, an impossibility because I was backed up against the door. I spun around, but saw nothing. The voices followed me, and I turned in a complete circle, but again saw nothing. I leaned back against the door. The rough wood of the frame caught at my hair, which stank of soot and smoke. "I don't understand."

More whispers, still unintelligible. "I don't understand!" I screamed, suddenly frustrated and tired and so overwhelmed with terror I couldn't stand it any longer. "We're both going to die here, do you get that? I couldn't stop Santiago. I can't put out the fire. I'm *sorry*. I just don't know what else to do."

The whispering grew in intensity until it was nearly a shout, and yet still had the quality of a whisper. I wiped tears from my eyes. "I don't know how you're doing that. I'm sorry if I'm stupid. Maybe a different custodian would understand—"

An invisible hand slapped me across the face, rocking me back on my heels and making the pain in my nose flare. I blinked in surprise. The whispering faded briefly, and I heard a chattering sound, like someone going *tsk, tsk*. It was so unexpected I laughed. "All right, enough whining," I said. "What can I do? What can we do, together?"

The whispering returned, but this time it was coming from somewhere in front of me—in the direction of the bookcases. Of the oracle. I walked toward it. The smoke came more thickly now, and I wished I'd thought to wet a rag to cover my face, but my path to the back of the store was now blocked by smoke and flames and it was too late for that. Still, there wasn't as much smoke as I'd expected. Maybe the oracle had some control, after all. "I hope this isn't just a faster way to get me killed," I said, and took three steps and entered the silence of the oracle.

The air immediately cleared, and I took a moment to wipe my eyes. It was still hot, though, and I could hear the crackle of the flames coming from somewhere nearby. My nose felt swollen to three times its normal size, and dried blood flaked off on my fingers every time I scratched my dry, itchy face. I kept walking, with no real destination in mind, but I wasn't surprised when I ended up at the heart of the oracle. From there, the sound of the fire was quieter, and I had no doubt this would be the last place it devoured—and when it did, the oracle would be destroyed, and I would be dead.

The whispering rose up again. I stood still and listened with my whole body, straining to make out words. It was like being just far enough away from a conversation that you could tell the words had meaning, but not what it was. I stepped closer to the tallest of the bookcases and rested my ear against its side, hoping maybe that would clarify things. The whispering grew louder, but no more intelligible. I stepped away and wiped my forehead, which was damp with sweat. "It's not working. I still don't understand."

Golden light welled up from the books again, a mellow glow that would have been pleasant if I hadn't been so terrified. "All right, so something about these glowing letters helps bridge the distance between the real world and whatever this space is," I said. "How does that help?"

The glowing light continued to grow, spreading to the shelves and the floor and increasing in brightness until it became painful. I shaded my eyes with one arm. The air was hot and pressing down on me in all directions, like a giant fist squeezing me. I felt like I might pop. "Stop it," I gasped, "I can't take it." The pressure didn't ease up. Liquid ran from my ears and my battered nose, the hot, sharp smell of blood filling the air. Keening from the pain, I sank to my knees and curled into a ball, trying to get away from the terrible, inexorable pressure. My joints ground against each other. My keening turned into a scream, wordlessly begging the oracle for mercy. I screamed again, and exploded.

My vision blurred, then focused with a clarity beyond anything I'd ever experienced. I was emptiness, filled with light, floating above the bookcases near the ceiling. I looked down at my crumpled human body. I was the oracle again.

I couldn't see the flames, even from my new vantage point, but I could feel their heat, plucking at my immaterial body like importunate children. The books were screaming in terror and pain, breaking my heart. I swooped down to soothe them, but they were too far gone to listen. All those tiny voices, just like in my dreams...

I drifted back, up to where I could see most of the room. My sense of urgency was gone, though a panicked back corner of my mind battered at me, shrieking *Do something!* No one was coming to my rescue. I had to save myself and the oracle. But how?

The golden light still filled the store. It drew me in, tethered me to the books as if I were a duck with a billion ducklings all scrabbling to fit under my wings. Toward the back of the store, where the fire was, the golden light flickered, all but extinguished. I turned my attention that way and flinched from the heat of the invisible flames. *Don't be a coward. You don't want to die here.*

Tentatively, I drifted toward the fire. The heat was visible as wavering currents of air, like a mirage over a summer pavement. The tiny golden letters burned brighter than a fire, their strands still attached to the books at one end and waving free at the other like seaweed fronds. I brushed up against one and felt an electric thrill sing through me. It was pure, innocent joy, and it made me angry that Santiago wanted to destroy it out of spite or selfishness.

The cut strands of the letters were fading, and I grasped them, wishing I knew how to keep them alive—surely they were alive, in some fashion. My immaterial body withered from the heat. Strands slipped from my grasp, fading away as the currents of heat grew stronger. The books screamed, and I screamed with them, the sound echoing through me and building inside me to a greater pressure than the one that had joined me with the oracle. For a moment, I saw the flames as if on a television screen, real and yet separated from me by glass.

Something snapped. The glass shattered, and I was in the real world, facing a wall of flame that crisped my immaterial body and made me scream again from pain. Golden letters still flickered all around me. The fire had spread a few rows further, and I felt it tugging at me, felt how the oracle was containing it through a vast effort of supernatural will. This close, it was a mass of color, reds and oranges and golds the same color as the tiny letters, and it deformed the space it filled, pushing the air aside to find a place to burn. It hurt, and yet I couldn't look away from it.

The raging wind tore through me again. It couldn't be a real wind, because it touched the fire not at all, but I felt its pressure on me and heard its howling voice: *...burn...transform...change...*

"Change what?" I shouted, or tried to—I had no lungs to draw air for speech. I let the words fill me and pour into the wind.

...fire...transform...

I stared into the fire. Part of me had already shriveled from the heat, and I didn't dare move closer. The remaining golden chains of letters outlined the dark edges of the fire—but dark, how? The fire burned so brightly I couldn't look at its heart.

And with that thought, I knew what the oracle wanted me to do.

I encompassed a whole row of shelves with my immaterial body and *lifted*, heaving hundreds of glowing, shimmering books into the air. I built a wall of books and moved it forward to encompass the heart of the fire. It crackled in triumph, thinking I had given it more fuel. I had other plans.

I gathered up all the moving strands of glowing letters. In this state, they made sense, though the words were still in no human language. They spoke of unity, of connection, of bridging the gap between what was and what might be. I knew almost nothing of magic, but I knew in my heart that the oracle's magic was like nothing else in the world.

I spread those chains of letters wide, stretching them far beyond the books into a net that glowed brighter than the heart of the fire. I wrapped the net around the flames and whispered to it, words in that strange language I wouldn't be able to remember when I regained my human form. They blazed so brightly I couldn't see anything around them, but I felt their presence, and it made me shiver with awe at being able to touch such a power, even indirectly.

For a long, infinite moment, we all three hung in a balance, the fire, the golden magic, and my immaterial self. I wondered if this was the end for me, if I'd have to stay in this position, holding off the flames, for the rest of eternity. But—was it growing cooler? I dared to extend my awareness toward the fire, hesitating in my fear of being burned again. I felt only the lingering touch of heat on my light-filled skin. The radiance was fading. I relaxed my hold on the magic and tried to breathe in a sigh of relief, then panicked briefly at remembering I had no lungs.

Where the fire had been, a light dusting of crystal powder sifted across the floor and shelves. The blackened husks of the burned bookcases were an empty spot in my mind, like the gap of a missing tooth. I rolled backwards and stretched myself thin and wide to encompass the whole store. The fire was gone. Perhaps a quarter of the bookcases had been destroyed. But the oracle remained.

I did another slow backflip into the heart of the oracle. Peace filled me as much as the light did. I could stay like this forever—

Something trembled inside me. I couldn't stay like this forever. I was human, not a magical being. And yet for right now, I was the oracle, and I didn't know what that meant. *Am I you?* I thought.

There was a long pause. Then I thought, **I am myself.**

I convulsed in horror. That had been my thought, and yet I was utterly certain I hadn't done the thinking. *Stay out of my head!* I screamed silently.

My head.

I looked down at where my human body lay motionless amid the drifts of books. That was me. I couldn't stay like this forever. I dove at my body and fluttered around it, trying to remember how I'd gotten back into it the last time I'd become the oracle.

I am not afraid of me, the oracle thought through my head.

Stop it!

I cannot hurt me. This is not forever.

I paused in my fluttering. There had been sorrow in that last thought, and despite myself I hesitated. *Why couldn't you work the magic yourself?* I thought, directing it deep inside.

I am the hands, I thought. This time I wasn't sure if that had been the oracle, or if I'd realized it for myself. **I am helpless without the hands.**

Then...you're trapped.

I am not trapped. I am encompassed. I am the hands.

A sudden flurry of movement startled me into drifting upward. Malcolm crouched beside my limp body, straightening my limbs and beginning CPR. A woman I didn't recognize stood nearby, staring up at my immaterial self. I wondered what I looked like from the outside. *I can't stay.*

I can stay.

No, I can't. I'm human.

I am myself.

The last thought struck me with such powerful loneliness I would have cried if I'd had eyes to cry with. *But I'm always here,* I thought, imbuing it with feelings of comfort. *Just because I'm not you doesn't mean I'm not with you, every day.*

There was another long pause. Then I thought, **I must go.**

Darting down to the floor, I gathered myself in as tightly as I could manage, shoving between Malcolm and my body. If I could make myself small enough, I could fit back inside, however impossible that seemed, with as huge as I was—

I blinked. Then I drew in a deep breath and started hacking and wheezing uncontrollably. Malcolm supported me to a sitting position, with one arm around my shoulders, and I grabbed hold of his other arm and steadied myself on it. When I could breathe normally, I flung my arms around his neck and held him tightly, felt him draw me close and stroke my hair. "Thank you," I whispered. My throat hurt too badly for anything louder. "I'm glad you came."

"We almost couldn't," Malcolm said. "The Mercy pressed us hard at the Gunther Node. It wasn't until I received your text that I realized the real danger was here. I thought I might go mad before I found a stone magus who could ward-step me here."

"Did Mr. Santiago not...I don't know what you call it. Make it impossible to step through Abernathy's wards? He thought of everything else."

"The only way to block a ward is to increase its strength," said the stranger. She was staring at me unblinkingly, like I was some alien creature. "He couldn't have had a stone magus with him, or he'd likely have done that. Were you that creature of light? That was—"

"Yes. It was me. And the oracle." My head and nose throbbed. The memory of what I'd done was already fading. "It knew how to put out the fire. But I had to do it. I'm its hands."

Malcolm helped me stand, then supported me when my legs wobbled. My vision swam with my exhaustion. "I'll take you home, then I have to return to the fight."

"But—what if Mr. Santiago returns?"

"Once you're out, I'll ward Abernathy's so well it will seal out any outside incursions," the woman said. "You'll need someone to take down the wards once the battle is over and the Mercy has been driven out, but for now it will be safe against anything up to and including a direct nuclear strike."

I wobbled again, and suddenly I was in Malcolm's arms, cradled tenderly like a baby. "Are we?" I asked. My voice sounded so faint. "Driving them out?"

"We are," Malcolm said, and that was the last thing I heard.

21

I crept silently through the stacks, sidling between the bookcases. Something was following me, something that flickered at the edges of my vision. My heart beat so rapidly it hurt. Fear filled me—

I woke, gasping for breath, to a darkened room. The smell of jasmine and the feel of the pillows told me I was in our bedroom in the apartment, wearing nothing but my underwear, and the silence told me I was alone. Terror propelled me upright. The Mercy. They'd come back and had invaded the store. I needed to get over there *now*.

I swung my legs over the side of the bed and tried to stand, but I was shaking too hard. I fell to my knees and pressed my face against the mattress, breathing in the scented sheets and trying to regain my wits. It was a warning, just a warning, like the others. There was time.

Finally I pushed myself to my feet and wobbled to my closet. It was practically a room to itself, with a chest of drawers and two poles for hanging clothes. I snatched a button-down shirt and jeans out of the drawers and fumbled around dressing in the dark. The sense of urgency was building. I needed to move more quickly.

When I emerged from the bedroom, I was surprised to find the rest of the apartment well-lit. Curious, I hurried to the kitchen, where I found Malcolm sitting at the center island dressed in jeans and a T-shirt, his gun laid out in pieces in front of him. He looked up, and an expression of pure relief crossed his face. "You're awake," he said, and kissed me with a sweet intensity that made the urgency of the moment fade. "This doesn't hurt?" He tweaked my nose.

"No, I—it's healed!"

"I realize Tinsley is extremely skilled, but you looked like a victim from a slasher movie, your face and front covered in gore, so I felt the need to verify your health for myself." His hand slid under my shirt to brush the skin of my belly, which made me tingle all over. "I think further investigation is warranted, don't you?"

I gently moved away from him. "I have to go to the store. The Mercy is coming back—they're invading Abernathy's—"

Malcolm took my hand. "The Mercy has been decisively routed," he said, "and won't be coming back. And Cole's wards are still in place. They couldn't get into the store if they tried."

"But I dreamed...Malcolm, it felt so real. And it was true the last time."

"Yes, but this time, it's impossible."

I sat on an adjacent bar stool and stared at our linked hands. "I don't understand. Why is Abernathy's still trying to warn me of danger when there isn't any?"

"Maybe it's not that kind of danger. Maybe that's just the only language it speaks."

I tried to recall everything that had happened that afternoon—or was it that afternoon? "Malcolm, what time is it? What *day* is it?"

Malcolm laughed and kissed my knuckles. "It's almost ten o'clock in the evening, and it's still Monday, Rip Van Winkle. Though you slept soundly enough I was going to wake you when I came to bed, to make sure you were still alive."

"Then—what happened at the node?"

"Our efforts at matching the timing of the weavers' movements in and out of space were successful. With their elite forces disabled, their steel and wood magi could not make up the difference. The battle lasted several hours, but in the end, we were victorious. When Tinsley and I left the node, Lucia was preparing to retake the other occupied nodes and sending communications to South and Central America, instructing them in how to defeat the weavers."

"If you take their masks off, they die," I said. "Or—maybe not. It might just be that they can't survive within the oracle without their masks. I saved one for Mr. Wallach to look at."

"What makes you say that?"

"I fought them off."

Malcolm's eyebrows rose. "You what?"

"I had some help from the oracle. And weaponized books."

"Weaponized—" Malcolm laughed. "I have to remember not to underestimate you."

"You don't do that often, do you?"

"Almost never. You are amazing, and I love the woman you are."

The look in his eyes made me warm all over. "I don't want to have to do it again, though. I hope that doesn't make me weak."

"Not at all. It's not weak to abhor violence." Malcolm went back to cleaning his gun. "Why don't you shower, and I'll finish this and make you something to eat."

"Thanks. I still feel so weary."

I hurried in the shower, the remembered urgency making me disinclined to linger, and returned to find Malcolm just reassembling his gun. I watched his agile hands put it back together. What had Judy thought when she returned to the store? Had she even gotten my text? "I hope Judy's all right."

"She sent several increasingly agitated texts, so I called her to explain the situation. She knew the fight at the Gunther Node was happening because her date had to cut their lunch short to return there, but believed the store had burned down. I told her she could return in the morning. I hope that was right."

"We're going to have to do a lot of cleaning tomorrow. And buy replacement books, eventually." I remembered those tiny voices crying out in pain and fear and blinked away tears. The oracle was strong enough to resist this damage, I was sure of it, but the memory of how forlorn it had sounded still made my heart ache for it. Even now, I could feel its loneliness.

I propped my elbows on the counter and rested my chin in my interlaced hands. "Malcolm," I said. "Do you remember what you said about my last dream? Not the one I just had, the one before?"

"Not really," Malcolm said, holstering his gun. He went to the sink to wash his hands. The sound of the water rushing reminded me of the roaring of the wind, filled with the voice of the oracle.

I got up from the stool. "I think I need to go to the store, after all."

"Helena, it was just a dream."

"It's not about the Mercy. Something else is wrong. And I think I know what."

———

It didn't look like the stone magus, who I knew only as Cole, did anything. She just stood there staring up at the back side of Abernathy's like she was interested in its architecture. Malcolm put his arm around me and drew me close against his side. "You're being awfully cryptic about this," he whispered.

"That's because I'm not sure I'm right. If I'm not, I don't want to look stupid."

"I would never think you stupid just for being wrong."

"I know. But this is a private thing...look, I promise I'll explain it all later."

"That's it," Cole said. "Do you want me to hang around and put them back up when you're done?"

"The Mercy aren't coming back," I said, "so the wards just need to be at their regular strength. Thanks for coming out so late."

"No problem. Abernathy's has stretched my abilities today, and I always like that." She nodded at Malcolm, one fighter to another, and got into her little Volkswagen and drove away.

I unlocked the back door, and Malcolm and I walked through the quiet, stinking darkness. The store smelled of smoke and char that left a film of grime on everything, even the places the fire hadn't actually touched. I ran my fingers along the wall in the hallway outside the break room and grimaced at how they came away black. "This is going to take some *major* cleaning."

"I'll give you a number to call," Malcolm said. "They're a magi cleaning service, so they perform magical as well as mundane cleaning. I'm not sure you'll get those books clean otherwise."

"Yeah, well, the first thing I'm buying in the morning is half a dozen fire extinguishers and setting them out all over the store."

We came to the front desk, where the cash register, for a miracle, was unsullied by the soot. "Wait here," I said. "I'm not sure how long this will take. No more than fifteen minutes, I hope."

"I will wait in great anticipation of an explanation," Malcolm said, kissing me.

I walked forward with measured steps, closed my eyes—and stepped into the oracle.

That was one hurdle down. I had felt, in thinking about everything that had passed that day, I would now be able to enter the oracle whenever I chose, not just with an augury request. But I hadn't been sure. Guessing right heartened me.

Light sprang up around me, not the bright glow of the letters but a softer light that seemed to come from the air itself. I strode quickly through the oracle's corridors with the wind whispering in my ear. I was also fairly certain I could do this from anywhere within the oracle's boundaries, but I wanted to show I was taking this seriously, and that meant the heart of the oracle. The wind snaked around my body, disappearing for a time but always returning to me, like a friendly dog. After what I'd gone through, I wondered how literal an image that was.

The heart of the oracle was darker than the rest, without the ambient light the other shelves had been filled with. I stood in the center of the space and turned around in a slow circle. In the darkness, the four bookcases seemed taller than they were in daylight, tall enough that their tops were invisible. They felt like a stone circle, redolent with ancient magic. "I received your dream," I said. "I wish I knew how you did that. Can you send a dream into anyone's head, or does it have to be your custodian? Not that I'd be able to make anything of it if it was the first option. Just curious."

The wind made another loop around my body and whistled off into the far corners. "So here's the thing," I said. "I appreciate that you're capable of giving warnings. I could wish them to be a little less ambiguous, but I appreciate it. But for those warnings to be effective, I have to be able to trust them. And that means you can't send out false warnings like you did tonight."

Perfect silence. But it felt like *something* was listening to me intently. "I think I understand now. Malcolm guessed it—you got used to having me around, and you didn't like it when I left. And when I became you, that satisfied some need I can barely comprehend. But *I'm not you*. Even when I take on your form, I'm still myself. I'm sorry you're lonely, but you just can't...co-opt my consciousness so you'll have a friend."

The wind returned. *...alone...*

"You're not alone. You have Judy and me. And you have all these Wardens who depend on you. Look, you're stronger than this, I know you are. You have more power than anyone's ever dreamed of. I've seen it. And I'm not going anywhere. Though I think we should be able to think of a better way for me to become you, when that's needed. Something that doesn't make me bleed at the ears."

The wind laughed, dizzying me. I felt something brush my face, something gentler than the wind. Then the sense of presence was gone, and I stood alone at the center of the oracle.

I brushed a tear from my eye and made my way to the storefront, where Malcolm lounged against the counter, looking not at all bored. "Did you succeed?"

"I talked to the oracle, Malcolm. And it listened. I don't know how, but it did."

Malcolm straightened, looking concerned. "What does that mean?"

"I have no idea. But there's more to the oracle than just a magical field that chooses auguries. It's...I think it's a creature. And it was lonely."

"That's astonishing. I wish I could tell you I've heard of things like this before. I think you should talk to your counterparts. If Abernathy's is a living thing, maybe the labyrinth and the fountain are too. Or the others."

"I will. Tomorrow." I let out a jaw-cracking yawn. "Let's go home."

22

Malcolm held the car door for me, a habit of his I appreciated more at times like this when I felt too tired for physical exertion. As he pulled out of the parking lot, he said, "It's not really home, is it?"

"Malcolm, I promised I would try! And it's feeling more homelike all the time."

"Oh, Helena. 'That's probably the sweetest lie you've ever told.'"

"I can't believe you're quoting *How to Marry a Millionaire* at me. And it's not a lie." I scrunched up in my seat and folded my arms across my chest. "All right. So it's a...a creative untruth. But I really am trying."

Malcolm sighed. "You shouldn't have to try, love. More to the point, I shouldn't have ignored your wishes. I owe you an apology."

"You wanted to make me happy. I understand that."

"No, I wanted to make *myself* happy by showering you with luxuries, even though I know you don't care about things like state-of-the-art kitchens and thermally adaptive bathrobes. *I* don't care about those things—it's true, I like having money, but I try not to let it cross the line. And I think this last week, I did."

"You were enthusiastic. It makes sense. But...thanks. I've just felt so out of place these last few days. Though I did like the music system." He'd never mentioned thermally adaptive bathrobes before and I decided not to ask what they were.

"I promise I'll never fall into that trap again. But that's not the only problem, as I'm sure you're aware."

"You mean Madeleine."

"I had words with my mother today, when the battle was over. About her harassing you. I've let this go on far too long, and again, I apologize. You're far more important to me than she is."

"Well...she is your mother..."

"That's not a reason to allow someone as nasty and vicious as she's become to interfere in our lives. I confronted her directly about her treatment of you, and she made it abundantly clear that she wasn't going to give up trying to get rid of you. And I thought—we're never going to be able to get away from her so long as we're in my apartment."

"I can ignore her. It's really not a big deal."

"Of course it is. We're talking about our home. It should be a haven, not a source of friction. But the big deal, Helena, is that I thought of it as *my* apartment. Not ours. And I realized I've been thinking of myself as your host, trying to make my apartment appealing to you. Even if the unnecessary luxuries weren't a problem, that's not how it should work."

I sat up further in my seat. "And when it was at the apartment over the store, it was *my* apartment. You're right. What we need is *our* apartment."

"Something that suits us both. I like my home gym."

"And I'll want a nice kitchen. I still mean to learn how to cook."

"And a room for guests."

"And a place for children. You know, someday."

Malcolm was silent. I looked at him and saw he was intent on the road ahead. I replayed my idle words in my head and felt my whole body go hot with embarrassment. "That is...I suppose that's something we should talk about, right? Maybe you don't want children.

Sorry, that sounded like I'd already made the decision for both of us. We can talk about it some other time."

"Let's take a detour," Malcolm said, and took a rapid right turn.

We drove through a neighborhood I didn't recognize. The houses were tall, some three stories tall, and sprawling on large lots bordered by hedges of arborvitae or rhododendron. In the light of the half-moon their façades were shades of gray, some dark brick, others lighter stone. Malcolm pulled up in front of one of the latter. Its double front doors were shaded by a stone portico supported by four white pillars glimmering in the moonlight. Ironwork grilles covered the lower halves of the upstairs windows, and rosebushes like the Kellers' lined the driveway, which circled around to the side of the house. No lights burned within; even the porch light was off. I had no way to tell, but it felt unoccupied.

Malcolm turned off the ignition and we sat there in silence. I had so many questions I couldn't think which one to ask first. Before I could come up with anything, Malcolm got out of the car and came around to my side to open my door. I took his hand and stepped out of the car. Malcolm kept hold of my hand, but stood looking up at the dark house. I examined it again. More rosebushes grew beneath the wide ground floor windows, their colors indistinct in the low light. I felt a sudden urge to explore the grounds that I had to suppress. "It's beautiful," I said, hoping this would elicit some explanation from Malcolm.

"Want to see the backyard?"

"Oh, Malcolm, we shouldn't trespass—"

"It's not trespassing. No one lives here. Come on, let's look around."

I wasn't sure he was right about the trespassing, but I nervously let him lead me along the driveway. There was a three-car garage at the side of the house, and a path of large white stones with rounded tops that went farther back behind the garage. The backyard, unlike the pleasant flowery crowdedness of the front, was a sweep of lawn easily as big as the house's footprint, bordered by a white vinyl fence that lit the yard with reflected moonlight. The fresh green smell of new-cut grass tickled my nostrils. I closed my eyes and listened to the breeze ruffle the blades of grass, imagining I could hear the sound of children running and laughing. The lawn had been mown recently, and the rosebushes were neatly pruned, so *someone* was caring for the house, but why wasn't something so beautiful being lived in?

"Let's go inside." Malcolm tugged at my hand.

"We *really* shouldn't, Malcolm, someone owns this place—"

"I promise it's all right."

I wavered. Trespassing was wrong, but the house was so beautiful, I couldn't resist the idea of taking just a quick peek. And no one would find out.

The back door led to a mud room tiled in rough red squares about two feet across. One wall was nothing but cubbies for shoes and boots and hats. It was completely empty. So Malcolm was right, and no one lived here.

One short step up from the mud room was a short hallway with a single door that turned out to be a washroom. At the end of the hall-way, it opened up into a kitchen that made me gasp. My kitchen at Abernathy's was small and antique, Malcolm's kitchen was ultra-modern, but this was big and yet cozy at the same time. Dozens of cupboards in a pale wood I couldn't identify covered the walls, filling my imagination with what they might contain, and I looked inside one, but of course found only emptiness. That made me feel an unnamed sadness; this kitchen should be filled with spices and plates in some bold color and thick glass tumblers.

The refrigerator was a modestly-sized stainless steel one, matching the dishwasher, and the stove top was one of those solid glass-topped ones I'd gotten so used to at Malcolm's apartment. The sink with two faucets was set in an island in the center of the stone-tiled floor, a perfect surface for preparing food. I ran my hand over the black countertop, which felt like granite, and opened a few more cupboards. "This, I could get used to," I whispered, but I no longer felt like an intruder.

For an empty house twice the size of my parents', it didn't echo or feel intimidating. Malcolm pointed out the dining room, the living room, the smaller living room off the front door, the breakfast nook, and the den before escorting me upstairs. I counted the bedrooms (four) and made note of a second living room on the second floor. *And it's not at all like Madeleine and her two sitting rooms.*

We wound up in the master suite, which was on a corner and had windows all along two adjacent walls. "The suite is really beautiful," I said, admiring the tub and the glass-walled shower in the master bathroom. "It's not quite as big as yours, but it feels welcoming. The whole house does."

"I think so, too."

"So how do you know about it? Whose property are we invading?"

"Mine, actually," Malcolm said. "This is the house I grew up in."

I gasped. "This—then we really aren't trespassing."

"I told you we weren't. Let's go outside. I want to show you something else."

We walked hand in hand through the beautiful house—"That was my bedroom," Malcolm said, pointing—and across the lawn to sit on the grass near the fence. The spot gave us a perfect view of the house. Malcolm put his arm around me, and we sat in peaceful silence for a while. I idly walked through the house in memory and wondered what it had looked like when Malcolm had lived there. I thought about who might have lived in it since then; it couldn't have lain empty for five years and still looked this nice. *That second-floor sitting room would be perfect for a home gym. And there are enough bedrooms to have one just as a playroom for the kids.*

"It doesn't look quite as nice in the daylight," Malcolm said, startling me out of my reverie. "The renovation starts on Wednesday. The renters were careful, but you never treat things the same when they aren't yours. And in the dark I can pretend everything's the way it used to be."

"Do you come here often?"

"It's only been empty for about a month. This is the second time I've been back." He shifted position, turning to face me. "But that's not why we're here."

The moonlight lit his face beautifully, highlighting the angularity of his jaw and cheekbones and the smooth curve of his lips. The intensity of his gaze made me nervous. "Why are we here?" I asked, trying for a light tone.

He said nothing for a long moment. "You want children, yours and mine," he finally said.

"Sometime in the distant future, but...yes."

"And you want to go on living with me. Somewhere that belongs to both of us."

"Yes. More than anything."

"Even though my mother is awful and will do her best to break us up."

"I don't care about your mother. I only care about you."

He reached out to caress my cheek. "I want to spend the rest of my life with you. I want to wake, every morning, with you by my side. I want to raise a family and grow old together. So—" He reached behind my ear and brought out, as if by magic, a little gray box. "Helena, will you marry me?"

The world spun. I clutched his free hand to keep from falling over. "What?"

He smiled. "I've been carrying this box around all week, waiting for the right moment. I think I chose well."

I focused on the ring box in his hand. Dazedly, I took it, but held it unopened near my heart. "I—" Everything he'd said, the beauty of the quiet house and the still, perfect evening, rang in my ears. "Yes," I said. "Yes, of course I will!"

A fierce, brilliant smile touched Malcolm's lips, and then we were kissing wildly, touching each other everywhere with a passionate urgency. Malcolm lowered me to the grass and we lay together, lips exploring lips as if for the first time. I tugged his T-shirt out of his waistband and put my hands on his bare skin. It was warm and smooth and I was struck by an insane desire to make love with him, right there on the grass where anyone could see. "We can't do this," I murmured into his ear. "Even if it is your house."

Malcolm lowered his hands from where he'd been unfastening my shirt. "You're right. And you haven't even looked at it."

"At what? Oh!" I cracked open the box and let out a long sigh of appreciation. "*Malcolm.* It's beautiful." It was antique gold, with a square setting etched with leaves holding a round diamond that was probably a full carat in size. Two leaves extended down from the diamond on each side as if they were supporting it, and two smaller round diamonds lay in the centers of the leaves. I held the ring close to my eyes—yes, tiny etched leaves decorated the band, like a laurel wreath.

"I thought about getting a replica of some famous actress's engagement ring, but it turns out most of them had big, gaudy things I knew you wouldn't wear," Malcolm said. He took the ring from my hand and gently slipped it over my finger. It was a perfect fit.

"This *must* be magic," I said, admiring it.

"The magic of asking your parents your ring size. You didn't think I would ask you to marry me without getting their blessing, did you?"

I gasped. "Malcolm, when did you do that?"

"Two days before we moved into the apartment."

"Then—my parents knew the whole time!" And my mother had managed to act surprised when Madeleine had said we were engaged. "I can't believe they were able to keep it a secret."

"So you like the ring?"

"I love it."

"I'm glad." Malcolm stood and helped me to my feet. "Now let's get back to the apartment and celebrate our engagement with a romantic tryst on the wonderful bed. And tomorrow we can start looking for a new place to live."

"I've already decided. I want to live here."

Malcolm stopped and turned to face me. "Helena, that's not why I brought you here."

"I know. I never thought that."

"I thought the point was to choose something that was ours, not mine or yours."

"It is. But I already love this place. It feels like home. Maybe that's because it's connected to you, maybe because it's so beautiful, but I can see us raising a family here. Do you mind? It should be a shared decision."

Malcolm picked me up and swung me, shrieking with laughter, around in a wide circle. "I would love to make this our home. It means so much to me that you feel welcomed by it. I like to think my father's presence is still here, watching over it."

"I can imagine." I'd never seen so much as a picture of Alastair Campbell, but having seen his sons, I thought of him as an older Malcolm, distinguished-looking with salt-and-pepper hair and a kind smile. And the dimple. "He'd make a wonderful guardian."

We drove back to the apartment—now that I'd seen the house, I couldn't think of the apartment as home any longer—in silence, though I couldn't stop looking at my ring and grinning like a fool. "How did you know this was the right time to ask me?"

"I knew you wouldn't be thinking of children, however far in the future, without thinking of marriage." Malcolm parked the car in the numbered spot and took my hand, rubbing his thumb over the diamond. "And...it felt right."

"It was. It absolutely was."

I hooked my arm around his elbow as we rode up in the elevator, still grinning like mad. I was getting married. It felt like a dream, except I had the ring as a reminder. It was perfect. Malcolm was perfect. Everything was perfect.

The elevator door slid open, revealing Madeleine, dressed in the formal business pantsuit that was her version of fighter's fatigues. She took a step back when she saw us. "I came to wish you good health," she told me. The expression on her face said she'd prefer to wish me to hell.

"Thank you, Madeleine, I feel very well." I couldn't stop myself; I wiggled my fingers so the diamond caught the light and fractured it into a dozen broken rainbows.

As I'd hoped, it caught Madeleine's eye. Quicker than thought, she seized my hand and brought it up to her eye. "What is this?"

"Helena and I are going to be married, Mother," Malcolm said. His words were pleasant enough, but there was a tension behind them I didn't like. I retrieved my hand without snatching it away and smiled at Madeleine.

"*Quel désastre!*" Madeleine shouted, following it with a torrent of French in which I couldn't make out individual words. Malcolm tried to cut across her words, but Madeleine was in full voice.

Finally, Malcolm gave up. "Good night, Mother," he said, escorting me down the hall. Behind us, the words cut off, presumably thanks to the elevator doors, and I relaxed my shoulders. I'd been anticipating Madeleine throwing something at me. "I'm sorry, love," Malcolm said. "That's the last time we have anything to do with her."

"How soon can we move out?"

"Not soon enough." Malcolm opened the door and drew me inside, then put his arms around me. "I love you."

I kissed him, slow and sweet. His mouth tasted like honey, and I breathed in the woody scent that was his alone. "I love you," I said. "Let me show you how much."

THE AUGURIES, AND THE MOVIE LIST

ABERNATHY'S AUGURIES:
    Ben Aaronovitch, *Broken Homes*

Heidi Murkoff and Sharon Mazel, *What to Expect When You're Expecting*

Alex Comfort, *The Joy of Sex*

Mike Resnick, *Santiago*

Maggie Lane, *Jane Austen's England*

Matt Ridley, *The Rational Optimist*

Umberto Eco, *The Name of the Rose*

Gabrielle Zevin, *The Storied Life of A.J. Fikry*

Jasper Fforde, *The Eyre Affair*

Susan Hill, *Howards End is On the Landing*

Sasha Abramsky, *The House of Twenty Thousand Books*

MOVIES CITED:

Mr. Blandings Builds His Dream House

Mr. and Mrs. Smith

Breakfast at Tiffany's

The Seven-Year Itch
How to Marry a Millionaire
Bringing Up Baby
Bring It On

ABOUT THE AUTHOR

In addition to The Last Oracle series, Melissa McShane is the author of The Extraordinaries series, beginning with BURNING BRIGHT, the Crown of Tremontane series, beginning with SERVANT OF THE CROWN, as well as COMPANY OF STRANGERS, and many others.

After a childhood spent roaming the United States, she settled in Utah with her husband, four children and a niece, four very needy cats, and a library that continues to grow out of control. She wrote reviews and critical essays for many years before turning to fiction, which is much more fun than anyone ought to be allowed to have.

You can visit her at her website www.melissamcshanewrites.com for more information on other books.

For information on new releases, fun extras, and more, sign up for Melissa's newsletter: http://eepurl.com/brannP

ALSO BY MELISSA MCSHANE

THE CROWN OF TREMONTANE

Servant of the Crown

Exile of the Crown

Rider of the Crown

Agent of the Crown

Voyager of the Crown

Tales of the Crown

THE SAGA OF WILLOW NORTH

Pretender to the Crown

Guardian of the Crown

Champion of the Crown

THE HEIRS OF WILLOW NORTH

Ally of the Crown

Stranger to the Crown (forthcoming)

THE EXTRAORDINARIES

Burning Bright

Wondering Sight

Abounding Might

Whispering Twilight (forthcoming)

THE LAST ORACLE

The Book of Secrets

The Book of Peril

The Book of Mayhem

The Book of Lies

The Book of Betrayal

The Book of Havoc

The Book of Harmony (forthcoming)

COMPANY OF STRANGERS

Company of Strangers

Stone of Inheritance

Mortal Rites

Shifting Loyalties

Sands of Memory

Call of Wizardry

THE CONVERGENCE TRILOGY

The Summoned Mage

The Wandering Mage

The Unconquered Mage

THE BOOKS OF DALANINE

The Smoke-Scented Girl

The God-Touched Man

Emissary

Warts and All: A Fairy Tale Collection

The View from Castle Always

Printed in Great Britain
by Amazon